ALWAYS THE BRIDESMAID

BRITS IN MANHATTAN BOOK FOUR

LAURA CARTER

Boldwood

First published in Great Britain in 2023 by Boldwood Books Ltd.

Copyright © Laura Carter, 2023

Cover Design by Rachel Lawston

Cover Illustration by Rachel Lawston

A CIP catalogue record for this book is available from the British Library.

Paperback ISBN 978-1-78513-560-6

Large Print ISBN 978-1-78513-559-0

Hardback ISBN 978-1-78513-558-3

Ebook ISBN 978-1-78513-561-3

Kindle ISBN 978-1-78513-562-0

Audio CD ISBN 978-1-78513-553-8

MP3 CD ISBN 978-1-78513-554-5

Digital audio download ISBN 978-1-78513-555-2

Boldwood Books Ltd
23 Bowerdean Street
London SW6 3TN
www.boldwoodbooks.com

For my youngest baby

SARAH'S STORY

IF YOU NEVER LOOK FOR LOVE, YOU CAN'T EVER GET HURT

1

SARAH

'Oh yeah, God that's good,' I groan.

'I told you I'd find the spot.'

'You have. You really have.'

I'm suspended from a reclaimed teak frame in Izzy's recently renovated dance studio. What used to be a stage for her 'Salsa Yourself Fit' classes has been replaced by an aerial yoga set-up.

As I shift to see myself in the wall of mirrors that line one side of the studio, I can see the effect hanging upside-down is having on my body: tomato-red face, long brown locks escaping the knot I had tied on the top of my head, the flesh of my cheeks sagging with gravity. It defies logic that Izzy makes this look immensely glamorous on TikTok.

My unsightly appearance aside, Izzy has found the exact spot on my lower back that has been playing up recently from too many hours spent lifting boxes of files and paper at work.

Drew – lawyer, boss and one of my best friends – has taken a case defending his longstanding client, vehicle-manufacturing giant Rolando. As his legal secretary of more than a decade, Drew trusts me more than any paralegal or junior associate at the firm. And so I have spent the last twelve days straight trawling through box after box of paperwork disclosed by the other side – a minority shareholder in Rolando – looking for one tiny receipt. The smoking gun that will prove that the applicant couldn't have been where he said he was at the precise moment the applicant's entire case hinges on.

I lugged those boxes up and down from tabletops and carried the heavy files home to keep going through the night, meaning I had to abandon my near-daily yoga practice and tweaked my back.

'Breathe through it,' Izzy says as she stands behind me, holding onto my thighs and leaning into my hips, getting straight to that sweet spot around my spine.

'I'm having a head rush,' I tell her, my voice

sounding peculiar in my ears, as if I'm speaking in a fish bowl.

'Whoa!'

The shout follows my other friend (and Drew's fiancée) Becky crashing to the soft floor beneath her as her silk ropes have somehow twisted, turned, and flipped her out onto the surface.

'Ouch,' she says, lying in the exaggerated position that a cartoon character who has been knocked over by a truck might lie in.

'What on earth!' Izzy says, as she ditches me and moves to collect her fellow Brit and friend from floor. 'What were you doing?'

'I've no idea,' Becky says, coming up to sit with Izzy's help. 'I think maybe that's part of the problem.'

I can't help but laugh. I laugh so hard my own gangly legs somehow unravel from their holstered position and I too fall into a heap on the ground.

Glancing sideways to Becky, I reach out to take hold of her hand and laugh harder.

'What a calamity you both are,' Izzy says, trying to maintain professionalism for the benefit of the other five women attending her class, each of whom looks remarkably more chic than Becky and me.

'Is this what you meant by being transformed into a butterfly from our cocoons?' I ask.

Despite her efforts, Izzy's voice breaks and the corners of her lips defy her, turning upward right before she too folds over and we are all laughing together – the very definition of lasting friendship.

* * *

I'm sitting on a stool at the food bar in the gym, flanked by Becky and Izzy, where a large coconut-milk latte and a slice of French toast with berries and maple syrup have been placed in front of me. Izzy has just been handed a green detox smoothie.

'Sorry, Izzy,' I say, digging the side of a fork into my French toast. 'I was willing to rouse from my hard-earned slumber and make the trek to Brooklyn for a nine-fifteen class on a Sunday morning, but I draw the line at having a vegetable-packed smoothie for breakfast.'

Below where we are sitting, we can see men and women swimming laps of the gym pool. The Williamsburg franchise is the latest addition to the Brooks Adams gym empire.

Despite Brooks's insistence that he pay for the legal advice and the discount that Drew gave, I happen to know that it actually *cost* the firm money. But Drew is a partner in the firm, he has the power to do that, and I fully endorse him supporting Brooks, who has been his best friend since kindergarten and one of my best friends for almost as long as I have known Drew.

What pleases me more is that I genuinely love Becky and Izzy. Both Brooks and Drew have previously had relationships that I did *not* approve of, ones which I knew were doomed from the start, and which were ultimately only about the bedroom. It's not as if I have the final say, or any say *really*, in who my friends date, but I more than encouraged them both to find their happily ever afters with Becky and Izzy.

I suppose you could say that is one of my *things* – matchmaking. In particular, matchmaking for my friends. And the next two weeks are further proof of just how skilled I am in coupling people up.

'I'm so excited for the wedding,' I say, untying my hair from my knot and letting it fall down my back, tickling my shoulders, which are exposed in my workout vest. 'I can't wait to see Jess in her bridal gown.'

Jess is marrying Drew's younger brother Jake next weekend and I credit myself with ultimately having nudged the couple from friends with benefits to life partners – or I at least played a significant role in helping them get their acts together.

We'll all be staying in a house I've arranged for us (using Drew's credit card to pay the rent) in Surrey – apparently a ceremonial county in southeast England, according to Wikipedia – in the week running up to the wedding. The week after, I'm staying in London to see the British sights.

'And I can't wait for us all to be together again,' I add, shielding the half-eaten breakfast in my mouth with my hand as I speak. 'My first trip to England! I know I say this all the time but it's crazy that all of the guys fell for Brits. I love it! Are you excited to be going home?'

While I sip my latte and take another inelegant bite of French toast, dabbing excess icing sugar from the side of my mouth with a napkin, I note the exchange of apprehensive looks between Becky and Izzy.

'Come on, it won't be so bad,' I say, attempting to sound reassuring.

'Won't it?' Izzy asks, one eyebrow raised in question. 'My sister let slip to my parents that I'll be back in the country. They want to have lunch.'

'Lunch sounds... nice, no?' I can feel my face

twist, as if I'm bracing myself for falling debris landing on my head.

'Not just lunch. Lunch with Brooks and his daughter. They're still grieving the career they always wanted me to have, using the degree that *they* paid for. They still think music, health and fitness is like my gap-year career. They don't get TikTok and Insta, they don't realize I have a brand now. Or maybe they do and they still don't care because I'm not some kind of literary correspondent for *The Guardian*.'

'Hmm... You never know, maybe they've missed you and thought about things, and—'

'Sarah, I assure you, it would be... the worst lunch imaginable.'

'I'm not sure where to go with this. I don't think I have a strong message of positivity off the cuff, so in a while I'm going to come back to you with some kind of Sarah affirmation. For now, there's always French toast, if you would indulge just one time. It's worth the cals, I promise.'

I take another bite of my toast and purr as if I'm making love to it.

Izzy rolls her eyes but her amusement is evident.

'How about you, Becky? Are you looking forward to it?' Izzy asks.

'The wedding? Massively.' Becky swallows a

mouthful of smashed avocado on sourdough, rubbing a spot of green mush from the tip of her nose with the back of her hand. 'I'm so happy for Jake and Jess and we haven't seen much of Drew's parents and sister recently, so it will be lovely to catch up with the family. But being in England? Having to pretend that every place I see isn't a trigger from my past? Nope, zero excitement about that.'

'Okay, I usually pride myself on choosing my audience but it seems long hours and an early morning have messed with my mojo,' I say jokingly. 'Seriously though, if either of you feels anxious or down about the trip, please, please talk to me. I have no purpose in life if I'm not trying to fix things.'

Becky smiles. 'A week of hanging out with my best friends will be all the fixing I need.'

'I second that,' Izzy says.

'Eek, it's going to be fabulous!' I say, rubbing my hands together. 'Now, I must go home and pack for our flight.' I rise from my stool and brush sugar from my yoga leggings, then finish my latte. 'I'm so pleased it worked out that we can all travel together.'

2

SARAH

The alarm on my coffee machine chimes, then the distinct sound of grinding beans filters through to the one bedroom of my apartment in West Village. Drew and Becky bought me the machine as a Christmas gift last year and I love the smell that fills my home every morning but I truly hate the offensively loud noise it makes.

It's Monday and the start of my ten working days of vacation from the office. It's the longest block of leave I've taken since my honeymoon. The thought comes to me as I walk into the kitchen of my open-plan living space, stilling me momentarily as I reach for a mug. It kills the giddiness I have been feeling about my trip.

I read the message written in Script font on the mug – *You've Got This*. I nod, as if the mug has physically rather than metaphorically spoken to me, and I tell myself what I always try to remind myself in these moments of melancholy – *at least you met him and enjoyed four beautiful years together.*

My husband was stolen from me far too soon. Before any of our life plans and dreams had come to fruition. I have been without him now for double the length of time I was with him and still the pain of his loss is ever-present, ever-real. It catches me off-guard. Something as simple as my mind acknowledging the last time I took a two-week break from work can thrust me back into darkness in an instant.

'London, London, London,' I whisper to myself as I set about pouring filter coffee into my mug and adding oat milk from the refrigerator. But it doesn't stop me from thinking of him. *You would have been so excited, Danny.*

I remind myself that I'll be enjoying the sights and sounds of London for both of us. That is why I have booked to stay an extra week after the wedding, when all my friends will be heading back across the Atlantic. I'll carry him with me, in my head and in my heart.

Turning my back on the coffee machine, I lean

against the benchtop and savor my first mouthful of coffee, sighing around the creamy caffeinated drink.

'That's better. Let's get you ready and Newark Airport bound, lady,' I tell myself.

An hour later, my hair is washed, dried, and whipped into a loose chignon to fend off the static that always makes it go wild on a long-haul flight. I've bought a travel outfit specifically for the flight out: a wide-legged black jumpsuit, which looks smart but has the essential elasticated waistband I need to absorb the forty-thousand feet airplane bloat.

There have been many times in my life that I have resented the height I was born with – at nearly six feet tall and with a personal preference that women should always be taller than their male partners, it lessened the available partner pool significantly in my singleton days, pre-Danny – but today, my ability to pull off a wide-legged jumpsuit with comfy flats is undoubtedly a perk of being lanky.

I do a last check in my shoulder bag for my passport (tick), wallet (tick) and smartphone – on which I double check I have all necessary QR codes (tick). Then I re-check that I have removed all plugs from sockets in the apartment, with the exception of the refrigerator.

Finally, I drag all thirty-two kilos of suitcase (not a

gram of my luggage allowance wasted) into the elevator of my old townhouse-style apartment block, bump it down the ten concrete steps from the red-brick building and make it to the cobblestoned sidewalk.

Heading east onto West 14th Street, I raise a hand, still lugging the case, and watch a yellow cab swerve toward the sidewalk to pick me up. Feeling guilty after the driver near breaks his back lifting my luggage into the trunk, I decide not to complain when he forces it over the lip with a strong battering from his knee.

I let out a happy sigh as the cab heads toward New Jersey and Newark Airport, where I will be meeting the gang ahead of our flight. The seven of us – Drew and Becky, Brooks and Izzy, Jake and Jess, and I – haven't been together for more than a few hours since our mini-break in the Hamptons last summer.

We had been staying in Drew's beachside holiday home to celebrate his engagement to Becky, which was ultimately gatecrashed by Jake's realization that he was in love with Jess. With a little nudge from moi, he had accepted Jess wasn't just his flat mate, his best friend, or even his friend with benefits. Nope, she is his soulmate.

On arrival at Terminal B, I feel bad enough about

the weight of my luggage to tip the driver more than usual. I settle the fare using my smart watch, then hand him thirty dollars in notes.

I fluff the strands of hair I've left hanging loose to shape my face – which is akin to a basketball shape without framing – and, struggling into the terminal, I locate a screen to confirm my luggage check-in point. As I make for the drop-off, I'm surprised to see a twenty-year-old woman with a funky new haircut, wearing workout leggings and a top that exposes a toned but not-really-required-to-be-on-show midriff, charging toward me.

During breaks from college, Cady, Brooks's daughter, ordinarily lives with her mom, Brooks's ex-childhood sweetheart, but in recent times she has been spending increasing amounts of time with her dad and Izzy.

Cady's relationship with Brooks was rocky throughout her preadolescent and adolescent years, as she went through every phase a girl of her age goes through: from gothic to emo, from nerd to class clown, from stubborn tantrums to grown-up forgiveness. Brooks found those years difficult, partly because he recognized himself when he had been through some of those same phases.

Since meeting Izzy, though, he's reconciled his

relationship with Cady and she has become a huge fan of Izzy's, no doubt connecting over cool things that I don't understand like Instagram, TikTok and whatever the latest social media trends are now. Only a year ago, Cady hated the way her dad was constantly dressed in workout attire, often marked with his own branding: *BA* or *Brooks Adams*. But now, seemingly Cady's latest trend is to wear workout gear too, perhaps inspired by Brooks and Izzy, or more likely the front page of every magazine focused at young women and MTV viewers.

'Sarah, I'm so pleased you're here. Dad and Izzy are on one,' she says, rolling her eyes. 'Izzy took an eternity to get ready apparently, but you know what Dad's like, Mr Impatient. He probably packed seven pairs of boxer shorts, two gym kits to put on rotation, and by force of being a groomsman only, a shirt and suit. Anyway, we've only been here for ten minutes and already they're driving everyone mad. You'll calm everything down, I know you will.'

I'm very much aware of the fire between Izzy and Brooks, which they will doubtless resolve between the sheets once they've landed in London, if not the bathroom of the airplane.

I hug Cady, kissing her cropped, highlighted and spiked hair. 'I like the new look,' I say, more to be kind than because I think it's the best look for Cady. 'Why are you all still this side of security?'

I look over to the small Starbucks where everyone is sitting – Brooks, Izzy, Drew, Becky, Drew's parents, his sister Millie, her husband Eddie and their two young kids – surrounded by small cases and bags of hand luggage on the floor.

I can see from a distance that Drew is stressed and I hope it has nothing to do with the wedding or the trip.

'That's the next drama,' Cady says. 'Uncle Drew isn't coming.'

'What do you mean he isn't coming? Why?'

'Something to do with work. Some case and boxes of documents or something. Why don't you drop your bags and I'll get Dad to buy you a coffee, then you can find out for yourself?'

I smile. Cady will force Brooks to buy coffee and it hasn't even occurred to her that she could do so herself. *Ah, to be young and dependent.*

Something tells me, perhaps the look on Drew's face and the hand that he is currently dragging through his short hair, that I ought to find out what is going on before handing over my luggage to be Heathrow Airport bound.

My eyes connect with his as I am hugged and

welcomed by everyone else. I've worked for him long enough to know that, right now, there is something pressing he needs to do before he can go to London. When I finally get to hugging him, I ask quietly, 'How big is it?'

He presses his lips together and, once again, his hand goes to his hair: his stress tell.

'The other side in the Rolando case have made a last-minute disclosure. Turns out the damn thing is six boxes' worth.'

'Six boxes! That's not last minute, that's burying us in paperwork.'

'You don't need to tell me that,' he says. 'And you just know that the smoking gun we're looking for will be in one of those six boxes.'

'So what are we going to do?' I whisper, mindful of the others. 'Can't one of the associates or parale-gals go through the boxes for you?'

'You know I don't trust anyone to find this needle in a haystack. No one except you and me. I'm going to stay until I find that damn weapon, then I'll get a later flight out. I'll be in good time for the wedding. I'll hopefully sort this today and fly out tomorrow.'

'Jake's stag night is tomorrow,' I tell him, fully au fait with the week's schedule since I created it. 'You can't miss your brother's last hurrah.'

I look around at the faces of my nearest and dearest, and Drew's family, and there's no way I can let Drew stay back.

'I'll stay,' I say, trying to hide that my entire mood just deflated. I hold my shoulders upright and back and force a smile on my glossed lips. 'Like you say, it'll be a quick job, we'll find the weapon, settle the case, and I'll be on the next flight out to London.'

'I can't let you do that,' Drew says, though we both know that I will ultimately be the person staying behind.

I hold up one hand. *Stop. Wait.*

'You haven't heard my condition yet,' I say. 'The firm can bump me up to first class.'

I wink at him playfully but neither one of us believes for a second that I'm joking.

3

CHARLIE

There's sweat running down my chest, between my moobs, making a little puddle in my belly button, which is bedded into my ever-so-slightly-too-chubby beer belly. I have a dad bod but without having a kid to justify the look – unless a Peroni baby counts.

I am coming into the final five minutes of my set at the comedy club in Camden, which *Time Out* recently named in its top three comedy venues in London. My set has developed into its current form over a gestation period of nine months or so. I can therefore call it my comedy child.

But this child is still a new-born and my nerves reflect the infancy of my professional career. It has only been since the inception of this latest material that I have started being paid regularly for gigs. Though I have worked the comedy circuit – the dingiest, smelliest, stickiest, most questionable pubs and clubs – part time alongside a swathe of low-skilled and poor-paying jobs since dropping out of university a decade ago, it took the first nine years to hone my craft and establish myself sufficiently to warrant half-decent payment, and now I headline slots in some of the best comedy clubs in the city.

Despite this recognition that I have a modicum of talent, I still get nervous to the point of throwing-up before most of my gigs. Maybe years of rejection, imposter syndrome or my innate introvert (which I have the ability to hide well but which is ever-present) are to blame. I think of myself as a social extrovert. Sort of like a social smoker – I can perform for crowds, I can be the life and soul of a night out, but once the drinks stop flowing, so too does my habitual joviality.

Tonight, I hurled my guts up just minutes before coming on stage as the headline act – less fancy than it sounds on a Tuesday night, of course, but I have aspirations of headlining this particular venue in a weekend slot. One day, maybe even being invited on shows like *Mock the Week, 8 Out of Ten Cats, Never Mind the Buzzcocks*... One can dream.

What has raised the stakes for my slot tonight is

that one of my best mates, Jake, is sitting in the audience, admittedly well-leathered, with nine of his closest pals, which includes his brother and his dad, who are over from the USA for his wedding this coming weekend. It's his stag night and, though Jake left the organization of the day and night's pub crawl to his three ushers, one of whom is me, he had insisted on the night ending at my gig.

I've tinkered with my cracks tonight, tailoring them for the stags. So whilst I have been with the group since lunchtime today, I have paced my drinking, only *appearing* to drink in some of the pubs that formed the eighteen-hole 'pub golf course', to ensure I am the right level of drunk-enough-to-perform this amended set but not so drunk my performance is a damp squib.

I rub my hairy forearm across my forehead, collecting beads of sweat and wiping them down my signature Hawaiian stage shirt. Unusually, I am finishing my set largely off-the-cuff tonight.

'Ladies, gents, say hello to my mate Jake down on the heckling table at the front here. Cocks, by the way, the lot of you!'

I am pleased the rest of the table laugh along with Jake. The stag guys have been good sports all night, actually, which is a relief, as I am well aware that British humor often doesn't translate for an American audience. I always use Rebel Wilson at the BAFTAs in 2022 as a particularly disastrous example of comedians from different territories just not able to land their jokes. Those put-downs didn't pack any punch.

'It's Jake's stag night, folks, which means by tomorrow morning, we'll be able to congratulate his bride-to-be on her near miss.'

The crowd responds appropriately.

'After all, what is a stag if not a male mammal looking to buck a load of hinds and add to his harem?' I pull a face of surprise and clamp a hand over my mouth, then remove my palm and ask the audience rhetorically, 'Is that too much in this age of post-Me Too apocalypse? I'm looking specifically at one of Jake's mates here, who is built like an absolute brick shit house, covered in ink and, frankly, looks a bit unstable. Essentially, he looks like a US Marine.'

The guy, Brooks, takes it well.

'Have you ever noticed how the US Marines are so much bigger than our British Royal Marines? They're like Vikings to our garden gnomes.'

I take a strategic drink from my pint of beer, which I have placed on a small table nearby the X marking center stage, where I'm standing. I wait for the laughter and murmurings of the two hundred or so people in the crowd to subside.

'In all seriousness, which is what you've come here for tonight, right, seriousness? I have known Jake and his bride-to-be Jess for a while now, though seemingly not long enough to be invited to be his best man, which is why I'm having to deliver that speech to you all tonight to end my set.' More laughter. 'I love them both dearly but I have been questioning Jess's judgement of late, in particular since their engagement. I had always thought of her as a smart woman. Attractive and quirky in the best way. Now, I question how smart she is, having settled for the obvious choice. Six feet two inches of tall, broad, dark, handsome, well-paid, mildly amusing, athletic...

'Where was I? Oh yes, having chosen someone like Jake over someone...' I gesture to myself. 'Chubbier, quirkier, perhaps with a slightly receding hairline under sort of out of control, not wavy, not straight, strawberry blond locks, and about ten feet shorter. What was she thinking?'

The room is amused but nobody more so than the group sitting around Jake.

'This might be news to Jake but I did try it on with Jess once.'

The crowd gasp and 'ooh' playfully in participation, all well-humored, I think.

'I sidled up to Jess in a Soho bar and I delivered that line every woman wants to hear. "Is your father a thief? Because he stole the stars and put them in your eyes".' I take another strategic drink of beer. 'Unsmiling, Jess told me, "My dad died when I was a girl".' I pause, contorting my face in the way someone might after sucking on a lime – exaggerated for stage. 'You might call me Maverick, the way I spectacularly crashed and burned.'

As the room settles, and after one final swig of beer, I say, 'I wish Jake and Jess well and I wish you all well. You've been a wonderful crowd and now I can finally drink myself into oblivion with the rest of the stags.'

I finish the set the way I always do: by reaching for my acoustic guitar from where it is perched on a stand to one side of the stage. I start to sing, the way one might tell folklore around a campfire.

> *'Thank you all for coming out to Camden*
> *Lock,*
> *To see Charlie Cook's new show.*
> *I hope your assessment isn't that he's a*
> *ginormous cock,*

With as much talent as your big toe.

I've been writing comedy lyrics since I
    was a boy,
So I'm pleased I've gotten through a line
    or two.
Because my guitar was always my fa-
    vorite toy,
And you've not yet started to boo.

You've been a wonderful crowd,
You've made me feel paternalistic and
    proud.
And as a father figure, I'm allowed to give
    you gyp,
Unless you head up to the stage and leave
    me a tip.'

I take a bow, hold up a hand in a wave, and say, 'Goodnight.' Then I lift a tin can from the stage, on which I have painted the word *TIPS*, and jingle the ten or so two-pence pieces into the microphone, garnering my last laugh of the evening.

* * *

Having splashed my face with cold water in the toilets and swapped my shirt for an equally offensive but less sweaty version, I take a seat with Jake and the rest of the stag do. With an air of arrogance befitting of my on-stage persona, I accept the pats on the back in the actual and figurative sense, and other variations of congratulations on a good show.

Once the guys have resumed conversations, banter and pints, I make all the right noises and actions to appear part of the conversation, but in actual fact I am enjoying the quarter of an hour of calm in my own mind, recovering from the show.

I can only liken the way I feel after being on stage to coming around after fainting or allowing yourself to get so hungry, your body is energy-less. I feel weak and drained, sleepy, and I know from experience that I won't feel 100 per cent until I've slept it off.

Hearing my name being spoken drags me from where I've been staring without thought.

'Come again?' I say in Jake's direction, realizing that it was Jake who spoke to me.

'A shhhed...' Hiccup. 'Yourappy to pick sup Shh-harah from the airport tomorrow.' Hiccup.

Jake's exaggerated gestures, slightly wonky-looking facial expressions and very slurred speech make clear he is exactly as rat-arsed as a stag should be by this time of night. It isn't often that Jake is the most drunk of our group of friends in London but when he overdoes it, he goes from zero to sixty, from absolutely fine to melting into the furniture. That is the state of play tonight. Fortunately, I have spent enough drunken nights in Jake's company to understand every word he is saying.

'Yeah,' I tell him. 'Absolutely fine to pick up Sarah from the airport, buddy.'

Given the groomsmen who travelled over from America yesterday are yet to be fitted for their suits for the weekend, Jake has asked me if I can collect Sarah and drive her out to Surrey, where Jake's brother has hired a large house for Jake and Jess's American friends, plus me (flattered much!), in the run-up to the wedding.

Apparently, Sarah is tall, beautiful, funny and totally together. Why wouldn't I have offered to collect her? It's a no-brainer.

I feel, rather than see, the eyes of both Drew and Brooks boring into me and I know instinctively they would be like pit-bulls if I tried anything untoward with her.

The thing is, when people tell me not to do something, I am generally inclined to pursue that very thing.

4

SARAH

After another very sleepless night spent trying to find Drew's needle in a haystack (which had been buried in the final bundle of the final disclosure box, number six of six), I am regretting not having caught up on some sleep during the extremely early morning flight to London. Sluggishly, I collect my luggage from the arrivals carousel in Heathrow Airport.

It was after 11 p.m. Eastern time last night when I called Drew with the good news. He was still up and I could hear music in the background, albeit drunken renditions of well-known songs being played on the guitar by what sounded like a worse for wear Brooks and a very drunk Jake.

Drew's usual business calm was more business excitable as he gushed and told me what an amazing secretary I am... And an amazing woman and all the rest of the slurred compliments he had offered. Most importantly, he gave me the greenlight to book myself a fancy class ticket on the flight over to London.

I started out my swanky pants flight with a complimentary glass of champagne and soon found myself four glasses in, having eaten far too much overly salted and overly sweet (deliciously so) food, and watched three good movies in place of sleep.

So, whilst I might have enjoyed re-watching *Top Gun: Maverick* and *Where the Crawdads Sing*, and being glued to *Elvis* from my swish recliner seat, I do wish I had closed my eyes instead.

If there is one thing I am certain of receiving this coming week, it is late night, boozy renditions of Elvis's hit songs – obligatory amongst the group when we get together – most likely acapella from Jake. His rendition of 'Suspicious Minds' is a close second to the real thing, not least because it's hilarious. In fact, I am certain too that his version of 'Suspicious Minds' was what finally clinched the deal between him and Jess.

I yawn as I exit arrivals and look for an old Ford Fiesta in bottle green. Whilst I was adamant on the phone to Drew last night that I am more than capable of getting from Heathrow into London and then out to Surrey Hills myself, I can't deny how grateful I am to have a lift instead.

A man with slightly crazy, strawberry-blond hair and wearing an un-fancy jogging suit makes strides toward me from his Fiesta, which is blinking its hazard lights and parked on a wonky angle to the sidewalk.

I move in for a hug and air kisses (after all, I am in Europe).

But my friendly greeting is met with a less than gentlemanly 'Hi' grunted from the Englishman picking me up.

'You'll have to hurry,' he says, almost panicky. 'I'm parked illegally. This place is only for taxis and I'm not in the market for a fine.'

At least he took my bag, I think, as I drop my arms to my sides and follow him to the car.

'I'm Charlie,' the guy says eventually. He glances at me, then quickly gets back to focusing on the road ahead as he moves off in front of the arrivals traffic, receiving tooting horns from numerous cab drivers.

He wears the look of a mole as he grips the steering wheel with two hands and leans forward over it, approaching what I know from reading

British novels to be a roundabout. Afraid for my life, I close my eyes as Charlie pulls out in front of a car coming from his right, until I remember that Brits drive on the opposite side of the road to Americans and he is turning left, too, in the same direction of travel as the other car.

'Sorry,' Charlie says. 'I'm not one for talking and driving, especially at a roundabout. You might not appreciate me telling you this, but I don't drive very often. There's no need when you live in the city.'

'You know, I couldn't tell,' I say with sarcasm.

In truth, I don't often drive because there's no need in Manhattan either, and if you do drive, parking in the city is through-the-roof expensive. Yet, I drive enough to know that Charlie is an appalling driver.

'I'll hopefully get you there in one piece,' he says.

It's impossible to tell whether he is trying to be funny or whether I should really fear for my life.

It's very unlike me to find it difficult to make conversation or to struggle to get a read on someone's personality, but that is the case today. Perhaps tiredness is to blame, but for once I can't think of a single topic to bring up.

Thankfully, Charlie seems adept in making small talk, in that way actual cab drivers can.

'Good flight?' he asks.

'It was smooth and I watched some good movies.'

That could've led to a discussion about which movies, I think, but once again, a deafening silence descends in the car.

If my peripheral vision isn't playing tricks on me, I'm fairly sure Charlie makes a gun with his fingers and thumb and fires it at his temple.

This may be the longest drive of both our lives, especially at the snail's pace Charlie is driving.

I watch four minutes tick by on the old-style dashboard clock before Charlie says, 'I'm pleased to see you can get a good real fake in Manhattan.'

I have no idea what he's referring to and Charlie must realize because he feels the need to explain.

'Your luggage. Louis Vuitton, is it?' And he ends the insult with a wink.

I feel my lower jaw hang loose as I wonder whether this guy is entirely, or just partly, socially inept. Is he trying to be funny, maybe?

But then he adds, 'Is it from Turkey or China?' His face is deadpan.

Irritability and lack of sleep mean I am incapable of exercising the level of empathy I usually pride my-self on having for others. Unable to help myself snapping my next words, I tell him, 'My luggage came directly from Saks Fifth Avenue, thanks.'

I turn away from him, looking out of the passenger window as we drive onto a highway, which I remember has another name in England but what that is has escaped me. As we head down a ramp to merge into multiple lanes of fast-flowing traffic, I cast a glance over my right shoulder and see an oncoming truck with *Eddie Stobart* written on the front. Charlie apparently sees nothing coming and swings his wheel right.

I scream, gripping the edge of my seat, knuckles white, as Charlie lets out a yelp himself and swings the wheel back left. Only once he has indicated and moved into an open space on the highway do I release my hands, close my eyes and take a breath of relief.

If I were a cat, I would have just lost one of my nine lives for sure.

Now I know that Charlie isn't making jokes, he really can't drive, and he really does believe that the luggage I bought with my annual bonus last year is a real fake from eBay.

Surely this isn't the guy my best friends have spoken so highly of.

Surely this isn't the guy Jess said I would adore.

Thankfully, concentration, nerves or a combination of both render Charlie speechless. I rest my head against my seat and watch out of the window as roadside shrubs present as blurred green and brown lines and eventually fade to the darkness of my own eyelids.

* * *

The first thing I do on opening my eyes is check the clock on the dashboard. The second thing is to wipe my mouth, just in case, as I calculate that I have been in a doze for nearly fifteen minutes.

Charlie glances my way as I sit up straighter, smoothing my hair back into my hair tie. 'Enjoy that?'

'I'm so sorry,' I say. 'That's hardly in the passenger brief, falling asleep.'

For the first time since he uttered a crabby greeting at the airport, Charlie smiles. His lips gently turn up in a childish sort of grin, showing a nice set of nearly white teeth. The kind that suggests he enjoys a coffee, maybe a glass of red wine, and whilst keeping up his oral hygiene, isn't the kind of man to entertain cosmetic whitening.

He may be rude, slightly obnoxious and ill-humored, but he is clean and seemingly not into *fake*, the way too many people are in the times of the Kardashians. It turns out we have *one* thing in common.

'Where are we?' I ask.

'Not far now.'

The landscape changed whilst I was dreaming. Smooth, fast, endless tarmac has been replaced with bumpier, slower, narrower roads lined with trees, hedges and open planes.

In the distance, I see fields of crops being sprayed by farm vehicles. Birds are flying as the sun begins to lower but still shines brightly in the evening sky. Charlie has lowered the driver-side visor over his window and appears to have relaxed in his seat now that there are just two rows of traffic passing each other.

'You're from New York then?' he asks.

I steal myself from the serenity of the view and look at him. 'Born and bred. My mum is from Michigan actually and my dad Seattle, but they both ended up in New York for work, found each other and here I am.'

'And Jake tells me you're single.'

For the second time on this trip, my mouth opens in shock. Not only is Charlie socially inappropriate, but he is brazen with it.

'Single but unavailable,' I tell him, just in case I have misread the unfriendliness between us.

Charlie gives one firm nod, focusing intently on the road ahead, whilst I turn back to the scenery and appreciate the horses that are merrily grazing in a field we pass.

Charlie and I don't speak again until we're near our final destination and he pulls over. He reaches into the back pocket of his seat, pulling out a large book that says *A to Z Roadmap*. He squints like someone who needs reading glasses but isn't wearing them, and traces the tattered map with his index finger. Eventually, he replaces the book and drives on ahead in silence.

There is palpable relief from us both when we turn onto the long gravel driveway of the large country home our party has rented for the week.

5

SARAH

Three black Range Rovers, which I know to be rental cars because I made arrangements for them, are parked in the turning circle around a water feature in front of the house. The building looks like something out of a British period drama. The reason I booked the house (albeit paid for by Drew and sanctioned by Jake and Jess) is that it reminds me of something out of a Jane Austen novel, and what better time to appreciate a Jane Austen romance than at a wedding celebration?

A large oak tree, lush green, stands tall to one side of the property and a similarly bountiful willow tree stands to the opposite edge. Green ivy is growing up past Georgian sash windows on the ground floor and shaping Juliet balconies on the first floor, finally rounding off at the roof. Each balcony is decorated with flower boxes, which are in full bloom: mixed red, pink and purple trailing flowers.

It is idyllic and my satisfaction grows when the front door opens and Jess appears.

Everything about Jess is ethereal. Her long waves of dark hair are always clean but never blow dried to perfection. Her bohemian-style, Asian-inspired patterned dress – probably her own creation – seems to sway in a non-existent breeze, dreamlike, as she opens her arms and walks barefoot under the porch archway in my direction.

'I'm so happy to see you,' I say, stepping into Jess's hold. We hug for the first time in months.

'You're finally here! I hope the flight was okay and Charlie looked after you,' Jess says, casting her eyes, playfully questioning, in Charlie's direction.

I glance across my shoulder to Charlie, where he is taking my luggage out of the trunk of his car.

Perhaps my initial perception of him has been a little harsh.

On the journey here, I rehearsed asking Jess whether this is really the same Charlie she has spoken of on the phone to me, singing his praises.

But now that I'm here, I decide to simply smile obligingly and tell her, 'The perfect gentleman.'

'Good lad,' Jess says, light-heartedly patting Charlie on the shoulder as he kisses her cheek.

'Good day, ma'am,' he says, James Bond like. 'Good to see you. Is the big man inside?'

Jess nods and steps to the side. Charlie gestures for me to walk into the house ahead of him.

'Let's go and say hi to everyone, then I'll show you guys to your room,' Jess says.

The vestibule of the house has retained antique wood paneling and large, grey-beige slate tiles, which might be cold in winter but today are helping retain some cool in the unseasonable – even for July – summer heat. Craning my neck, I look up to see a large cast-iron chandelier, which I remember from my virtual tour of the property in advance of negotiating a deal for the wedding party.

'This place is sweet,' Charlie says as we step into one of four lounge-living spaces. He has left our luggage in the vestibule and turns in circles, unburdened, appreciating the space.

The ornate coving and ceiling artwork feel vintage but I can tell they have recently been painted white – the fresh paint smell still lingers subtly in the air. Two mocha-colored leather sofas and two tall, checked, wing-back chairs hold court in the space, each turned to face an extravagant open fireplace that would be wonderfully cozy and romantic on a cold winter's night. Cow-skin rugs cover large swathes of the dark wood flooring and stag antlers decorate alcoves either side of the fireplace.

'Fitting,' Charlie says, pointing out the deer décor.

I follow his pointed finger.

'They're stags,' he explains, as if I'm clueless. 'Jake's a stag,' he adds in a tone of voice that sounds like Homer Simpson: *doh*.

'I'm American, not stupid,' I snipe under my breath, thankfully quietly enough for Jess not to hear; unfortunately, not sufficiently quiet for Charlie to miss it, which I can tell from his smirking lips.

We follow Jess through a vast, modernized kitchen-dining space, which was presumably separate rooms at one time and now, with the use of archways and pillars beneath the tall ceilings, is open plan and twice the width of the large lounge area we have just left.

The kitchen, by contrast to the lounge, is bright and modern. High gloss white cupboards serve as a contrast to the shiny black tiles on the floor. An island I would aspire to own, with stools around all four sides and pans hanging like in a celebrity chef kitchen above the oven centerpiece, steals the show.

In the dining area of the space, there is a large wood table with two benches down the length of one long side and eight wood seats down the other side. The table has been set with crockery, cutlery and glasses. I suspect Becky will have taken the lead in dressing the table, knowing that I have arranged for outside caterers to provide a private dining experience for the group this evening.

Bi-folding glass doors lead out to pristine grey decking and before we head outside, I can already hear the animated chatter and laughter of my friends by the pool, buoying my mood further.

Jess, who is usually more reserved in expressing her excitement, announces to the group, 'The Matron of Honor has finally arrived!'

'And Sarah is here too,' Charlie adds with a grin.

Whilst he receives some chuckles from the others around the pool, most of whom stand to come over and welcome us, I find him utterly annoying.

Why does he feel the need to spoil the moment for Jess and me?

Brushing away thoughts of my irritating-as-hell ride from the airport (grateful that I no longer have to provide day-care services to a man-child who acts like a pre-pubescent teenager), I accept the warm embraces of Becky and Izzy, both wearing fancy two-piece swimwear. I squeal when Jake, fresh out of the pool, shakes his hair like a dog with wet fur in my direction, then hugs me, wetting through my lower half with his saturated swim shorts.

'You're trouble, Jake Harrington,' I tell him with a playful scowl, one hand perched on my hip.

Drew is next in line to give me a hug. 'I owe you one.'

'You do!' I say, giving him a mock look of disapproval. 'Just so you know, I like the new Lady D bag from Dior, in peony pink.'

I receive a thick chortle from Drew in return.

From his reclined position on a sun lounger, Brooks holds up a bottled light beer and says, 'We can finally get the party started. I'd get up, Sarah, but this hair of the dog hasn't kicked in just yet.'

'I take it the stag was a good night, then?'

'You need to get in the pool, buddy,' Jake says, leaving my side, tapping his brother on the shoulder and making his way with Drew toward Brooks.

I see it coming and I'm only surprised that Brooks doesn't – which shows how bad his hangover must be. Brooks yells as he is rolled off the edge of his sun lounger, crashing into the pool with an enormous splash, his beer and shades going in with him. When he resurfaces, he is guffawing.

This is what I've been so excited about coming into this week, perhaps even more so than the wedding itself. Time with my friends, together as a group – my favorite time in the world.

Amongst the melee, Edmond appears. Whilst not as old a friend as the others, Edmond – who by happy coincidence is the executive chef at a Michelin restaurant just a few blocks away from the law firm where I work – has become a fixture at gatherings of our tribe. He is the reason Becky moved to New York, transferring from his London restaurant to his Manhattan venture after the breakdown of her first marriage.

Edmond is five feet eleven but has a Mediterranean svelteness that makes him look taller. Much like his wife, Amy, who now rises from her rattan seat at a poolside table to greet me, Edmond is elegant and refined in that stereotypical way we expect of the French. Parisienne chic.

Whilst the others around the pool are lounging topless (the men) and in swimwear (the women), Edmond is wearing a white T-shirt with Bermuda-style shorts and Amy wears a chic kimono over a one-piece, a large wide-brim hat and Chanel cat-eye shades.

After saying their *bonjours* and *saluts*, Edmond and Amy resume their positions at the table, both sipping blush under the cover of a parasol.

'I have anticipated an extra glass,' Edmond says with his French-American lilt, his native tongue mixed with years of New York twang. He fills a wine glass with blush as he speaks, then holds up a second empty glass and asks Charlie, 'Will you join us?'

Charlie makes a show of looking at the watch on his wrist. 'Well, the sun is over the yard's arm. Go on then, Eddie.'

Eddie? Yard's arm what now?

Rolling my eyes behind my tinted glasses, I make my way to the table, trying not to get splashed as Brooks pops up on his arms and leaps out of the pool in one easy, smooth move.

'Ah, this must be the infamous Sarah we've heard so much about.'

The owner of the voice I don't recognize comes walking out of the house through the bi-folding doors behind me, causing me to turn and be confronted with what I can only describe as a very beautiful specimen.

A new person.

I beam as I hold out my hand, shamelessly en-joying the view of the man's deliciously dark skin, kind teddy-bear eyes and, yes, his toned body that could rival that of Brooks. I am pleased for the covers over my eyes and only hope they disguise my ogling.

'All good, I hope,' I say, finishing with a reflexive giggle that I recognize from my hormonal teenage years.

'In all the right places,' the man says with a smile, revealing perfect, *perfect* teeth. 'I'm Cash.' He twists toward the door, where another very attractive man is stepping onto the decking. 'And this is Will.'

Will is also tall but much less buff and heads over to us holding two flutes of something bubbly. He hands off one glass to Cash.

Ah, I think. *The best ones are always gay.*

'I'm Sarah,' I say with a smile. 'It's a pleasure to meet you.'

'It's all ours,' Will says, leaning in to kiss my cheek, smelling divine.

As I take my seat at the poolside table, I accept the glass of blush from Edmond, pleased that Charlie takes his glass and goes to sit on the end of Jake's sun lounger, rather than sitting at the table. I hum my appreciation of the wine and the situation.

From my seat, I cast my gaze across fields of green

surrounding the property, which lead to hillsides of vines. This has been a great choice of accommodation, but mostly I'm grateful to be with my best friends, and thankful that there are no available, single men in the vicinity to distract me. Well, there is Charlie but he is possibly the last man on earth with whom I could ever imagine a romance (I think this in the voice of Colin Firth as Mr Darcy because it's befitting of the theme of the week).

I sit there for less than five minutes before I ask the group, 'Did the online shopping arrive? Does everyone have a drink? Should I make us some plates of snacks and nibbles?'

6

CHARLIE

She never sits down. She's like a blue bottle, buzzing around noisily *all* the time. Okay, not a blue bottle, more like a ladybird or something prettier still – a butterfly, perhaps. But all that fluttering *does* get annoying. Moreover, it's distracting. She makes me lose my train of thought, stops me from being able to hold a conversation. So much so, I have decided to take up a spot reclining on a lounger and pretend to sleep.

She finally stops bringing people refills and topping up bowls of snacks. There are pretzels, 'chips' of the crisp variety, hummus and veggie sticks, cheese, all kinds around the pool edge. Jake, Brooks, Drew, Izzy and Cash are lazily drifting around on inflatables – a crocodile, a flamingo, a unicorn and two Lilos, apparently all purchased and delivered ahead of time by none other than the Matron of Honor.

It is irritating me that I'm irritated, making me massively irritated that no one is stopping this incessant display of fussing. I want to yell at the group, *Get your own drinks*. Sarah reminds me of my first ever foster mother, who could never do enough for the tribe of foster kids she had, who could never do enough for her biological kids, and who was never stopped or assisted or just told to slow down by her husband.

Barbara was my preferred carer in the long line of foster carers and foster homes I went through as a kid. Before my parents adopted me in my mid-teens, Barbara had been my longest reigning temporary mother. She had provided a warm, welcoming home for me for two years, two birthdays, from ages six to eight years old. She was the only carer I had ever called Mum, before my adoption. The only one who wasn't just in it for the money. The first and last of them who seemed to really give a toss about me. But ultimately, she had let me go, too.

I waited another seven long years and nine more carers before I found someone who genuinely wanted to do good by me, and that was my adoptive parents, who took me in alongside their own son and daughter.

It has been a long time since I've thought about that first family. It's only now, as an adult, that I appreciate them and realize how grateful I should have been at the time, rather than the cheeky shit I was. But I was a child, a small child, and all I had wanted at that stage was to be back living in squalor with my addict birth mother.

I squeeze my eyes tightly behind my sunglasses, wishing I was truly sleeping so that my ill-temper would dissipate. I hope I won't spend the entire week watching Sarah be so bloody accommodating that it's the equivalent of listening to a teacher dragging her nails down a blackboard.

But there it is again: her unmistakable laughter. It's big and bright, innocent and silly, and it takes all my strength not to give the game away with a smile. The sound of Sarah's laughter is like the sun in the summer sky when it's raining, the finest pink rose in the garden which is forbidden, the last piece of chocolate cake in the café when it's closed. I'm not much of a poet but suffice to say, it is a nice laugh. I like hearing it, even though the owner increasingly grates on my nerves.

Alanis Morrissette's 'Ironic' comes into my head

and I start to sing the lines in my mind. I don't realize I am wiggling my toes to the beat until Jess is standing at the bottom of my sun lounger, casting a shadow over me.

'You're awake! Great. Shall I show you to your room now?'

I pretend to wipe slaver from my chin. *Why?* I'm not sure. I'm not sure why anyone would *fake* having drooled down their face, but I do and I watch as Sarah's expression twists into disgust watching me do so. As if she's so perfect. Didn't she slobber down her chops in my car?

'Yeah, grand,' I say, having forgotten entirely that my small weekend bag and Sarah's beast-sized designer luggage are still where I left them in the vestibule.

* * *

'You don't have to carry those,' Sarah says as I grunt my way up the staircase, laden like a working donkey.

One heave-ho at a time, I think of a gag for a show...

'Have you ever noticed how women never really mean it when they say "you really don't have to", all doe-eyed and beautiful? I mean, imagine if I stopped mid-staircase and said, "Actually, darlin', here's your luggage, carry it yourself," and handed over the Louis Vuitton suitcase that the airline had dubbed *heavy baggage*.'

Clearly, I haven't just *thought* of that joke, I have accidentally uttered it aloud, because Jess, who is walking ahead of me, hears me and chuckles. Sarah, by contrast, draws her head back into her shoulders and looks like a puppy has just taken a dump in her mouth.

It is true, see... British jokes so often don't land with our neighbors from across the pond. Nevertheless, I am too grouchy and breathless to apologize. And so, I lug on like a Sherpa until Jess stops on the landing outside the first white wood door we come to.

I have known Jess long enough and know her well enough to recognize her sudden sheepishness, to read her fidgeting of her own hands, and to know she feels awkward.

'I have a small confession,' she says, glancing to Sarah, then firmly planting her focus on her own feet. 'Last night, on his stag-do, well, Jake was drunk and he sort of asked Cash and Will to be ushers at the wedding.'

'Another two? Christ, I really mean nothing to him, do I?' I say, dropping the luggage to my sides dramatically.

Jess smiles, then chews one side of her mouth, which is another of her awkward tells. As an aside, Jess really is a shocking poker player, though her honesty is, incidentally, one of the things I respect most about her.

'Obviously everyone else in the bridal party is staying in this house and now Cash is part of the bridal party and—'

'There aren't enough rooms for Charlie and me to have one each,' Sarah says with a look of sheer terror on her face, as if *Beetlejuice* met *Scream* in a dimly lit alleyway.

I'd be Beetlejuice, I think, kind of cool in a badass way, though with sort of mad hair and questionable dress sense.

Jess bites her lip and shakes her head. 'But... There's a gorgeous big king bed in this room and a very comfy looking double sofa-bed.'

'Bagsy the king,' I say, relishing Sarah's attempt at a *subtle* gasp. 'I carried the luggage,' I add, straight faced, meeting her eye for added fun, knowing full well that I will never ask a woman to take the sofa bed.

To my surprise, Sarah's face turns into a beaming smile as she places a hand on Jess's shoulder. 'Hey, don't worry about it. This is Jake, I should have foreseen something like this happening. Charlie and I will be fine sharing, won't we, Charlie?'

I want to laugh so much, it is physically hurting my internal organs. 'Yeah, great. I hope there's an en-suite we can share, too.'

Garghhh, I'm dying. This is hilarious.

'Oh, yeah,' Jess says, missing entirely the way Sarah's shoulders have risen to her ears and her hands are balled into fists at her sides. 'It's gorgeous, too, come and see.'

'After you,' I tell Sarah, failing to suppress a smirk.

I set down our luggage inside the door. If this was a BnB, and Sarah and I were dating, the room would be just the ticket. It is like it's out of a brochure for the world's top ten most romantic breaks. It is unfortunate then that I'll be sharing it with someone who seems to hate my guts.

One feature wall has birdcages on the wallpaper, and when I run my fingers across it, I realize it is velour. The bed is not just a large king, it is a swish four post bed, which would be ideal if this was *Fifty Shades of Grey* and I had a six-pack and could lift my legs in a straight line whilst balancing on a pommel horse.

I watch as Sarah absorbs the details of the room. If she wasn't already livid at the idea of sharing, she really will be at the sight of the red velvet chaise longue sitting beneath one of three Georgian sash windows. Especially so when she realizes that the ensuite is not a small room off to one side, but an area visible through an archway. In the center of the archway, acting as a feature, there is a freestanding cast-iron bathtub. I laugh out loud.

'This is brilliant,' I whisper, though not quietly enough, receiving a thump on my arm from Jess. 'Ouch!'

Sarah clears her throat, her face placid now. 'It's a beautiful room.'

'It really is,' Jess says, rightly nervous.

Resting my hand on Sarah's shoulder, I ask, 'Shall we draw straws for the bed?'

Sarah moves her gaze from my face to my hand on her shoulder, then flicks off my touch, the way she might flick bird shit off her clothes.

'And don't worry about the bath,' I add. 'I've brought an eye mask for sleeping, which I can wear when you bathe. It only covers one eye but I can do a long wink with the other one.'

I can tell Jess is holding in her amusement. 'I'll leave you guys to it,' she says, making a swift exit from the room and closing the door behind her.

The whole time, Sarah smiles like a Cheshire cat, not at all displaying the true level of her vexation.

When we hear Jess descend the stairs, Sarah asks, 'What will we use as makeshift straws?'

She's cracking me up. She's totally livid.

'Don't worry,' I tell her. 'You can take the bed. Chivalry isn't entirely dead.'

'That's surprisingly decent of you, thank you. As for the bathtub, there'll be no one-eyed-peeping-Toms; I'll ask one of the girls if I can use their shower. But you should feel free to have a soak; just be mindful that I don't have any eyepatches.'

She winks, and I have to hand it to her: that was genuinely quite funny. At least there is one effective comedian between us because she clearly doesn't find me entertaining in the slightest.

We unpack in silence, which for me takes less than five minutes – the length of time it takes me to put one pair of shorts, one pair of trousers, a pair of jeans, a pair of lounge bottoms, some underwear, a few tops and a shirt into a drawer. Sarah has kindly (sarcasm intended) allocated to me the smallest drawer of five in a chest, whilst she has commandeered the other four and spread her clothes, it seems, into categories of casual wear, pool wear, fancy stuff and, I assume in the smallest drawer, her underwear.

I try not to speculate what she might wear beneath her clothes, but testosterone is testosterone and I can't help wondering if she is a silk lady or a lace lady.

I also know that my imagination is the closest I'll ever come to finding out.

I spend most of the time we are in the room together making up the sofa bed. It's comfy enough, I suppose. I have certainly slept in worse places in my time, from sprung mattresses and sometimes floors during my foster days to sofa surfing when I first moved to the city.

After my show last night and a day spent so far in the company of others, all whilst nursing a mild but present hangover, all I want to do is lie on the sofa bed for an hour and close my eyes. Not necessarily to sleep but just to have a moment to myself, without having to speak to or entertain anyone else. A chance to drop my extrovert façade.

I'm pleased when Sarah, with her arms full of garments and one of the four towels that have been rolled into a sausage shape and placed on the bottom of the bed, tells me she is going to take a shower.

'I need to wash off that airplane grime and get ready for dinner. The catering company will be here in an hour and I'd like to make sure everything is to plan whilst the others are getting ready.'

'God,' I say with exasperation. 'All you've done since we arrived is run around after the others. Don't you need a rest?'

With a look of scorn that I have to admit looks good on her, Sarah places one hand on her hip and tells me in the way a school teacher might address a pupil, 'I like helping others. Jake and Jess are my friends and I want this week to be as perfect as it can be for them. If arranging and overseeing the catering team helps them create special memories together, then yes, I'm very happy to run around after people.' She makes for the door and, placing her hand on the handle, swings back around to face me. '*Some* people. *Grateful* people.'

With that, she leaves the room and the door slowly closes behind her, slow enough for me to hear her clearly when she says, 'I'm assuming you take no time at all to get ready and I'll have the room to myself when I come back from the shower.'

It isn't a question.

The thing about me is, I don't take orders well. Never have. Especially from those who I know will be temporary features in my life. And tonight, I'm feeling increasingly agitated. Agitation, unfortunately for Sarah, usually makes me act out.

7

SARAH

Gosh, I needed that shower. Finally free of the grime of travelling and cleansed of my increasing levels of irritability, I pad barefoot across the landing from Drew and Becky's room, carrying the clothes I have changed out of. My Japanese-style silk kimono is wrapped around my body, and I've twisted a towel around my wet hair.

There are oil paintings lining the ivory-painted walls, each depicting a British countryside scene. The one that grabs my attention most shows a field of golden haybales, the sky clear and bright blue in the background. A young girl wearing red dungarees and a red and white checked shirt has her back to the painter. Her long blonde hair hangs down to her sacrum and on top of her head is a red bow, tied with ribbon.

I begin to hum the tune to 'Fields of Gold' – Eva Cassidy's version.

I know I'm in much brighter spirits now because I always hum, sing or whistle when I'm in a good mood, like a reflexive reaction to happiness. I'm still humming as I place my hand on the handle of my bedroom door, noticing that I am building an appetite for the fancy dinner I've organized to start in a couple of hours' time.

Reaching the chorus, I open the bedroom door and am struck by the scent of what I think is black pepper and ginseng body wash. It's a scent my husband used to wash with in the shower.

Holding my blink longer than usual, I inhale deeply. When I open my eyes...

I scream at the sight of a naked man lying, unashamedly, in the fancy bathtub that is a focal point of the room.

'What the actual fuck is happening?' I shriek like a banshee.

'I'm taking a bath, what does it look like?' There is a ghost of amused arrogance around Charlie's lips and a glint of mischievousness in his eyes, both of which add fuel to the fire that is already raging inside me.

'Naked? In all your glory? In our shared tub? What are you, some kind of exhibitionist?'

I don't mean to look but it's impossible not to notice his man-piece under the clear water. It's not bad, actually. Unexpectedly neat and tidy. Perfectly adequate. Not too large, not too small.

Sarah, stop! Not the point here.

'There were strategically placed bubbles covering my important parts but you spent so long contributing to the world's water shortage that they've dispersed.'

I open my mouth to protest but it did occur to me whilst I was in the shower that I was using too much water. That said... 'And how much water do you think *you're* wasting by lying in a bathtub purely out of spite?'

'It hasn't escaped my attention that you've looked at my – how did you put it? – glorious member,' Charlie says, dismissing my retort entirely.

'I didn't!'

'Yes, you did. But not to worry, I'm looking forward to getting my own back.'

'Getting your own back? There's no way you're going to see my important parts, ever!'

'We've all seen that episode of *Friends*. "The One with the Boobies". You know, the one where Chandler walks in on Rachel in the shower and sees—'

I hold up my hand in a bid to stop his relentless ramblings. Of course I have seen that episode. *Friends* is one of my favorite sitcoms. A classic. But I am not in the mood to enter into a conversation about that now.

'*Friends* is a sitcom in which scenes are scripted for comedic effect.'

Charlie raises his arms out of the water, drips landing all over the grey tiled floor. 'And I'm a comedian,' he says.

'Really?'

Fascinating.

I had pictured him as some kind of annoying tech guy, like those in the law firm I work for. The kind who don't get out much, make bad jokes to attract attention, and tend to dip their hand in the candy drawer too often.

'Well, there's nothing funny about this.'

I turn on my heels to storm away but with my back to Charlie, I realize I have nowhere to go. This is our room. *Jointly. Together. Urghhhhh!*

'How long will you be?' I snap. 'I need to blow-dry my hair and make sure all the arrangements are in place for dinner.'

'More jobs for Sarah. Tell me, do you take on the role of chief organizer because you want to or because you're addicted to people pleasing?'

Who is this guy?

I like organizing. I love my friends. I want to do things to make them happy. They'd do the same for me, in a heartbeat. I know they would.

'Could you just... hurry up!'

'Will do.' He reaches for his phone, which he has placed on a stool on top of a towel at the head of the bathtub. He presses play and a voice I don't recognize begins to sing what is admittedly an attractive melody. Then he lies his head back against the end of the tub and closes his eyes, with a look on his face that's so smug, a person of violent tendencies might fill a bucket with his dirty tub water and empty it right across his floppy hair.

Lucky for Charlie, I am not a person of such tendencies, but what I do do is take out my hairdryer, locate the plug socket nearest the bathtub, and turn the noise-maker on full power.

'Sorry, I hope you can still hear your tunes,' I say pathetically sweetly through the most disingenuous smile I can muster.

I miss his next – doubtless choice – words. As I tip my head upside down to dry my stubborn, thick hair, I shout, 'P.S. When a grown man uses the word "boobies", it's all kinds of ick.'

He leans over the edge of the bathtub, closer to me. 'Yeah, well, P.S. stands for postscript. When people use it in speech, it sounds all kinds of idiotic.'

I close my eyes and grin, delighting in the fact that I have rattled him, at last, and that his mock take on an American accent is utter trash.

* * *

With the room to myself, finally, I slip into a pink and purple snake-print maxi dress. I always feel nice in this dress. The A-line cut accentuates my height, which is the one thing about myself I have grown to appreciate in my thirties. Like most women, there isn't a lot about my appearance I can say I love, or even like a lot, so to find clothes that make me feel good is a treat. And this dress has been worn rarely, on holidays only.

After speaking with the catering team, I have left them to do their thing in the large kitchen and as I make my way out to the rear decking, I'm ruminating on when I last wore this dress.

Stepping outside, I see the backs of all the men in the house, watching the sun begin its descent behind the distant hillside, all wearing various iterations of a Bermuda shorts and shirt combo. And it comes to me, watching the guys lean across the glass panes of the fencing around the deck: the last time I wore this dress I was on a Caribbean cruise with Danny. It had turned out to be our last holiday before he died.

I look at the sun now, spots dazzling my vision despite my shades, and I remember how Danny had stood behind me on our cabin balcony, his arms around my waist, his chin on my shoulder. We stood like that as we watched the setting sun, St Kitts in the foreground.

'Here she is, guys,' Jake says, stealing my attention. 'Hide your members.'

I scowl. 'It's not funny, Jake.'

'Ah come on, Sarah.' He laughs as he makes his way over to me and hangs an arm around my shoulder. 'It's no more than Brooks would have done to Izzy or I would have done to Jess.'

I pinch Jake's chin between my index finger and thumb, ignoring Charlie in my peripheral vision, his back now to the sun as he watches the interchange play out.

'You are *marrying* Jess. I have zero interest in seeing Charlie's member.'

'That's not the story we heard,' Brooks says, his shoulders chugging on a laugh.

'Ignore them, Sarah, they're so grim,' Cady says.

Cady has spent the day with Drew's family – his parents, sister, brother-in-law and their young kids. She has got into photography whilst studying at college and now loves a scenic daytrip – far from the girl who Brooks was having to rescue from house parties, completely inebriated, at eighteen.

Cady is staying in the house with us – and has a room to herself – but sadly it's the smallest room, with one single bed, otherwise I'd be jumping in with her instead of Charlie. The rest of Drew's family are staying in a nearby guest house and partaking in some of the plans I have made for the group throughout the week. Millie and Eddie decided their kids are too young to enjoy our plans in the house, telling me, 'The little pickles are feral; they'll get under everyone's feet and on everyone's nerves.' So I arranged the guest house for them, and Drew's parents said they would prefer to stay there to help Millie.

'You're back,' I say to Cady. 'How was your day?'

'Beautiful.'

'It really was,' Drew's mum adds, who's sitting with his dad at a poolside table, and, I notice, is drinking a martini. *Classy.* 'Thank you for organizing the day for us.'

For some reason, before I say, 'You're all *so* welcome,' I glance at Charlie, who shakes his head, bottle of beer to his lips.

Okay, I planned something else for someone else, I get it. But they *do* appreciate it, as I said they would. So, it's my win, not his.

'Would you ever consider life photography, Cady? Charlie over there is quite the exhibitionist!' I say, tongue-in-cheek.

The men laugh.

'Would you photograph me like one of your French boys, Cady?' Charlie jokes, getting a bigger laugh. *Damn.*

'I have zero idea what's going on here, but you're all being weird,' Cady says. 'I will absolutely not photograph you, French-style or otherwise, and I'm going to sit myself back over there with the grown-ups.'

'Not to side with the men...' Izzy's voice comes from behind me as she steps outside onto the deck, 'but they're right. Brooks would pull that prank on me.' She leans into my ear and whispers, 'Have you considered that Charlie maybe has a *thing* for you?'

I almost choke on air. 'Unlikely! He hates me.'

'Like people who hate each other don't learn to love each other,' she adds, raising her eyebrows.

It's true. Brooks and Izzy had been hate at first sight. Until they weren't.

'Fine. But I seriously dislike him, too. Oh, don't tell Jess or Jake, though. I don't want them to worry about the room situation, or anything else for that matter.'

Izzy draws closed an imaginary zip across her lips. 'Your secret is safe with me.'

One of the catering staff approaches us with a mango daquiri for Izzy and a Long Island Iced Tea for me. We take our drinks from the waiter's tray and head over to the guys.

Izzy slips into the line next to Brooks and receives a kiss on her temple. I wiggle into a space next to Jake, who nudges his hip into mine and clinks his bottle of beer against my cocktail glass.

'So, what's going on over here in the boys' club?' I ask.

'Well, I didn't want to ruin the surprise for anyone else either but I'm currently pondering how in the hell I'm supposed to find time to go into London to get Jess's wedding present without her knowing that I'm getting her wedding present.' Jake leans forward and rests his elbows on the rail. 'You know Jess; she doesn't want any fuss. I had to convince her to have something bigger than a registry office for our wedding. But we agreed no wedding gifts.'

'Usually, I'd go all girls' club on you, Jake, but I am with you. I think that girl deserves a wedding gift. But why on earth have you left it until three days before the wedding to collect it?'

'You wouldn't believe the lengths I've had to go to to get this.'

'Tell her what it is,' Drew says. 'Sarah will love it.'

Jake swigs from his bottle and sniggers. 'You know the only thing she loves more than Elvis himself is me impersonating Elvis. But not just any Elvis. She really gets off on that leather pant suit from his nineteen sixty-nine comeback. You know the one?'

I fan myself with my hand. 'Show me a woman who doesn't.'

'See! So tell me why no costume shop wants to give me Elvis's suit from his comeback show! They all want to give me the white Vegas jumpsuit. Anyway, I've managed to track one down. It was already on loan to an impersonator for the whole of summer, so

I had to get in touch with him personally and make a whole load of deals with him to get it. He's only just agreed that I can borrow it for the wedding and now I've got no time to get into the city unless I cancel on something we already have planned. In which case, I'll have to give Jess an excuse as to why I'm cancelling. I'm already having to sneak some time in with Izzy because she's choreographing some moves for me. And Jess knows me far too well to believe any bullshit I spin.'

'Can't you just get up early and go first thing?' Charlie asks.

I shake my head. 'No, tomorrow he has breakfast at a vineyard with Jess's aunt and uncle and his parents. It's the first meeting of the families; he can't cancel. On Thursday, he has a hot air balloon champagne breakfast with Jess, their last alone time before the big day. And on Friday morning, you guys all have your final fitting for your suits, and given they've only been altered this week, it has to be first thing so there's time to adjust them again during the day if needs be.'

'Naturally, you know his entire schedule,' Charlie mutters. I try to ignore his unhelpful sarcasm and think of a solution to the real problem at hand.

'I'll go,' I say in a snap decision. 'I'm the only

person who can be free without Jess thinking it's a big deal. I can tell her I'm dealing with florists or catering or something. And I don't have the family piece to juggle. Plus, I've taken next week as vacation, too, so I can run myself ragged this week if needs be.'

I can feel rather than see Charlie's eyes boring holes in me.

Why should it bother me? Why does he care? Yet, it does bother me. It annoys me, actually.

'How do I get to London from here?' I ask Jake.

Leaning further forward on the rail so that he's looking around me and in Charlie's direction, he says, 'What do you say, Charlie? Can you give her a ride?'

'What is it worth?'

I look between the two of them.

'How about a free meal and booze on Saturday?' Jake says, much to Charlie's amusement.

Charlie looks from Jake to me. 'I have a gig tomorrow night in London. I'm driving into the city for it. We can leave earlier and pick up the suit but you'll have to either come to my gig or occupy yourself until I'm done.'

I force a smile. *It's for Jake and Jess*, I tell myself. Then through gritted teeth, I say, 'That would be great, thanks.'

Charlie snorts – *ick* – and is still snickering when Jess and Becky come out of the house, Jess floating like an angel in a long white dress, which would have looked hippy on someone else but on Jess looks like a television advert for a luxury resort in the Seychelles.

'Here she is, the love of my life!' Jake announces.

Jess rolls her eyes and accepts a cocktail from one of the wait staff before coming to join us.

The pre-dinner cocktails are subsequently un-eventful, the usual fun that we always have as a group together. I make sure to integrate Drew's parents and his sister's family when they arrive, as well as our new friends, as much as possible, circling the decking to chat with everyone.

At 8.59 p.m., pleased that a shower and a couple of sugary cocktails have lifted my travel weariness, I check my watch. I built in time for us to enjoy the sunset and dinner should be served promptly at—

'Ladies and gentlemen, if you would like to make your way into the dining room, the chef is about to serve your amuse bouche.'

Nine o'clock. Punctual is exactly how I like people when I'm running to a timetable.

We follow the waitress into the dining room, with me last to leave the decking. As I do, I notice an en-tirely untouched Manhattan cocktail on one of the side tables. Only Becky has been drinking Manhattan cocktails and it is not like her to leave a full drink.

Ruminating as to why Becky might have sneakily left her drink, I follow the others inside to the dinner table.

I'd decided not to go so far as to prepare a seating plan for dinner but I'm pleased to find myself wedged between Becky to my left and Cady to my right. Happily at the opposite end of the table to Charlie.

Finally, I have some breathing space from that man.

I decide to blank any thought of him and the trip I will have to endure with him tomorrow.

The dinner has been paired with matching wines, and an English sparkling rosé from Surrey Downs is presented to the table by the sommelier to accompany our amuse bouche.

When the waiter comes to pour for Becky, I detect nervousness from her. She asks for a small pour.

And a figurative light bulb is switched on above my head...

This is going to be a long old meal if Becky is going to try to conceal the fact she isn't drinking alcohol for the entire night.

I subtly shift my glass from the right side of my place sitting to the left, where it is now right next to Becky's. Looking my friend in the eye, I take a sip from her half-full glass, then one from my own.

I also realize that I'm going to have a humongous hangover if I help Becky keep up this pretense all night. But if I am right, the reason behind this sudden turn of events will be worth it less than nine months from now.

8

CHARLIE

Sarah is definitely drinking for two. I have been watching her surreptitiously (I hope) and every time a new wine is presented by the sommelier, she drinks from her own glass first and then from Becky's. I respect whatever loyalty she is showing to her friend in helping to keep up a smokescreen, but in my opinion Sarah is either incredibly brave or incredibly stupid. This is a six-course tasting menu and the fine-dining courses are far from the size of the pub grub plates I'm used to eating – the kind that soak up liquor.

Still, she seems relaxed, at last. Her true smile, I have noticed, is wide and lights up her entire face, making it sparkle. And her authentic laughter is contagious – loud but feminine, even though I have twice caught her covering a snort with the tips of her fingers, which only made her laugh harder each time.

Perhaps I've been wrong about her – partially. She is *definitely* a people pleaser. Obsessively so. But maybe I have been wrong to think she is taken for granted. It seems like every person at the table adores her.

Maybe her brusqueness with me is more of a reflection of my behavior and my failings. Very possible. I do tend to rub people up the wrong way. Hell, I aggravate myself half the time.

I'm almost jealous of Sarah's likeability.

I have always had to work hard to gain friends and even harder to keep them. For anyone in my life to like me enough to keep me around, for that matter. Some things never change.

But in honesty, I'm not sure what I have done to alienate Sarah so badly already.

I take a sip of the Sancerre to my right.

Okay, maybe the naked tub joke was a bridge too far. But come on, it *was* funny.

I chuckle into my glass.

I was chatting with Jake and Cash when we were called inside to be seated for dinner, so happily, while I have engaged in banter from around the table, I have spent most of the time conversing with my bud-dies. They know me well enough and me them that I haven't had to perform for the last two hours, which is a welcome relief.

The number of people staying in the house and the back-to-back socializing is starting to drain my energy. And thanks to The King himself, my respite time tomorrow – a nice long drive into London and back with only music for company – has been com-mandeered by Sarah.

The pouring of dessert wine signals the end of our meal and I am truly devastated. I'm still waiting to feel full and satisfied.

Why people are willing to pay a fortune for a ball of foam on a tiny plate is beyond my comprehension. *Foam. Is. Not. Food. It's air!*

With a bit of luck, Edmond might have left some of his fancy bread in the kitchen that I can seek out for a midnight binge.

I'm also devastated because my relative peace sit-ting next to my friends is about to be shattered by a group game of charades.

Organized fun... The absolute bliss of it... Said no one ever!

In what seems to be her obsessive style, Sarah has already divided the group into four teams. Probably a good thing, I think, as I watch her rise unsteadily from the table and undertake an almost graceful wobble into the living room.

The couples in the group – which is basically everyone except Sarah, Brooks's daughter and me – have been separated. I've been teamed with Jess, Drew's sister Millie, Drew, Edmond's wife, Amy, and Sarah.

We might as well consider ourselves one very tipsy teammate down.

Our four teams are sitting around two sofas and two large armchairs, utilizing ottomans and the floor for extra seating. In the middle of the room, covering an attractive but pointless wood-burner, is an art easel – I truly hope we aren't playing Pictionary, too.

I still can't quite believe I've been forced into a dress code for the evening and want badly to ditch my buttoned bottoms and shirt for an elasticated waistband and one of my Marvel comic T-shirts.

The waitstaff bring around espresso martinis for everyone – regardless of whether people would have preferred a straightforward beer from a bottle. Jake's parents excuse themselves (and carry out Millie's sleeping kids, who, on grounds of being asleep, behaved impeccably well through dinner) when their pre-booked taxi arrives to take them to their nearby guest house. Foresight at its best! I bet they have a stash of sandwiches and crisps there, too.

The rest of the group oblige by taking a martini – all except Izzy, who declares herself too boozy from dinner already, and Becky, whom my spidey senses tell me is pregnant. I'm not the most astute man in the world but there is only one reason to my mind that a woman who was drinking hours before is no longer touching a drop.

A braver man than me might have suggested to Sarah that she oughtn't have a martini, but she takes her drink from a tray, declaring, 'Just the one.'

That one turns into a second as we watch the first two teams make an appallingly bad effort at charades.

We're up...

Sarah holds up her hand like Hermione Granger bursting to recite a mind-boggling spell in class.

'I'm a guesser, it's my thing.'

'Charlie should be the actor,' Jess says. 'What?' she asks, disingenuously innocent as she sees my thunderous expression and giggles in that way she does when she's tipsy. 'You're used to being on stage, especially now you've hit the big time.'

She giggles again, making it impossible for me to be mad at her.

Performing for the group is the last thing I feel like doing, but I can't say that and spoil the joviality so I take my espresso martini and stand by the fire, all eyes on me.

'Okay, okay, your category is...' Izzy shuffles a pack of charades cards and slips one from the top. 'Romantic comedies.'

Drew throws up his arms in dismay. 'Come on! That's a fix.' He shakes his head. 'I'll just be over here with another drink, completely useless.'

His sister rolls her eyes. 'Me thinks thou doth protest too much,' she sings.

'Are you a closet romcom watcher, Drew?' Izzy asks, finding herself hilarious.

'Let's do it,' Sarah says, patting the sofa either side of her. Jess and Millie move closer to her.

Well, I either throw the game, or I expose my secret indulgence: I love nothing more than sitting home alone with a tub of ice cream, streaming a romcom.

'Okay,' I say, thinking of how to demonstrate the first card. I hold up two fingers.

'Two words!' Jess and Sarah shout in unison. 'Second word!'

I bend to one knee and mime opening a ring box.

'*The Proposal!*' Sarah yells.

Nice.

I think again when I see the second card, then I hold up three fingers. Then I point first to Jake, then Jess.

'Wedding. To Be Weds. Marriage. Engagement. The Engagement,' Jess reels off.

'Are these even movie titles?' I ask, shaking my head and once again receiving Jess's tipsy giggle.

I point once more to Jake, then Jess, more aggressive in my gestures now.

'Ooh, *Friends with Benefits!*' Sarah shouts.

Wow, she's good.

'Is anyone else on the team, here?' I ask jokingly.

Next, I mime picking up two handfuls of shopping bags and have only just commenced a strut like a woman wearing heels – or as near as I can do – when Sarah lazily wafts a hand through the air and says breezily, '*Pretty Woman*. Next.'

By the end of our minute, we have achieved seven romcoms and by the end of two rounds, we have thwarted the other teams.

I hold up my hands and Sarah gives me a double high five.

'And to the rest of you,' I say, looking at our other team members. 'Thanks for turning up.'

Jess, Millie, Amy and Drew raise their most recent cocktails to that. Everyone is in good spirits.

'Another round. We're warming up now,' Jake announces.

Sarah rises from the sofa unsteadily and places her near-untouched cocktail on a side table. 'I'm just stepping out for some air,' she says.

But whilst the others continue their banter, I watch Sarah make her way to the staircase rather than the garden.

I set down my own cocktail and follow her. By the time I reach our bedroom, Sarah is already throwing up her foam and basil gel drops into our ensuite loo. For a woman who oozes femininity and, I will admit, pheromones, she throws up like an animal. I've only heard Gelada monkeys make more noise than this.

'Go away,' she groans on seeing me. 'Don't even look at me.'

'We've all been here. I lived with Jake for a while, remember.'

She groans again. 'Please don't compare me to Jake. He's a man-child.'

I notice a hairband on top of Sarah's beauty bag on the side of our fancy his 'n' hers sinks. I reach for it and as Sarah fumbles around, head down, arm extended above her, searching for the flush, I gently draw her hair back and tie it up.

'Why isn't it ever woman-child? We never say that, do we? If a man acts out, he's a man-child. When a woman acts out—'

'People call her difficult, or worse,' Sarah croaks, slightly more comprehensible now.

I bring myself down to sit on the floor, trying not to inhale through my nose as I let my legs flop out in front of me, my back against the mosaic tiled wall.

'Oh God, don't sit next to me. Leave me to die here alone.'

'Imagine the headlines,' I say, drawing an imaginary scrawl in the air with my hand. 'Matron of Honor dies in pool of espresso-martini vomit. One guest said he would never be able to drink coffee again.'

Sarah looks up, mascara smudged around her eyes, a speck of brown vomit on her cheek. For the briefest of moments, she meets my gaze and laughs. Then her mouth closes and turns down like an exaggerated animation making a sad face. Her chin wobbles, then she is crying into the loo.

Ah Christ. Crying women are *not* my forte.

Then she throws up again, heaving into the ceramic pot, and all I can think is – I took a dump in there just hours ago.

Wincing, I rub her back. 'Get it all up; you'll feel better for it tomorrow.'

She weeps harder.

'Don't cry over spilled ceviche,' I say. Anything I can think of to try to bring that smile back.

It doesn't work.

'Am I allowed to ask if you're crying because you're being sick or for some other reason?'

Sarah sniffs with zero elegance. 'No.'

Nodding, I move back to my position propped against the wall.

'Maybe taking one for Becky wasn't the best idea,' I venture.

'You saw that? Huh. Isn't hindsight a marvelous thing.'

Always.

'Charlie?' she says to the bottom of the loo.

'Yeah.'

'I just want to go to bed.'

Me too.

I help her stand and take her weight across my shoulder. 'Come on, then. Let's be having you.'

She leans into me sleepily.

'Teeth first,' I say, bringing her to lean against the

sink, where I put toothpaste on her brush and hand it to her.

Once she has paid lip-service to cleaning her teeth and given her face a cat's-lick wash, I help her into bed, pulling the covers over her fully clothed body. Then I do my own ablutions, strip down to my boxers, and settle onto the sofa bed.

''Night,' I call out.

Sarah responds with a snore of the kind I have only heard coming from old men who still enjoyed snuff in the nineties.

Not so perfect after all. Yet significantly more relatable.

9

SARAH

'Here,' Brooks says as I enter the kitchen. He hands me a mug of filter coffee. 'You need this more than I do.'

I hold up a hand – *stop*. 'Please don't.'

The character lines on Brooks's face betray his amusement. 'I've not seen you that drunk for a long time.'

'Yes, ha ha, very funny. Let's joke at my expense, then move on.'

'Oh boy. Tetchy Sarah is here. It's going to be a long day for you.'

I inhale deeply, my nostrils flaring with my exhale, and take a long mouthful of coffee, needing the caffeine hit but not enjoying the memory of too many espresso martinis.

I notice Brooks is wearing running shorts and a vest. 'Tell me you're not exercising at this ungodly hour,' I mumble into my mug as he pours himself a second coffee from the machine.

He checks his watch. 'It's eight thirty, and I've just finished.'

Urgh. Ordinarily, spritely is something I like in people in the mornings. Today, not so much.

'Why are you up if you're hanging this badly?' he asks.

'I've got to go on a search for The King.' The caffeine is moving directly to my head and marginally relieving the fog.

'Ah, yeah, the Elvis suit. Trust Jakey.'

I smile the way a mother might over her child. Because that is how Drew, Brooks and I view Jake – he is Drew's baby brother.

'And Charlie's driving you?'

I nod.

Unfortunately.

'He seems like a really nice guy,' Brooks says. 'A bit British but decent.'

I make a non-committal noise through my next mouthful of my warm necessity.

'You two seem to have hit it off,' he adds.

I really ought to have stayed in drama school.

Before I can reply, the comedian himself comes into the kitchen, fully dressed for a change.

'Morning, morning,' he says nauseatingly brightly.

'Morning, buddy,' Brooks replies. 'There's coffee in the pot. I'm going to take a shower. Good luck in your quest today. Oh, and have a good gig tonight, Charlie-boy – or break a leg, is it?'

'Something like that,' he replies.

Garrrrrrgh, I have to endure his comedy show later. Urgh, this day is going to be looooooong.

Once Brooks has left the room, placing a hand that feels both mocking and sympathetic on my shoulder as he moves past, Charlie begins to sing.

'Wise men say, only fools drink for two. But I can't help, holding your hair back for you.'

'Ha. Ha.' I swivel on my bare heels and go in search of my handbag and sandals.

Of all the people who could have witnessed my demise, it had to be him. FML.

* * *

'Here,' Charlie says, handing me a brown paper bag as he gets into the driver's side of his car. 'It won't hold for long but if you need to puke, catch it in there, would you?'

I desperately want to wipe his supercilious look right off his face. But I accept the bag huffily, knowing I may well need it.

Next, he hands me another brown paper bag from which I can smell just-baked pastries from the frozen selection I had delivered to the house. 'I grabbed us one each on the way out. Croissant or pain au chocolat? You can have first dibs. Whichever one makes you less likely to vomit in my car.'

I take the bag – I am actually a carb-loader when I have a hangover – and press my temple against the cool glass window as Charlie drives us away from the house.

'It's hardly a palace in here,' I mumble, knowingly pathetically.

'If it's good enough for Elvis...'

He presses a button on his old-fashioned dash and, too loudly, starts to sing 'Hound Dog'.

Kill. Me. Now.

Despite the racket, I close my eyes and feel myself drift into a semi-lucid sleep.

* * *

'Argh, shit. Not again.'

I open my eyes to see Charlie pulling into the side of the road. As far as I can see, we are in the middle of nothingness.

Green swathes of space surround us and trees line the seemingly endless road. There are hardly any other cars around. No buildings. Two horses in a field to our left and four goats in a field to our right.

'What are we doing?' I ask.

He kills the engine and I see smoke coming from the front of the car. I'm no mechanic but this can't be a good thing.

'I thought it was fixed,' Charlie says, unclipping his belt and getting out.

I follow him onto the side of the road. 'You're joking, right? As if today wasn't already bad enough.'

'Sorry, princess, I can't predict when my car will break down.'

I take a breath – in for four, out for four. He's right. I'm hungover and crabby as hell, but the only thing he has done wrong is drive a shitty car.

'Sorry, that was uncalled for. Do you have some kind of pick up or breakdown cover or something? Can we, like, get an Uber or something?'

'To drive us around London all day?' he asks. 'I need the car. I'll call the AA.'

'Ha. Ha. Back to this. Look, I hardly ever drink. Or not to excess, at least. I was tired and wired and—'

'Hi, is that AA breakdown recovery service?' Charlie speaks into his phone, clearly saying the full name for my benefit.

Ohhhhhhh. Not Alcoholics' Anonymous, then.

'I've broken down... somewhere near Chessington. No, the country roads, there was an accident on the carriageway.'

It takes nearly two hours for roadside assistance to arrive and the heat of the day is bringing me out in devastatingly unattractive alcohol sweats.

When the recovery guy arrives, he offers both Charlie and me a cold bottle of water from a cooler in his truck. I sit on the grass verge and hold the bottle to my forehead. This is so unlike me. I hate being hungover – and don't particularly enjoy the feeling of being drunk either.

But it had come easily. And sitting alone with my thoughts now, I know it wasn't just because I had been tired from a long day of travel and being sociable. It wasn't just that I had been helping Becky out with her wine tastings.

No, there was a deeper reason lingering and in

the melancholy of my hangover, staring at the pebbles in the road, I know it's because all of my friends are moving on with their lives. Izzy and Brooks are settled, with Izzy and Cady functioning well as a step-family. Drew and Becky are engaged and now *pregnant*. Jake is the baby of the group and even *he* is growing up.

Everyone is making huge life gallops and my life is stagnant. Indefinitely so.

I have *been* married. Danny and I wanted a family one day and that day will never come. I used to thrive in my job, always wanting more and pushing for it, but now there's nowhere else to climb, or I just don't have the energy to climb anymore.

My vision blurs as I wonder how much of that I am still clinging on to.

'All sorted,' Charlie says, standing over me and, thankfully, dragging me from my reverie.

'Finally.' *Stop. Being. So. Shitty.* 'What was wrong with it?'

'Do you understand mechanic speak?'

'I resent that stereotyping,' I say, not really feeling affronted at all. 'But no, I don't. I'm a blue car, red car kind of person.'

'Good, because it would be like me trying to translate Mandarin to German to tell you.'

'Do you speak Mandarin?'

'Nope. Nor German.' He swigs from his water bottle and I notice sweat patches turning his Marvel T-shirt a darker shade of blue under his armpits. 'I've zero idea what was wrong with it but for a ridiculous sum of money, it's now roadworthy again.'

It's the first joke he has cracked that I genuinely want to laugh at but the murderous look on his face makes me refrain.

'So,' I say. 'Elvis.'

He sighs. 'Fucking Elvis.'

Momentarily, I feel sorry for his predicament.

My sympathy lasts only so long as it takes him to start belting out 'Jailhouse Rock'.

'Do you *ever* give the play-acting a rest?'

He completely ignores my question, which I take to mean no.

* * *

The analogue clock in the car confirms that my rumbling tummy is not unreasonable. The short arm has ticked past twelve and I have been running on one pastry for three hours now. Pastries to me are like fresh flowers in a vase – attractive and temporarily mood lifting but lacking any real substance. What I

need now is a tree – some long-lasting carbs and pro-
tein. I am ravenous.

But it seems that lunch is still far away...

'I live near Clapham Junction,' Charlie says,
which means absolutely nothing to me, since I don't
know London at all. 'We'll drop off the car at my
place, then take the Tube into Soho.'

My heart sinks. 'The Tube? That's like a subway,
right?'

He glances at me and must register my dismay.
'It's fairly quick. Are you hungry?'

'A little.'

'Me too. I know a great Vietnamese. A family-run
place.' He leans far over the steering wheel, too far,
and squints in that way he does, as he indicates and
takes a right at a junction.

Ooh, Vietnamese. I could definitely do
Vietnamese.

'I thought we were meeting the Elvis suit guy in
Camden, though – or are Soho and Camden one and
the same place?'

'*You* are meeting the Elvis guy – Joe, I think he's
called – in Camden. After lunch, I need to go to the
club where my gig is tonight.'

'Do you sound check for comedy gigs?' I ask, both
surprised and curious. Whenever I've been to an

open mic night for these things, it has seemed very casual and off-the-cuff.

'Nah, it's just me. I like to make sure everything is ready and get a feel for the stage and whatnot.'

'I hadn't figured you to be a *prepared* kind of guy.'

He scoffs but doesn't speak, for a change. And because of that, I have no idea what he's thinking. In honesty, neither do I care.

We turn into a residential street of the ilk I have seen in London-based movies. Victorian terraces – not those fancy white ones where billionaires reside but the yellow brick ones that normal people live in – four floors high, with bay windows on the ground floor and, oddly, even on the basement floor too.

Charlie parks on the street and I follow him up some steps to a blue door that has a gold 38 sign on the front. Inside, he picks up a small pile of what looks like spam post and opens one of four postboxes on the wall of the plain painted hallway.

I can distinctly smell fried onions and curry powder, which serve as a reminder to my stomach that it contains nothing but acid right now.

Interior stairs lead up from the hallway, and to their left is one white door, which Charlie opens with a key.

I follow him inside to find a blue futon on laminate flooring in an open plan lounge-cum-diner-cum-kitchen space. There is a glass television stand in the corner of the room which has a charger plugged in that I recognize as being for a Mac, but there is no laptop or television in sight.

Brown boxes are stacked on top of each other in the lounge and on top of a small glass-top table in the area that appears to serve as the diner. I can see down a short corridor that has two open doors – a toilet and a bedroom – where more boxes are stacked.

'Are you coming or going?' I ask.

'Coming,' Charlie says, now opening the refrigerator in the kitchen and taking out two cartons of what looks like children's fruit smoothies. 'Want one?'

'Please.' I'm not in a position to be picky.

'I've recently moved in, hence the boxes. It's the first place I've actually rented on my own – I've always been in shares – so it might not look much but I'm pretty proud of it.'

I smile. 'A lick of paint and some pictures and it will look great.'

He nods as he slurps his smoothie through the straw. 'I've only recently started earning the kind of money from my gigs that means I can afford a place like this to myself.'

'Oh, so being a comedian is your job, then?' I don't mean to sound as shocked as I do.

He does that scoffing thing again but doesn't answer. He throws his empty carton into a pedal bin.

'Right, I need a wee, then we can head off. Want to go first?'

'Erm, yes, actually, thanks.'

'Take ten steps forward, two to the right, and Bob's your uncle,' he says.

'Excuse me?'

'The toilet. It's that first door on the right.'

'Oh. Thanks.'

Who the hell is Bob?

I can tell a lot about a person from the state of their toilet. In this case, I am unexpectedly pleased with the cleanliness of the bathroom, the neatness of the toiletries stacked in the shower bucket, and the immaculate toothbrush holder and soap dish. I am even more delighted with the clean, folded hand towels in a basket on the basin top, the luxury brand handwash and moisturizer combo, and the finely perfumed automatic freshener that sprays from the corner of the room when I close the door.

Who knew?

10

SARAH

The Tube is marginally less grungy than New York's subway system but it is similarly hot, smelly and congested. We follow a black line on the Tube map, which is apparently the Northern Line. We stand for the duration of the ride, clinging on for dear life every time the train chugs out of a new station.

We get off at Leicester Square and I follow Charlie, weaving in and out of people, sidewalk repairs and other random hazards like trash bags waiting for collection, in much the same way as I would through Midtown Manhattan.

We turn into a street where people are standing outside of pubs, drinking light beer in pint glasses, and queuing outside of Asian restaurants. There's a wonderful buzz and thrum in the area, smells of fragrant Thai and Vietnamese restaurants, even the smell of British 'chips' coming from the pubs.

'What is that man eating?' I ask, watching a hefty man shoving a ball of something bread-crumbed into his mouth with one hand, whilst the other holds onto a pint of what I suspect is Guinness.

It's more of an aloud curiosity than a real question but Charlie answers, 'It's a Scotch egg.' Then on seeing my confusion, he adds, 'Boiled egg wrapped in sausage meat and breadcrumbs then deep fried.'

'That sounds disgusting.' Still looking at the stranger, I trip on a loose paving slab. I would have fallen but Charlie catches me by the shoulder.

'Okay?' he asks, his hand still on me, his touch unexpectedly gentle and, in the circumstances, welcome. I nod and he lets go.

'They're far from disgusting,' he continues, as if my near accident never happened. 'Trust me. That's *proper* food right there. I'll get you one to try.'

'Oh, I'm good, thanks.'

He half-smiles, which is as good-humored as I have seen him for hours.

His tone has been clipped and his entire demeanor uptight and wired since we got off the Tube. I wonder whether it's the crowds he doesn't like, or my company. Probably both.

We stop outside a dark-grey-fronted restaurant. There is a short line of people waiting to be seated and I pray it won't be long until we have food in our mouths.

Happily, two small wood stools and a similarly styled dinky table become free under an awning out front – Parisian café style. Two men Charlie describes as 'scenesters' settle their check and head out into the bustling street, both wearing skinny-fit jogging suits and chunky sneakers.

Occasionally, I follow fashion trends but this whole pretense that jogging suits are acceptable smart-wear is not something I can get on board with. Even Charlie, in his Marvel tops, is smarter than that. Oddly, Charlie's T-shirts are starting to grow on me. Who doesn't love a superhero? Today's choice is a comic strip logo that simply says 'MARVEL'. It is sort of nerd-chic.

As soon as we are seated, Charlie pours us both an ice-cold glass of water from a bottle a waiter has placed on the table after wiping down the surface top.

'The *bún thịt nướng* is amazing from here,' Charlie says.

'It all sounds good and I'm so hungry, the choice is killing me.'

'Shall I order us a few dishes to share?'

I'm thrilled to have someone do the thinking for me and ecstatic when one of those choices is summer rolls, which are cold and so arrive almost instantaneously.

I grab one and dunk it in sauce, two bites and a full mouth later mumbling my appreciation.

'And I thought I ate quickly,' Charlie says through half-masticated vegetables. 'Very impressive.'

'Why thank you.' I accept the mock-praise without shame and reach for another roll. 'It's my superpower,' I tell him, also speaking with my mouth full. 'Also, these are too good for more than two bites.'

'I agree wholeheartedly.'

Bún thịt nướng arrives next, followed by *cơm gà xào xả ớt* and finally, udon king prawns. We share each dish evenly, hardly coming up for air.

In less than twenty minutes, we are leaning back against the window panes of the restaurant, both talking longingly about stretchy waistbands and marveling at just how clean we have left the crockery.

It's the first time I haven't felt monstrously hungover today and Charlie's clipped edge seems to have relaxed, too.

'Sorry if I was a bit of a dick before,' he says.

When exactly before? I wonder, but in the interests of conciliation and, frankly, surprised to hear an apology, I decide to keep that thought to myself.

'I can't stand crowds. Or people, often, but mostly crowds,' he adds, looking out to the street.

'You live in London,' I note, stating the obvious.

'Yeah, well, you've got to live somewhere. London works for comedy.'

I nod. It makes sense. Though I am very much a city girl, I do like to escape from the hive of activity sometimes.

'I'm sorry, too. I'm not usually so crabby. And I should probably thank you for not making a fuss about last night... In the moment, at least.'

'You mean for holding your hair and rubbing your back as you purged yuzu foam from your nose?'

That mischievous glint is back in his eyes. I am less offended by it on a full stomach.

'I take back the apology,' I say, only half in jest.

'Sorry, no takie-backies on an apology,' he says, rising as he does and leaving fifty pounds on the table in notes, placing his empty water glass on top of them.

He flags to the nearest waiter that he has left the money and starts to walk away, expecting me to follow, not stopping until we reach the entrance to Leicester Square Tube station again.

'Do you remember how I told you to get to Camden?' Charlie asks. 'Joe is going to meet you outside The Lock Tavern pub. It's very... British looking. Wood entrance, gold writing, flower boxes and stuff.'

'With such a fine description, how could I possibly get lost?'

He sighs. 'Do you need me to come with you?'

I wouldn't have said no to the support – new city, clueless on the transport system, strange man acting as an Elvis impersonator. 'Don't you want to do a sound check?'

'Yeah, I do, but—'

I place a firm hand on his shoulder. 'I'm a grown woman. A city gal. I'll be fine.'

'Okay.' He turns to walk away but gets only so far as two steps before he turns back to me. 'Are you sure?'

'Go. I'll have fun. I'll see you at the club for the opening set.'

He nods but doesn't make to leave. 'Okay. See you then... then.' Once again, he takes two steps before turning back. 'Remember, the Chalk Farm stop is closest.'

'Sure.'

'And don't forget to try the churros.'

'I won't.'

'And the Amy Winehouse statue is pretty cool.'

'Got it.'

'And—'

'Charlie, go. Please. What I've learned in the last thirty-six years will stand me in good stead.'

He smiles, claps his hands together, does an odd, very uncool, finger point-cum-gun salute thing, and *finally* leaves me to it.

* * *

It takes the aid of Google Maps and a large chunk of my overseas data roaming bundle to locate The Lock Tavern pub on the corner of Chalk Farm Road and Harmood Street. Charlie's description, whilst un-helpful to a tourist, was accurate. The pub is as British looking as I could imagine.

I have made my meeting time with Joe with thirty-seven minutes to spare so decide to head in-side for a cool drink after suffering the heat of the Tube.

A young guy with a thick London accent – very Michael Caine in *Going in Style* – takes my order from behind the bar. He can't give me a club soda but can give me a soda water, which we suppose is the same thing.

The bar is stocked with bottles of spirits and more beer taps than I have seen in even an Irish bar in New York.

On the bartender's recommendation, I take my drink up to the roof terrace and find a cushioned seat on a bench, squeezed between two women chatting to one side and a group of boisterous, student-looking guys and girls to the other. From here, I watch Camden go by below.

For the first time, I have space to think. And whilst this isn't how I had intended to experience London, I am thrilled that I can help Jake pull off this gift for Jess. He is right, of course, that Jess is no-frills, but she will adore seeing Jake as a hunky Elvis, strutting his stuff at their wedding.

It strikes me how very different Jake and Jess are to Charlie, despite them being good friends. Jake is bold and vivacious, endearingly so, a big city guy and a money earner, like his brother. Jess is easy-going and immensely comfortable in her own skin, finally earning money from her own fashion line, which until recently has been a passion project.

Charlie shares certain traits with each of them, yet he isn't like either of them. Creative and clearly outgoing – he performs on stage for a living. He earns money from his passion but as far as I can tell, he is far from wealthy. The vocation means more to him than the pay. Perhaps success in his field means more than money to him.

Yet none of these labels quite fit neatly. After spending hours in forced proximity with him, I have decided that Charlie is somewhat an enigma.

Who is the *real* Charlie?

Suddenly remembering why I am sitting on a rooftop under the sun in Camden, I check the time on my watch, spring up from my seat and rush down to the street.

I all but run through the pub doors – I can't mess this up for Jake – and smack right into a wide, slightly rotund man, who smells strongly of peppery cologne.

'I'm so sorry, I'm—' Stepping back, I look up to see a man whose skin is almost orange with fake tan. He has long, onyx-black, bushy sideburns and thick hair of the same color, stiffened into a quiff. 'Joe?'

He raises his upper lip at just one side. 'It's Elvis, ma'am, thank you very much.'

I suppress a gargantuan laugh. Charlie will be sorry to have missed this. Very much Elvis of the seventies, rather than *hot* Elvis of the fifties and sixties,

Joe has a dubious Tennessee accent and an even worse impersonation of Elvis.

'Wow, you're just like him,' I lie (impressively so, I think).

The lip comes up again. 'Thank you very much.'

And his repertoire is limited, too.

I manage to keep a straight face whilst we exchange a wad of twenties for the suit.

After assuring Joe Elvis that the suit will be dry cleaned, not damaged, lost or stolen and returned to him by me personally the following week, I bid him farewell and wish him good luck at Graceland. Then I send a WhatsApp message to Jake:

Got it!

I wander in the warmth of the afternoon to the statue of Amy Winehouse.

The bronze statue is impressive. A real likeness. But I wonder what it is about Amy Winehouse that makes Charlie like it so much.

Pausing for a minute, staring at the talented woman who had been extremely troubled, I conclude I don't really know much about Charlie at all. Perhaps I'm looking for some deeper meaning and there isn't one. It is possible that Charlie simply likes the statue. Maybe he's a fan of sculptures.

I walk on to Camden Market. The market is fascinating. Not just because of the eclectic mix of shops – from antiques to upcycled clothes, from fancy dress to real fur – but because of the buildings themselves – old stables, a former equine hospital; they are full of hidden details and delights.

I wander through Italian Alley, Cuban Yard, the Basement, the Amphitheatre, North Yard, Saddle Row, Gibley's Row and Paddock Lane.

I try on an outrageously jazzy, upcycled denim jacket that I might have pulled off as a teenager in the nineties and early noughties. Looking at myself in the mirror now, I am reminded that I am not a young girl anymore. And that's okay. I've already lived a longer and fuller life by comparison to some.

In a hat store, I am encouraged by the store owner to try out a red beret, a green top hat, an orange bucket hat and a purple cloche hat with turquoise trim. The eccentric man turns me and twirls me around the compact and jam-packed store until I feel like an actress in a romance movie, where the girl and guy fall in love as they work their way through market stalls, trying on hats, scarves and funky shades, the more outrageous the better.

But when I stop twirling, this time in a grey homburg, I realize the man under whose arm I am turning is around seventy years old, an old punk rocker, and almost certainly gay. My life isn't a clichéd romance. I am a widow. Mid-thirties and alone. I have lost the love of my life. My soulmate. There are no more knights in shining armor for me and no more market stall meet-cutes.

I slide the homburg from my head and hand it back to the owner. 'Thank you,' I say. And because I have spent so long being wooed in the tiny store, I tell him, 'I'll take the beret,' and hope that Cady will like it as a gift.

I want to get back to Surrey and to my friends. Spending too long alone is never good for me and it isn't even 5 p.m. yet. It will be hours before Charlie and I are back in Surrey.

I have been wandering in contemplation until I realize I have stumbled into a food court. Assaulted by the smells of spice and sweet, my salivary glands go into meltdown. My mouth is like Olaf in the Caribbean sun.

Chickpea curry, chicken kebabs, falafel, Venezuelan pockets. Pakistani food, Nigerian food, Hungarian food. It all smells so good. Still far too full-up for savory, I reluctantly walk past the stalls, but find my second stomach – the one reserved for sweet treats only – has a little hole for something tasty.

Drawn to a food stand selling French crepes, I order a classic, with lemon juice and sugar. I thank the server and carry my carton away to find somewhere to sit and eat. But en route, I spot the churros Charlie told me to try.

I buy six and stack the box on top of my crepe box. Before I locate a suitable spot to eat, I smell, then see a Portuguese stand selling custard tarts.

Cinnamon wafts up my nostrils like magical dust, stopping my legs from carrying me forward and drawing me left. A minute later, I am walking away with desserts stacked three boxes high.

Finally, I see a seat on a bench, beside a little girl and her dad, each of whom is eating a scoop of fried ice-cream from a cardboard pot.

'Mm, strawberry,' the little girl says, smiling cheekily at me and rubbing her tummy to demonstrate its deliciousness.

'Yummy!' I say.

'Sorry,' her dad says, 'She'll talk to anyone.'

I smile. 'She's extremely cute.'

'Thanks. Gets her looks from her mum.'

And her mum, who now comes to join them,

holding a custard tart much like one of the two I have bought, is very beautiful.

I watch the family as they steal each other's desserts and laugh amongst themselves.

I open the box containing my crepe and see two small wood forks inside with the food. I shouldn't be binging alone and I know someone whom I'd bet would love a churro.

Closing the lid, I gather my bags, the Elvis suit and my food boxes and set off to make one last stop before heading back to Chalk Farm Tube station.

11

CHARLIE

I didn't need to do a sound check – ordinarily, my manager deals with technical details for my gigs – but I did want to scope out the place. More than that, I just needed an hour or so, some space to myself, with my own mind and my own thoughts. No one whining at me or speaking to me or expecting me to perform and turn on a smile. A moment's peace. I know Bill, the owner of the club, and I knew that he would let me come inside for a drink before the club opened at 5 p.m.

I feel bad about bailing on Sarah and sending her to Camden alone, in a city she doesn't know, but she is a New Yorker born and bred; you don't get much more city than that. And from what little I know of

Sarah, she is as independent and sharp-witted as she is feisty. I know she'll be fine. Nevertheless, I felt so bad that I almost changed my mind and went with her to meet Joe Elvis.

I'm onto my second bottle of alcohol-free beer, sitting alone on a stool, at a slightly sticky high table, staring at the stage on which I will be the main act tonight.

'Penny for them?' Bill asks as he approaches, a can of Diet Coke in his hand and his typical Nirvana hoody zipped up to his neck to combat the chill of the empty, dark space.

'Just running through my set in my head,' I lie.

'Want me to leave you to it?'

'Nah, I'm done.' I have sufficiently decompressed and I'm ready to resume civility.

Bill pulls out a cloth from the back pocket of his ripped jeans and picks up a bottle of spray from a nearby table. He squirts the cleaning product onto the tabletop and I oblige by lifting my bottle to allow him to wipe the surface.

'I didn't like to say but it was a bit sticky,' I say.

'I'm sure when you're a permanent fixture at the O2 Arena you'll have sparkling clean tables,' Bill teases.

I scoff my amusement into my bottle. I doubt I'll

ever be on the same level as the likes of comedic superstars Peter Kay and John Bishop, but I can dream.

Bill and I make small talk and share our usual banter until a slow but steady trickle of punters have come into the club and Bill excuses himself to help behind the bar.

I am watching the door, mindlessly observing the comings and goings, when a tall, rather beautiful woman I recognize, still wearing her jean shorts and fitted T-shirt from earlier, beams at me, entirely unexpectedly, and makes a beeline for my table. Sarah walks in with bags and boxes, flushed in the cheeks in a naturally pretty sort of way. In her hands she is holding what looks like three food cartons.

'Hey,' she says in that casual way that Americans seem to do. She seems much brighter and perkier than when I last saw her. 'How did the sound check go?'

I don't want to lie. There is nothing I hate more than liars. So I avoid the question altogether.

'What have you got there?'

Sarah looks first across her right shoulder then across her left, sheepish. 'Contraband?'

I laugh when she opens the top of one carton and inside are two custard tarts, one simple with cinnamon on top and the other with three raspberries pressed gently into the baked custard. There are also two wooden forks, one of which she hands to me.

'Do we dare?' she asks. 'I took your advice and saw the statue, then had a look around Camden Market but got distracted by sweet treats.'

She opens the lid on the second container and inside is a crêpe, grains of sugar sparkling atop the dessert. I laugh as she, once again, glances across her shoulder to the bartender. Then she opens the third container and I see the churros I would give life itself for.

'Phwoar! Now we're talking!'

'Do you think we'll get kicked out?' she asks.

I raise my fork to Bill and use it to point to the food cartons, then smile as he shakes his head and taps on his imaginary watch as if to say, *eat them quickly but go ahead.*

'We're good,' I tell Sarah. 'I'm the talent, remember.'

'Clearly your modesty knows no bounds.'

I'm laughing again, now around a mouthful of churro dipped in hazelnut chocolate sauce. The sugary, cinnamon fried dough makes me groan with delight.

'Calm down, Sally!' Sarah says.

My light laughter moves south from my chest

until it becomes a deep belly guffaw. Perhaps if Meg Ryan had been eating churros, the infamous scene Sarah is referencing from *When Harry Met Sally* would have made more sense.

Sobering, I thank Sarah for bringing the desserts. It was thoughtful and kind but mostly it has been a nice distraction from my building stage anxiety. Despite her cantankerousness, I can admit that Sarah does seem to be a genuinely nice person.

It's not that I have trouble warming to nice people. I have trouble warming to *all* people. In my experience, 99 per cent of people on the planet are a letdown.

'How was The King?' I ask, as Sarah straightens her back and presses her hands to her stomach in an expression of fullness.

'Very seventies Elvis rather than fifties.'

'Ouch. Will the suit fit Jake?'

'I hope so. His height will hopefully counterbalance Joe Elvis's waistline.'

I hold up crossed fingers.

'I just want to say, Charlie, I'm sorry I've been hard work today. I'm grateful for the ride. It means a lot to me to be able to help Jake and Jess.'

'Me too. And you're welcome.'

She smiles sweetly. 'Did we just agree on something?'

'You mean besides our love of romcoms and sweet things?'

She raises her eyebrows. 'You're right. For two people who rub each other up the wrong way, we do have some common ground.'

I stare at her for a beat too long without meaning to.

'So,' she says, edgy now. 'What time are you on?'

'Not until nine. Don't feel like you have to stay here. I won't be offended in the slightest.'

'Of course I'll stay. I mean, unless you don't want me to.'

I don't think I do. I'm not sure why. It seems to have just struck me that some of my stage content is quite personal and maybe I don't want to share it with Sarah. Then again, I share it with loads of people on a weekly basis.

'Yeah, sure, it's just a show, you know, open to everyone.'

Her brow furrows, unsurprisingly, since I am giving off a fairly mixed message.

'Right. Yeah.' She's too breezy now. Forced casual. 'Well, my feet are sore from walking around in sandals all afternoon, so it will give me a rest.'

'Yeah. 'Course. Good shout.'

Shit, I've offended her. This morning, that wouldn't have bothered me but after she bought desserts...

'Charlie, can I say something? I think we maybe got off on the wrong foot. I'm not usually so grumpy and uptight and I have a feeling you're not always so pig-headed either.'

'Wow, was that one of those backhanded compliments or backhanded insults?' I smirk in response to the apprehensive look on her face. 'Don't worry, I'm not really offended. I agree, actually. I'm sure nobody can be as uptight and grumpy all the time as you've seemed to be.'

I am pleased that she finds me amusing, for a change.

I hold out my hand in that cliché way like Channing Tatum in *The Vow* and say, 'Hi, I'm Charlie. How do you do?'

Sarah rolls her eyes but she shakes my hand. Her skin is soft, moisturized, well looked after. Though her hand is large, it fits neatly inside mine.

'Sarah,' she says. 'Just a regular girl from New York City. Not uptight, unless I feel insulted, and not grumpy, unless I don't like people.'

It is my turn to find amusement in her words.

'How about I get us a couple of drinks and you tell me what it's like living in the concrete jungle where dreams are boundless?'

She recognizes Alicia Keys's lyrics and tells me, 'There's nothing a girl can't do.'

We talk about everything from Broadway and the West End to how we make a living, from ways to escape the bustle of Manhattan and London to the places we would like to visit.

When the first comedian takes to the stage at 7 p.m., we are both drinking alcohol-free beer from the bottle and sharing a plate of spicy barbecue wings.

It's a tough crowd. The young woman, who must be new to the circuit given I have been working it for years now and don't recognize her, gets a rough ride.

Unfortunately, her jokes just aren't landing. Her nerves are making her voice tremble and throwing off her timing, which doesn't help the ill-judged jokes she's making.

In my opinion, the days of making jokes about race, gender and sexual orientation, even if the comedian is of ethnic minority or LGBTQ+ themselves, are gone. Extremely crass, crude and anything 'ist' jokes are no longer funny to the average punter who comes out for a bit of a laugh and a pleasant weeknight drink with friends or workmates.

Nevertheless, I can't stand hecklers. It's bad enough knowing you are dying on the stage from the silence of the audience when your punchline is dropped, without being thrown-off by dickheads who think they are funny, when all they really are is inconsiderate bullies.

I feel sorry for the girl on stage. I laugh where I know she has predicted a laugh. I laugh harder than necessary, like that guy in an office job on a work night out when they want to make clear they are the loudest and most powerful suit in the gang. And at times, even though I can tell she doesn't find the act funny, Sarah follows my lead, laughing loudly, showing just how empathetic she is.

When the break between comedians comes, she turns to me and says, 'I admire you guys. I couldn't get up on stage each night and expose myself like that, especially not knowing how the crowd will respond. How do you do it?'

I'm not sure I'm qualified to answer that question, given I have no idea how I myself manage to combat my anxiety every time I go on stage. I tell myself what many actors, comedians and sports stars seem to say in interviews or when 'writing' their autobiographies

(Ross Geller air-quotes intended): that nerves make me perform better. But if that was true for us all, if nerves make us all better, I wouldn't have just watched the first act of the night crash and burn.

Perhaps it was that long twenty minutes watching someone's demise on stage. Maybe it's that I am a little embarrassed and dreading that Sarah is probably wondering what she's got herself into and whether the rest of the night is going to be just as bad. Whatever the cause, my usual steady climb to a peak of anxiety just before my set has raced ahead to raging nerves. There are two more acts before I take to the stage and I can already feel my palms getting clammy. I can feel sweat forming under my armpits and on my brow.

'I'm going to get a pint of something with actual alcohol in it,' I tell Sarah. 'Can I tempt you with a hair of the dog?'

I watch her stifle a yawn in that way people do when they try not to open their mouths to show their overt boredom and the yawn comes out of their eyes, glazing over the irises.

'That sounds like a good idea to me. I've held off long enough on the basis I didn't want you to think I needed you to call the AA again.' She smiles. 'I'll take whatever the measure is – a pint, did you say? – of

London's finest light beer. Whatever you recommend.'

Now this is my kind of woman. None of those fluffy cocktails or fancy fizz like we've been having in Surrey. A proper drink.

Either the alcohol helps loosen us up, along with the rest of the audience, or the next two acts are genuinely funny. Their jokes are landing and I notice Sarah laughing heartily of her own accord, without having to give me a sideways glance to check if she ought to be laughing. Sometimes British humor is understood by Yanks.

Regardless, it only serves to lighten my mood and suppress my anxiety enough to hold polite but monosyllabic conversation.

Though once the third and penultimate act has finished, my anxiety is at fever pitch.

No longer able to think of anything banal to say, I make an excuse to spend the twenty minutes before I am due to go on stage alone. Not in a fancy green room but in a cold corridor off to the side of the stage.

With a second pint of beer in my hand, which will also act as a stage prop, I lean back against the cool, damp, slightly dirty and in-need-of-a-lick-of-paint wall, with a towel wrapped around my neck, catching any sweat to stop it from leaking onto my Hawaiian shirt, which I have pulled on over my Marvel T-shirt, again as a slightly eccentric stage prop. I asked for a glass of water with ice from the bar before coming backstage and having downed the cool liquid and wrapped the ice inside my towel, it is now pressed against the base of my neck, trying to cool both my nerves and my temperature.

I can feel my heart beating hard in my chest. If I didn't experience this every night before I went out to do a gig, I would be thinking I am having a heart attack. As I run through the highlights of my show in my mind, I feel my stomach churn and know my standard loose bottom will arrive soon. Hopefully, not until after my appearance.

It dawns on me, as I am running through the main gags, just how much of my real life I bare to the audience. It hasn't occurred to me before, other than as a good idea to both get the audience on side and take the piss out of myself rather than others, which is something I don't like to see comedians do. Generalist piss-taking is fine but specific is just nasty, using a platform to bully.

The realization brings my breaths thick and fast, something which doesn't usually come alongside my elevated heart rate. It's a new feeling and I don't like it.

Why now? Why tonight? Why when Sarah is out there?

Why does she want to stay? Does she think that she has to because I have driven her into London? God, I hope not.

I would actually like nothing more in this moment than to step out onto that stage and see that she has left and gone elsewhere for a drink or sightseeing of some sort whilst I perform. I don't tell people close to me about my life for a reason and only now it's occurring to me that it is wholly absurd that every night on stage, I tell strangers all about it. It doesn't bother me in front of people I don't know and will never see again; I use it to my advantage. It doesn't even bother me in front of people like Jake and Jess, who know about my upbringing in the system. Who know me well enough not to judge me for it.

Tonight, for some reason, it is bothering me. A lot.

I slide down the wall until my bum reaches the cold dirty tiles of the floor and I take control of my breathing.

'Charlie? Are you okay?' Sarah asks.

I look up and register her concern. Pasting on a

beaming smile, I spring to my feet, briefly seeing flashes of light in my vision. 'Yeah, yeah, absolutely. Just, you know, running through my lines.'

She nods but I don't know if she believes me.

'I'm sorry to interrupt,' she says. 'Your manager said it would be okay for me to pop back here. You left these on the table and I just thought you might need them.'

She is holding up several pieces of paper folded into a pocket-sized rectangle, which contain bullet points from my repertoire, on the off chance I have a mind blank and need them. Not that I ever have done.

'Right, yeah, no, it's great that you're back here. Great.'

I take the papers with thanks and endure an awkward moment of silence until Sarah says, 'Break a leg then.'

'Yep. Will do.' I sound like an idiot.

I am grateful for the interruption of my manager, which makes Sarah leave.

The presence of my Geordie mate, who has backed me since the start of my career, reminds me that this is my life, my bread and butter, and I've got this. I know this gig and I know I can rock that stage.

12

SARAH

The apprehension I have been feeling over watching Charlie tonight has made me nauseous. He is little more than a stranger to me but the anticipation of him *not* being funny and me being forced to fake a laugh – the way I have done a few times already listening to the preceding acts – has been oddly anxiety inducing. And to see him crouched on the ground behind the scenes and looking so incredibly nervous did nothing to alleviate my concerns.

I was surprised to find out he makes a living as a comedian, since I hadn't found him funny at all yesterday. Today, I feel like I'm *getting him* a bit more, though I still often wonder whether he is trying to make a joke or if he is just downright rude.

What surprises me even more, however, is that I am sitting in the club with a super-strong pint of beer in my hand, next to the empty stool where Charlie was sitting an hour ago, with tears streaming down my face. I can't remember the last time I laughed so hard that my entire abdomen ached.

Either beer has made Charlie funny or beer has made me *think* Charlie is funny. Whichever, it is working. I catch all of his punchlines and at one point, he has me squealing so loudly, I am drawing the attention of people sitting close by.

Any nerves Charlie had displayed before his set are gone now. He owns the stage. Fits it naturally. He oozes confidence and self-assurance but in a completely likeable way. I notice that his accent – 'melting-pot southern England,' he tells me – is stronger on stage and I guess this is intentional.

'Has anyone ever been told they could be the milk man's kid?' Charlie asks through his hand-held microphone.

While the audience respond with confirmations, shouted and mumbled, Charlie takes a drink of beer and nods.

'Well, I could have been,' he says. 'My mother genuinely had no idea who my father was. In the box on the birth certificate that says "Father", mine says, "Could have been Dave, Jonny, Simon or Pete".'

When the laughter subsides, he continues. 'I grew up in the system.' He raises an arm, as if to say *Louder*, and receives a chorus of 'awwwwwww' in response.

'Yeah, tough gig, especially for an overweight kid who has a sort of penguin waddle walk. My nose has been reset a few times, I can tell you. To make matters worse, I had to change my name to Charlie by deed poll because my mother had originally named me after her best friend... cocaine.'

I am still laughing along with the rest of the audience, mostly at the delivery of Charlie's words, but I am also wondering how much of this is true. Charlie doesn't at all seem like the kind of guy who grew up in the system.

'I know what you're thinking. Where are his tattoos? Where are the tear drops down his face and the scars from knife crime from his days incarcerated? It's called fake tan. Lather enough of that stuff on and you look more like a contestant on *Strictly Come Dancing* than a tough lad from the wrong side of the tracks.'

Charlie sets his microphone down on the floor and in the manner of a prima ballerina, he begins rising to his toes – naturally, not reaching the tips – and raises his arms above his head before prancing, completely uncoordinated, around the stage.

Laughing at himself, along with his fans, Charlie resumes his hold on his microphone and, a little breathlessly, says, 'My first foster family put me through ballet classes. See, my mother had never cut my hair. It wasn't until my foster mother saw me taking a stand-up piss months into our stint together that she realized I was a boy.' He holds up a hand. 'Wait, before anyone passes comment, I agree, boys can do ballet, too. Unfortunately for me, I'm not well equipped enough downstairs to pull off Lycra.'

He reaches for his pint and takes a drink.

'Seriously, though, do they stuff socks down there? What is it about male ballet dancers? It's like the criteria for entry to The Royal Ballet School are good feet, strong quads and a big, fat cock.' He waits for the crowd to settle and adds, 'I bet those lads don't get swiped left on Tinder.'

For another fifteen minutes, I hoot and snort, cry and squeal with zero grace, until I am completely exhausted. I haven't felt so light and fluffy since... Since before Danny died.

Without realizing it, I have needed that.

Charlie's show has been a release. Cathartic. He

had me completely immersed in his words, his jokes, his transformation on stage to this incredibly honest, funny, charming man. Those are not words I would have expected to put in the same thought bucket as Charlie just hours ago.

* * *

It is more than half an hour since his performance and Charlie hasn't yet reappeared. The bar has started to empty as people have finished their last drinks and I am beginning to wonder if he's abandoned me for the second time in one day. I stifle a yawn and check my watch, calculating that it's going to be the early hours of the morning before we are back at the house in Surrey.

I'm expecting – and hoping for – the chirpy, charismatic Charlie from stage but as I watch him finally appear, limply shaking some hands and blatantly forcing weak smiles at a few of the audience members who have stuck around to compliment him, I know *that* Charlie has gone.

He looks tired. Not in a sleepy, need-to-go-to-bed kind of way, but in an exhausted, drained, depleted-of-all-energy kind of way.

Despite my annoyance at the wait, I slip down

from my stool and hug him. 'You were amazing up there.'

He pats my back in a way that tells me to take my hug and flush it down the toilet.

'Cheers,' he says.

He picks up his satchel from underneath the table, with me still a bemused onlooker.

He raises his eyebrows. 'Are you ready to go?'

'I... Yes. Sure thing.'

Rude. Abrupt. Grumpy as hell. This is the Charlie I first met. One minute, he's the Devil and the next he is Stage Angel. Whiplash doesn't give justice to the car crash that is Charlie's ever-changing personality.

It's as if someone has taken out Charlie's proverbial batteries. He looks spent. His body is hunched as we walk to the underground station and when we get on the train, he slumps into a seat, leaning his head back, his eyes closed.

I find him impolite and feel sorry for him simultaneously. Whilst I am desperate to get back to my friends, in the luxurious house I have booked for us all, once Charlie and I are back in Clapham and making our way back to his place, I feel obliged to offer, 'We could stay here tonight, if you would rather not drive.'

I am devastated when he visibly perks up.

'Are you sure? We could head back first thing in the morning.'

'Well, I would need to be back super early. Before Jess wakes up and realizes I've been missing. It will defeat the point of the secret surprise if I have to tell her where—'

'Deal.'

I open my mouth to protest but given it was my idea to stay, what can I say now? My attempt to dissuade him with the early rise was an epic failure.

Back in his flat, we stand side by side in the single bedroom, staring at the double bed.

'I'll take the futon in the lounge,' I offer, not at all wanting to sleep on a hard, rickety futon.

'I can't let you do that. I'll take the futon,' Charlie says.

But as I stare at the dark-grey sheets on the bed, wondering how many nights Charlie has slept in them and, more importantly, what he might have done in them, I think the futon might be the lesser of two evils.

'I'll change the sheets,' Charlie says, shaking his head as he leaves the room, clearly having read my mind.

Sorry, not sorry. God only knows how gross single men living alone might be.

When I finally lie back on the bed, I sink into the mattress with a sigh. It has been another long day.

So far, this visit to England has not been at all what I had envisaged.

Lying in corpse pose and trying to visualize my yoga classes and how quickly I am able to relax at the end of them, I close my eyes and feel my limbs begin to sink into the mattress.

Then I hear the almighty roar of the grizzly bear snoring from the futon.

Pulling a pillow across my face, I speak loudly into it.

'You. Have. Got. To. Be. Kidding. Me!'

13

SARAH

'Charlie,' I whisper, gently rocking his shoulders where he lies on the futon, all crooked and looking like he's been hit by a truck, wearing only his boxers, and a passer-by has haphazardly thrown a blanket over his legs. 'Charlie. Wake up.'

Like an old banger of a car that has just been jumped, he goes from dead to sparking with life, springing bolt upright.

'What? What's happening?'

I'm crouched down on my haunches next to his make-shift bed and reach for a mug of coffee I have set down on the floor next to me. 'We need to get going. If we're much later, the others will be awake by the time we get back to the house.'

He scrunches his face like a squirrel might and rubs his eyes.

'What time is it?'

I don't dare tell him. Instead, I hold out the steaming mug as a peace offering.

'I made you coffee. I hope you like black instant coffee because that's all I could find in your cupboards.'

He takes the mug and gulps. 'Ouch, that's hot!'

'That's sort of the point.'

'Ha. Ha.' He brings his legs around to sit on the edge of the futon, in almost all his glory. 'Sorry, Your Highness, I'll stock my cupboards for the burglars next time I'm away for the week.'

I roll my eyes as I move away from his near-naked body, holding up a hand to shield my eyes.

'Haven't you heard of cupboard staples? Here, put these on, we need to get going.' I toss him the jeans and T-shirt he was wearing last night.

'Can I at least shower and put on some clean clothes? What's the big rush?'

'Come on, Charlie, we spent the night away. Just the two of us. If the others wake up and realize we didn't come back, they'll assume we were *together*.'

Charlie chuckles. 'We are adults.'

What?

Panic takes me by surprise, making me pace the unfurnished lounge.

'No! I don't want all the questions. And I don't for one second want them to think that I've—'

'Would it be the end of the world? Seriously? Might this be an overreaction?'

'Yes! And no!'

Charlie scratches his scalp and yawns as he pads through the lounge toward the bathroom. 'Don't spare my feelings here, will you?'

Exasperated, I shout after him, 'Oh please, it's not like you would go anywhere near me anyway.' I hear the bathroom door slam. 'You clearly can't tolerate me either!'

I regret my words within minutes. As soon as I've finished my coffee, coincidentally. Danny always used to say that it takes one coffee for me to come around in the mornings. I have proved him correct in this instance.

My worry about the others thinking I might contemplate a relationship with someone else, and how guilty that would make me feel, has made Charlie think I would be ashamed for that someone else to be him.

I have spent rare and emotionless nights with men since Danny. They've been few and far between, usually once alcohol has lowered my inhibitions. Those men fulfilled a physical need, nothing more. I didn't know them before the night I spent with them, not really. My friends certainly hadn't known them. Especially not Drew, who was friends with Danny before he had even met me. Drew was lost when Danny died, too. It brought the two of us even closer, joint in our grief.

Charlie would be an entirely different prospect. The whole group would know, and I've already spent too much time in his company for either one of us to simply be used physically.

To another woman, I am sure Charlie could be quite a catch. He isn't unattractive. He is surprisingly clean. And I am starting to understand his humor. Last night, he genuinely had me in kinks.

But he is appallingly arrogant, often grumpy and occasionally downright rude. He is completely emotionally unstable.

Nevertheless, my words hadn't been intended to hurt his feelings. In falling short of giving him my full truth – that I can never give away a heart that has already been given once before, wholly and completely – I have left him assuming an insult.

***

I needn't have worried about my words affecting Charlie.

He swans out of the shower, thankfully clothed in jeans and yet another take on a Marvel T-shirt (the giant Spider-Man, bright and outrageous), towel drying his hair and singing about only knowing you love a girl once you've let her go.

I am sitting on the futon, which I've cleared and turned back into a seat, my legs crossed, my second rancid coffee of the morning between my hands.

I find myself staring at Charlie's clean-shaven face and noticing his features are quite defined in the sunlight, which shines in streaks through the apartment windows.

'Ready to go?' he asks.

'Yes, please.'

We head out to the car and after hearing the engine splutter but come to life, I begin to apologize for my inadvertent nastiness earlier. Reluctantly, I start to explain, and am happy to be cut off by Charlie reeling off line after line of cliché statements.

He has the heart of the Tin Man, the skin of a rhino, my words were water off a duck's back...

Clearly my feelings of guilt have been pointless.

We drive much of the way in silence, happily

making good time. I am hopeful we'll be back before anyone notices we didn't return last night.

Until... Back in the surrounds of the countryside, Charlie takes a right turn at a junction...

'I think you should have turned left there,' I tell him.

'Doesn't God love a backseat driver,' he responds, leaning far over the steering wheel, his mole-y squint in place, until the road straightens out.

'First, I'm in the front seat. Secondly, while it busts the female stereotype, I'm like a homing beacon with directions.'

Despite his focus on the road ahead, I catch his dismissive expression.

'I remember this road,' he says.

Thirty minutes. Thirty minutes it takes for Charlie to give up the pretense, stop rabbiting on about short-cuts, and work his way in a loop back to the junction where I told him to turn left.

I want to scream at the top of my voice.

Men! Goddamn men! Stupid male egos!

By the time we come to a stop out front of the house, I know at least some of the others will be awake. I cringe as the stones of the forecourt scrunch and rattle under the weight of the car tires, announcing our return.

I thank Charlie for the ride and take the prized possession – Joe Elvis's suit – from the backseat.

Turning the key quietly in the front door, then tip-toeing inside, I don't hear voices.

'Come on, I'll make us both a decent coffee,' I say, my hackles softening now.

'And I'll get those frozen pastries in the oven.' Charlie pats his tummy comically.

We've got away with it and both of us seem lighter now that we are back on neutral territory, in the vicinity of our friends.

As we make our way toward the kitchen, I say, 'I didn't really get a chance to say last night, since you were Mr Grumpy, but your performance was great.'

I think I see his cheeks flush, uncharacteristically, and his mouth opens as if to respond but it remains open, like a shocked emoji, as his eyes shift from me to the three men standing around the kitchen island, stone-faced, arms folded across their chests.

Brooks. Drew. Jake.

Oh boy.

All three men are dressed in running gear and a sheen of sweat.

A quick scan of their faces and their pointed stares at Charlie confirms my worst fears. They suspect Charlie and I have been doing the hanky-panky!

Before anyone in the room can speak, Izzy rushes inside from the decking out back.

'Sarah! You're back. Great, I need your help.' She loops her arm through mine and ushers me out of the kitchen, calling 'Hi Charlie!' back across her shoulder.

On my way out of the room, I give Charlie a look which I intend to be both an apology and an 'I told you so'. Whether I achieve either or neither of those messages, I can't tell, for his face remains expressionless.

'I did try to tell them this isn't appropriate,' Izzy says. 'I told Brooks you don't even like Charlie, let alone want to start a *thing* with him.'

We reach the staircase.

'And they didn't listen at all?'

Izzy turns to look me in the eye and shrugs. 'Brooks said, quite rightly, that I hated him before we almost had sex in the showers at his gym.'

'Whoa! Too much information.'

Upstairs, Izzy leads me to her bedroom. I ought not to have been but I am taken aback to see Becky and Jess, still wearing their nightwear and sitting cross-legged on the bed.

'Oh, come on!' I exclaim, throwing my arms up.

In unison, all three of the other women sing at me to tell them more, tell them more—

'He's no Danny Zuko and I am definitely no Sandy Olsson.'

Jess gasps in jest, holding her hands in front of her wide-open mouth theatrically. 'You didn't put out on your first night away together, did you?'

I shake my head and try not to smile at the ridiculousness of the scene in front of me. 'I most certainly did not.'

Becky pats the bed next to her and raises aloft a plate of French bread with little ramekins of butter and jam. There's an offer I won't refuse.

I think of Charlie and the grilling he must be getting downstairs – certainly without the offer of breakfast for his troubles – while I tuck into decadent bread and receive a mug of fresh cafetiere coffee from Jess.

'So what *did* happen?' Izzy asks, now relaxing into a large rocking chair by the open window of the room's Juliette balcony. Like the guys, she is wearing workout gear and a ring of sweat has turned her pale-blue vest a darker shade around the neck. 'It's like a scene from *Fight Club* downstairs,' she says. 'The protective Dobermans are in full hangry mode.'

'Never cross those men when they're hungry.' Becky laughs.

Though I could allow myself to be irritated by the insinuation that I might jump into bed with another man, and another man I have just met for that matter, I find myself more entertained by the situation. It's like we are four teenagers discussing our first kiss.

'All right, all right, but I hate to tell you, there's no gossip to share.'

'Just take a step back, would you?' Jess holds up her palm. 'Why were you and Charlie in London anyway? You just fancied going to his gig, Jake said? But an entire day! I mean, he's funny but I'm not sure I would have taken the whole day for it.'

And, thanks to my final stop in Camden before taking my desserts back to Charlie at the club, I now don't have to lie to my friend. Or not lie in a very big way, at least.

Hindsight is bliss!

From the back pocket of my jean shorts – the same ones I have now been wearing for more than twenty-four hours – I remove a small, blue, velvet bag and hand it to Jess.

'I don't want to step on any toes or ruin any plans you might have, but these are for you.' As Jess opens the top of the small pouch and takes out the jewelry inside, I add, 'They're vintage and the stones are aquamarine. And they are new to you. So...'

Jess holds up the white-gold earrings and admires the feather shape with aquamarine teardrop stones on the end of each feather.

'My something new, something old and something blue,' Jess says.

'I hope you like them. If you already have other earrings planned then please don't feel like you have to wear them. They just reminded me so much of you, I would like you to have them to wear any time.'

Jess lunges forward and wraps her arms around my neck. 'I love them, Sarah, thank you so much. And I don't have plans to wear anything else. In fact, I was going to ask for your help to find something today, when we have a final dress fitting, but these are perfect.'

I relay the story of the broken-down car, skim over how pleasant my lunch with Charlie had been, so as to not have the girls reading anything further into it, and tell them how I went shopping in Camden, where I bought the earrings.

I tell them about all the desserts I tried at the market but leave out that I took them back to the comedy club to share with Charlie. I reflect on the poor girl who took to the stage as the first act of the night and how her jokes just didn't strike the chord of hilarity she was hoping for.

I tell them Charlie's performance was hilarious and then how I had felt so bad for him having such a long drive back here after the show that I had suggested we stay over at his place.

I describe in detail, so as to make a point, how empty and like a bachelor pad his flat is and how Charlie was kind enough to sleep on the futon. I make a joke of us having to change the sheets on his bed in the early hours of the morning, really driving home the point that Charlie I did not spend the night together, in any way, shape or form.

'So poor Charlie really is downstairs taking a verbal beating for no reason then?' Becky asks.

I nod solemnly, though not feeling truly terrible. 'I did tell him we needed to be back before the guys woke up.'

'I suppose it is nice that they're so protective over you, even if it's in a hugely oppressive way,' Jess says.

I am lucky to have such good friends in my life to look out for me. I am a big girl but doesn't everyone need a little support sometimes?

Keen to change the topic, I ask, 'How was lunch with your in-laws-to-be and your aunt and uncle, Jess? And how was the balloon ride with Drew,

Becky? And Izzy, what did you, Brooks and Cady get up to yesterday?'

'Hold the phone. Before we move on, can I just clarify, do you *like* Charlie?' Jess asks.

'Charlie in a good mood or bad mood?'

Jess scoffs. 'Understood. He's a complex character.'

Speaking of complex... 'Actually, Jess, he mentioned in his performance that he grew-up in foster care. Is that true or was that just for laughs?'

'I guess his past is his story to tell, just like everyone's is, but yes, that much is true. He had a pretty rough upbringing.'

It's unlike me to not give my friends my full attention but as I listen to their stories from the day before, the romance of Drew putting his arms around Becky in the hot air balloon because she is afraid of heights, how Jake pulled out all the stops to make Jess's family as comfortable as possible at the dinner table, and how Izzy and Brooks had strolled behind Cady hand-in-hand as they had wandered down rows of grapevines with Cady taking pictures as they went, I am distracted.

It strikes me, once more this trip, hearing about my friends living their lives, just how alone I am. They are building their families, and while I know they love me as a friend, I'm not part of those immediate families. At the same time, I'm having visions of Charlie as a boy, neglected, abandoned, hurt. Lonely.

I know I shouldn't write his past for him – I have no idea what he has been through – but I wonder about his gags, about his mother and her drug addiction. I wonder whether he has been in foster homes, how many families he had had during his upbringing, and I wonder if one of the reasons he puts himself through clear anxiety to get on a stage and make people laugh is because laughter has been his medicine throughout his youth.

I don't know the answers to these questions and I shouldn't make them up myself but my stomach is contracting with a sickly combination of feelings – love, loss, anger and sadness.

'Can I get another piece of that bread, Becky?'

If there is one thing that will help a sickly stomach, it is overloading on comforting carbohydrates.

14

SARAH

Jess has made clear from the beginning of wedding planning that she wants a small affair. She describes her style as 'Bohemian' and that is what she's had in mind during our months of planning.

As these events tend to do, the wedding has taken on a life of its own and is now much bigger than Jess intended, though she did always plan to have three bridesmaids: Becky, Izzy and me. All along, Jess has maintained that we should choose our own bridesmaid dresses, in any style we feel comfortable with, and that her choice of wildflower bouquets will naturally tie us all together and signify our importance.

Now, Jess, Becky, Izzy and I are standing in an exquisite bridal store, which is managed by another good friend of Jess's – Carrie, whom she knows through their joint connection to the fashion industry.

Carrie is more luxurious-chic in her style than Jess but the ease with which she makes conversation and makes all of us feel comfortable is a trait she shares with Jess.

Carrie fills five glasses with Spanish cava and hands them to each of us, raising a toast to Jess: 'The most beautiful bride the world will ever see.'

Becky, Izzy and I sent our measurements for our dresses in advance, months ago, in lieu of being able to visit the Surrey-based store. Today will be the first time we have tried on our dresses and I am praying that they fit. Not least because there is no time in the schedule for alterations.

'So, when you're ready, Jess,' says Carrie.

The rest of us take seats on a fine upholstered sofa with our drinks and listen to the pants, grunts and moans coming from behind a curtain as Jess wrestles her way into her bridal gown.

There is a moment in my mind where I wonder if she has surprised us all and gone for a very traditional style of dress. I remember being manipulated through similar grunts and yelps into my princess gown when I got married. But when Carrie steps out from behind the curtain with a beaming smile and reveals the bride-to-be, I see a remarkable looking bride, every bit in in her own style.

The dress has a bodice, buttoned from beneath Jess's shoulder blades all of the way down to her sacrum, which she shows off as she twirls, happiness making her eyes dazzle. The long flowing matte crêpe material swishes as it sweeps the floor and the small trail at the back twists the fabric about her ankles. It has a square neckline and long sleeves, which button at the wrists. It's stunning. Jess is stunning. And my stomach dances at the thought of Jake seeing his bride for the first time in less than forty-eight hours.

I don't realize I'm crying until Carrie holds out a box of tissues for me to take.

I'm not sobbing – snotty and ugly crying. Silent tears roll down my cheeks, a mixture of happiness and grief. As I celebrate the marriage of my friend, I am mourning the loss of my own.

Carrie asks Jess if she can try an accessory on her head and when Jess agrees, Carrie places a wreath of wildflowers on top of her long flowing locks. It looks wonderful.

'What do you think?' Carrie asks Jess, who looks at herself in the mirror and says, 'I love it.'

Carrie grins. 'Well, I'm pleased you do because I ordered this in especially. This is my wedding gift to you, if you'll take it.'

As Jess deservedly admires herself in the mirror one more time, I notice she is wearing the sparkling aquamarine earrings I bought her.

'Okay, which one of you is going to try your dress first?' Jess asks.

'Since I'm the only one not mid-blowing my nose, why don't I go,' Izzy suggests.

Whilst Carrie helps Izzy into her bridesmaid dress, I watch Becky place her untouched glass of bubbles on the glass coffee table in front of the sofa.

'While it's just us,' she says, 'I want to say thank you, for helping me out at the table on Tuesday night *and* being subtle about it.'

I discard my tissue into the wastepaper basket next to the sofa, the presence of which tells me that crying is a completely normal reaction to have in this store.

I take hold of Becky's hand. 'You're welcome. I won't ask for details unless you choose to tell me, but are you happy?'

Becky's eyes fill again and she reaches for another tissue, looking to the ceiling, mocking her own emotional meltdown.

'I'm pregnant. I guess I should get used to this.'

She nods, part laughing, part crying, and reaches for another tissue.

'I had only taken a test before dinner on Tuesday night and hadn't told Drew yet. I told him yesterday in the hot air balloon. He was ecstatic, though pretty annoyed that I had decided to go up in the balloon whilst pregnant.' She laughs harder now. 'All's well that ends well, right?'

I chuckle. I can just imagine Drew's face. He is extremely protective when it comes to his friends and family, especially so when it comes to Becky.

'Can I be honest with you, Sarah?' she says, already knowing the answer, I hope. 'I feel really mixed about it. I am thrilled at the thought of having a baby with Drew but I'm terrified, too. I lost a baby once, in the past, with my ex-husband. I suppose looking back, it was for the best but it still would've been my baby, you know?'

I squeeze her hand tighter. 'I'm so sorry, Becky, and I think your emotions are more than valid. But I have such a good feeling about this. I think you and Drew are going to have the most beautiful baby and I think you're going to be a remarkable mummy.'

Becky just about manages to nod her head as she blows her nose and wipes mascara from under her eyes. Then, coughing and snotty, she tells me, 'You're going to be the most fantastic auntie.'

Before I can melt alongside Becky, Izzy springs from behind the changing room curtain and strikes a dazzling red-carpet pose.

Izzy's dress is so very her. From the thin spaghetti straps that show her toned shoulders and arms, to the long, flowing, bright-pink silk that matches her baby-blonde hair and vivacious personality.

Becky tries on her dress next and has similarly chosen well. Her dress has capped sleeves and layers of sunshine-yellow fabric. It's a great fit to go with Izzy's and it seems symbolic to me that the mum-to-be wears a color as happy as a sunbeam.

So far, the dresses have all fit without need for adjustment and as I step into the dress that has been made for me, I am nervous that I might be the one who ruins the clean sweep.

Though Jess gave us girls free rein on what we would like to choose to wear for the big day, knowing how much Jess loves aquamarine, I have chosen an aquamarine dress.

It's a satin halter neck, held and fastened around my neck with a silver necklace. The fabric clings to my body but in only the right places, hiding my indiscretions. As I feared, when I slip on the shoes I have brought with me to wear on Saturday, the dress is slightly too long.

Rather than make a fuss, I subtly ask Carrie to let me try a taller heel and with that, the dress needs no adjustment.

Each armed with a dress in a dress bag – and me with a new pair of shoes hanging in a bag over my shoulder – we head to a fine dining restaurant I have pre-booked, for overpriced salads and more bubbles.

Becky, as designated driver for the afternoon, seems relaxed and happy, perhaps relieved to have confessed her wonderful news to me, and maybe too because driving has given her the perfect excuse to drink soda water and lime.

According to its website, the restaurant is new age while being sympathetic to the local area of out-standing natural beauty. It uses only locally pro-duced goods to make an exquisite dining experience. It was the outdoor area with its 360-degree panoramic views that I found most enticing, though the rosette awards were also attractive for a week I want to be perfect for my friends.

We are seated around a mosaic-topped table and all decide on having the three-course set lunch and a bottle of local white sparkling wine to share. I take my shades from my handbag and shield myself from the very welcome sun, which has cast a happy glow across the abundance of lush green land we can see in the distance. It's a far cry from the hustle and bustle, concrete buildings and loud traffic of Manhattan.

When we fall silent, we can hear chirping birds in the trees and overhead. Gentle orchestral music plays at a very low volume in the background. This is serenity at its best. Food for the soul, as much as any spa or meditation experience might have been.

I close my eyes and raise my face to the sky, breathing in the fresh air.

'This place is great, Sarah, thank you,' Jess says.

'You are so welcome. You guys are my family. I love you all.'

The starter of chicken parfait, various purees and a lemon and zucchini foam is served and I find myself cringing over the memory of vomiting into the toilet and Charlie holding my hair, making remarks about me throwing up yuzu foam.

As I set down my knife and fork at six o'clock on my now empty plate, I am startled by a small dog yapping a table away from us. Startled because I hadn't expected a small white dog to be sitting on a chair at a table in a fine dining restaurant. But my eyes aren't playing tricks – the little Scotty, with its pink encrusted collar, is sitting on a chair, front paws on the tabletop.

I chuckle as the memory of one of Charlie's jokes from his gig comes back to me. He had been talking about the love people have for their pets and how, in the extreme, people will share their clothes with them. Just as a waiter announces at the nearby table the arrival of a puppychino for the dog, I notice the pink crystal-encrusted handbag sitting on the floor next to the dog owner's chair. The owner's pink painted nails with little diamantes pressed into the gel are also a match for the dog's collar and the handbag.

Charlie will love this. And suddenly I am eager to get back to the house and tell him what I have seen. Perhaps he can use it in one of his routines.

'Sarah,' Becky says, grabbing my attention as I dab my lips clean from my starter. 'Drew tells me the officer manager at the firm is retiring and his job is coming available.'

'Oh, Gerald, yeah, he'll be a loss. He's a nice man. A bit archaic and set in his ways, so I think a new face will be good, but he'll definitely be missed.'

'Mmhmm. Soooo, Drew thinks you should apply for the role.'

I pause with my water glass midway between the table and my lips. 'He does?'

'Yep.'

Becky is smiling but I'm not sure what kind of response she expects to elicit from me.

Am I supposed to be happy that one of my best friends in the world, the man I run around endlessly for, work tireless hours for, the man I basically kept together in all aspects of his life before he met Becky and, for that matter, the man who wouldn't have seen sense when it came to asking Becky out without me, now wants rid of me?

'My best guess is that he blurted that out without thinking. I'm nowhere near qualified enough for the role but honestly, I'm needed where I am.'

I hope, on both counts, that I'm right.

I brush off the kind of comments girl pals give each other, like 'You've got way more transferable skills than you give yourself credit for' and 'You'd make a great manager, you're so organized,' and 'You deserve the title and the pay rise.'

I hope it won't be brought up again. I like my job. Moreover, Drew needs me.

We eat a main course of roast duck, served with locally grown baby potatoes, and a dessert of Eton mess, with freshly picked strawberries from the field right behind the restaurant. Afterward, homemade and hand painted chocolates accompany our coffee.

Thankfully, the conversation moves on to Izzy's latest exercise and nutrition book, and more wedding details.

When Becky and Jess make a trip to the ladies' room, Izzy asks me, 'How are you doing with all this?'

'The food?'

She smiles sweetly, gently. 'No, I mean the whole event. The wedding, being around couples. I don't know if I'm asking the right question, I just think that if it were me and I had lost Brooks, then I'd find these kinds of occasions difficult. I don't want to put a downer on anything but I want to make sure you're okay.'

I am both caught off-guard and touched by her sensitivity. So much so, it brings a lump to my throat. I have to swallow it down before I'm able to respond.

'I'm okay. It is hard, so thank you for asking. I am beyond happy for Jake and Jess and for all of you guys being in couples and so in love. I truly, genuinely couldn't be happier for all of you. And actually, I normally do quite well at these events. I've been to numerous weddings since Danny died but for some reason, this one has me feeling a little out of sorts.'

I pause for a drink, wondering why now, why this wedding. But... 'I'm not sure why. Maybe it's the rush of going back to the office and getting here late, then getting stuck in London. Sharing a room with a man who isn't Danny, which is completely bizarre. Or maybe it's none of that. I don't know. Maybe it's just that time of the month and things are getting me a little more choked than they might otherwise do.'

Izzy's smile is both empathetic and pitiful, I think. Pity I can't handle this week.

'We all love you so much, Sarah. If you need anything, even just five minutes of girl time, you let me know, okay?'

'I will but I'm fine, honestly.' I offer a smile that I hope looks more genuine than it feels.

* * *

Back at the house, I'm thrilled to see all of the other guests lying and frolicking around the pool. It is a gloriously sunny day and I would be happy to spend the evening – the last evening the bride and groom will spend together before the big day – just being on holiday, soaking up some R 'n' R.

Edmond and Becky are laying on a spread to eat

tonight and I have planned more silly games for us all to play.

First, I need to change into my bathing suit before I head out to the pool to chill with the others.

When I come back out, dressed for the water, Drew and Brooks are at a poolside table playing cards with Drew's parents. Millie, Amy, Jess, Cady and Izzy appear to be midway through a group manicure. Jake and Edmond are teasing each other as they make failed attempts to light a large coal grill. And apparently Drew's brother-in-law is back at his guest house winding down two hyper kids for the evening.

I want to tell Charlie about the dog at the restaurant but he seems much too busy to be interrupted as he floats around the pool in a giant pink flamingo, a bottle of beer tucked into each wing of the bird, chatting with Cash. Cash is lying on a blue Lilo on his tummy, his head resting on his arms.

I hold up a hand to say hello and hope he will float my way to chat but he doesn't react at all. It's impossible to tell from behind his polarized shades whether he has even seen me.

Considering the options, I decide I have spent less time with Drew, Brooks and Drew's parents than the others over the last couple of days, so I pull up a seat and ask to be dealt in to the next round of cards.

15

CHARLIE

I am floating around the pool in an inflatable, simultaneously chewing the fat with Cash about everything from political affairs to arts and culture, drinking beer and fantasizing about smoking a cigarette.

I smoked my first cigarette when I was nine years old, encouraged by another foster kid I was living with at the time who was fifteen and, to my juvenile mind, *really* cool.

At the height of my addiction, I was smoking a pack of twenty every day and an occasional joint, too.

I remember, vividly, the day I quit smoking. It was 2014 and my twenty-second year on the planet. It was the day the statue of Amy Winehouse was unveiled in Camden.

I had happened upon the unveiling by luck, rather than judgement. I liked Amy Winehouse's music – who doesn't, it's iconic – but I wasn't fascinated enough to go along to the event.

Nevertheless, when the statue was uncovered, I was struck by a sense of waste. The singer's life trashed by addiction. My birth mother's life also destroyed by addiction. My own life, thrust into the system, because of said addiction. Yet, there I was, a university drop out, fag in my hand, shortening my own life, letting myself and anyone who cared even a little bit about me down, *again*.

In that moment, as I stared at Amy Winehouse and thought about how much greater she could have been, I decided to stop. I quit smoking and decided to turn my life around that day.

As I float around the pool now, I know, no matter how much I fancy a smoke, I won't have one.

'I can't believe they've made a musical about *The Great British Bake Off*,' Cash says, drifting by my shoulder. 'I mean, what will they have, dancing fairies in wet trousers?'

'You'll have to explain that one to me,' I tell him.

'Fairy cakes with soggy bottoms.'

My amusement is cut short sharply as Sarah steps outside from the house.

Wow. Just wow.

She looks incredible. I don't want to sexualize her or objectify her or do anything that is deemed entirely unacceptable in the present climate. I sure as hell don't want to get the three amigos on my back for a second time in one day, after the dad-like talking to I had to endure in the kitchen this morning. But by God, she deserves some subtle admiration, even if it is from behind the shield of my sunglasses.

In fact, God will be disappointed in me as a man if I don't, at least in my own mind, comment on how good Sarah looks in her black swimsuit, legs reaching from the Earth's core to outer space, and that teasing floor-length lace robe tied around the middle, which allows me to see her slender neckline, kissable collarbones and subtle but taunting cleavage.

Whilst ever there is an ounce of testosterone in my blood, I won't be able to notice a woman as astoundingly sexy as she is without offering mental praise.

This isn't sexy in that way young girls think *Love Island* contestants are. No, Sarah is all woman. All sophistication. All glamour. All beautiful, classic, exquisite beauty.

'Are you listening to me or are you just undressing that woman with your eyes, man?' Cash asks.

Dammit. Maybe the polarized lenses aren't foolproof, after all.

'I am 100 per cent listening to you, Cash. I am in no way shape or form interested romantically, sexually, or any other *ly* way in anybody in this house,' I lie.

I risk one more decadent and naughty glance in Sarah's direction, then erase all prior thoughts and get on with my day, my primary task being to ignore her and stay out of trouble.

'And to your previous point,' I tell him, diverting the subject. 'I hear you, but I don't read a historical novel for the precise factual detail and minutiae of historical accuracy. I like to read a romantic thread that just happens to be set against the backdrop of a significant historical moment. For that reason, Sebastian Faulks remains my favorite author. And before you say it, that doesn't make me any more gay than you.'

Cash laughs so hard that his belly rocks him off balance on his Lilo and sends him crashing into the water. It's his reaction, as opposed to my own joke, that makes me laugh with such vigor that I almost fall out of my big pink bird.

Though I should have known I wouldn't escape the fall out entirely. As Cash kicks back up to the surface, he reaches up to one of my flamingo wings and with one hefty plunge, he drags me into the water.

I surface and jump onto his muscular shoulders, wrestling him under the water, with an awful lot of splashing from both of us.

'Would you two get a room?' Will shouts.

When I look, ready to issue a retort, I see he is now playing cards at the table where Sarah and the others are sitting. And so I also find Sarah's gaze, behind large tortoiseshell lenses, fixed on me.

I indulge myself in a nanosecond glance at her smile, then look away, hopefully without attracting the scrutiny of Brooks and Drew, to whom I have promised I will stay clear of Sarah. Or words to that effect.

Ever since they enlightened me as to her past this morning, I understand why they want to protect her. But as I pointed out to them this morning, her interest in me has been limited to my acting as a taxi driver and an unwanted squatter in her bedroom only.

True, we have shared moments of friendliness. And though, as I have been floating around the pool, I have allowed myself to be the smallest bit flattered that the people closest to Sarah might entertain, if only fleetingly, that she could fall for someone as unrefined and ordinary as me, there has been nothing romantic between us.

As the evening wears on, the temperature begins to cool slowly. Edmond and Becky, with the others chipping in here and there, prepare a finger buffet and the cards table becomes the hotspot.

As Sarah and Drew become increasingly competitive and animated, even those who aren't playing have gathered around to listen to the banter and laughter between them.

I keep my distance, staying in the pool, while the others dip in and out, or come to sit on the side of the pool with their legs dangling in the water to chat to me. All except the key card players, which suits me fine.

It's 8 p.m. before Drew and Sarah call a truce and agree to be joint cards champions. With the girls taking the lead, the group starts to head inside to change out of our swimwear and into warmer but still casual clothes for dinner.

I decide not to perform any naked bathtub antics

whilst Sarah uses our room tonight. Instead, I am one of two last men standing as Brooks and I watch the sun slowly making its descent for the day.

'This is exactly what my soul ordered for dinner,' he says.

'The beers or the quiet serenity of the setting sun as a backdrop to this resplendent landscape?' I ask.

Brooks shifts to look at me with something like astonishment on his face. 'That was almost poetic.'

I rest my chin on my hands, leaning on the lip of the infinity pool. 'What can I say? I'm an artist.'

We enjoy the view, occasionally making small talk, until Izzy and Sarah return, ready for dinner.

'Brooks, can you go get ready? You can't stay in soggy swim shorts all evening,' Izzy says, calling over.

'And just like that, the peace is broken,' he mumbles, for my ears only.

There's a part of me that's happy not to have another half to order me around and tell me when to get dressed for dinner. But as I watch Brooks plant a wet kiss on Izzy's cheek, then wrap his arm playfully around her shoulders, and Izzy squeal about him making her wet but giggling as she tries to wrestle free, there's also a part of me that is envious.

Under the guise of watching the exchange between Izzy and Brooks, I allow my eyes to follow

Sarah as she moves around the decking. She has changed into an all-in-one that's electric blue, pulled in at the waist with a belt and floating around her legs down to the ground. It accentuates her height and her figure. Her hair is somehow fixed up, in whatever way women manage to hold up their hair, doubtless precisely placed yet looking effortless.

Effortless. That is how Sarah looks always, actually. Effortlessly beautiful.

She is a disgusting drunk, cantankerous with a hangover, irritable after travel and as hangry as me.

Yet, the sight of her has increased my heart rate. I feel like I've had too much caffeine – that combination of excited and nervous energy.

And I realize, true to form, that I now really want what I have been told I cannot have.

I recall Drew's words from this morning. *She's been through too much to be messed around.*

In this instance, I have to heed the advice and let her be.

So, I finish my beer and without interacting with her at all, wrap a towel around my waist and head upstairs to change.

I don't own designer trousers and expensive Italian shirts like the other guys but I dress in my smartest pair of jeans and one of two shirts I own that isn't Hawaiian. This is still a floral number but it's blue and the white flowers are small and subtle, in my opinion. It has long sleeves and, believe it or not, I have decided to tuck it into my jeans. Not only this, but I am also wearing a belt.

My outfit choice has nothing to do with the fact I have seemingly developed a crush on Sarah.

Edmond and Becky's finger buffet is no ordinary finger buffet. In place of the eighties-style vol-au-vent that is still rolled out at wakes (as if a dollop of tuna mayo in a teaspoon-sized oval of puff pastry is a way to tell the dead how loved they are), Edmond and Becky have made giant love heart-shaped vol-au-vents.

One such delicacy has been filled with mixed roasted Mediterranean-style veg and topped with creamy, salty feta cheese and fresh herbs. A second has been filled with cream cheese, smoked salmon, dill and capers.

Rather than those packet dips I see at my mates' house parties – the cheap ones from the supermarket with sour cream and onion, cheese and chive, onion and garlic, and Thousand Island dips – Edmond and Becky have prepared a bright and fresh salsa verde, a mixed tomato, slightly smoky, slightly spicy salsa, and a creamy mushroom and tarragon whip.

Where I would usually snap and dip a cheap breadstick, on this table there are warm, light home-made flatbreads and rainbow-colored crudité on ice.

The off-duty chefs have slow roasted and shredded pork chipotle, served with all the trimmings to make burritos. There are home-made Scotch eggs, the centers oozing when they are cut – I wonder if Sarah will find them so disgusting now. There are spinach and ricotta filo parcels, which, despite being veggie, are mega tasty.

Basically, I am going to find it difficult to move from the table for the duration of the evening.

Everyone is in good spirits and whilst I don't want to seem mushy, I am warmed by how dizzily in love Jake and Jess appear to be. They are more of a subtle PDA couple usually, more likely to banter than hug in front of others, but tonight they are like loved-up teenagers. A stroke here or a pet there, with an occasional hug or a kiss. But most importantly, they are laughing together, and that is what I love most about the two of them.

They were friends with benefits for a while but when they finally saw what everybody else had been able to see for months, that they are perfect for each other, they transitioned seamlessly into being a couple, yet still retained that sense of fun and play-fulness.

I'm happy for them, though maybe the churning in my stomach that I am occasionally feeling tonight is also a bit of the green-eyed monster.

That, or I really need to move away from the finger buffet.

I'm beginning to see Sarah as the Monica of this friendship group. The woman loves a bit of organized fun. But I am also a fan of a party game, so when she declares it's time to pin the top hat on the groom and pin the veil on the bride, I am up for it.

Grabbing one more Scotch egg, I follow the co-hort into the lounge where, stuck to a wall (the owner of this place will not be happy about that) is a giant cardboard bride and a giant cardboard groom, each with movable limbs, attached with those little gold butterfly clips kids use to make Christmas decorations in school.

I remember making a Santa Claus one year with those kinds of clips. His arms and his legs moved, and I was super proud of him. My teacher had beamed when she said I could take my artwork home for Mummy and Daddy; they always forgot that I didn't come from a regular family, with a regular mum and dad, and always seemed to trip over their feet with me.

But the making of my dancing Santa Claus is such a vivid memory, not because my teachers told me to take it home to my parents, who I didn't have, but because that year I had been placed temporarily with a family who didn't believe in Christmas. There had been no tree, no church service or Christmas stories read by a fire. I had taken my dancing Santa Claus home and tucked it under my bed pillow. Then, whilst my foster parents and their other foster children had watched television and ate sausages and mashed potato for dinner, I had stayed in my room, hidden in the wardrobe so that the other children didn't see me and make fun of me. And I had sung Christmas songs that I had learned in school and made my Santa Claus dance to the music.

The memory causes me to look around the room and feel immeasurably grateful for being in this room full of love tonight. It also makes me mourn the inevitable loss of my friends, old and new, knowing this week, like all good things, will end.

There is something about silly party games when everyone is in a jovial mood that makes them funny when they would otherwise be ridiculous. As a group, we heckle and jeer as each person is blindfolded and the top hat is pinned on the bride's face, on the groom's feet, not on the bride or groom at all. As the bride's veil is pinned on the groom's abdomen, on the groom's elbow and on the bride's right leg.

'Okay, Charlie, you're up,' Sarah says.

It is legitimate, given she has addressed me, that I look at her. That smile. That sparkle she has in her eyes when she is organizing things and taking care of people.

I step up to the wall and face her. She moves her body to within inches of mine and her proximity overwhelms me. My entire body, from head to toe and every limb in between, is energized by her. By the feel of her fingertips as they graze my face when she ties a blindfold around my eyes. By her perfume, which I can't name but which doesn't stick in my nose and make my eyes water like others do because they're so overpowering. It is subtle yet intoxicating. Just like Sarah.

I inhale deeply through my nose but slowly, so as to not give me away. And when Sarah asks if I can see through the blindfold, I lie and tell her I can, just so I can feel her fingertips again as she adjusts the material.

Now, readjusted, I can in fact see.

All the better to play pranks, my dear, I think.

Peering beneath the blindfold, I lift my head slightly and pin the top hat on the groom's crotch, moving the groom's butterfly pinned arms to hold it in place. Then in my best impression of Jake, I say, 'Hey babe, what are you doing? It's bad luck to see my dick before the wedding!'

I then pin the veil on the bride's movable arms and whoosh it around dismissively. In my best impression of Jess, I say, 'Jake, honey, come on, it's not as if we didn't get pissed and shag each other one thousand times before we stopped pretending we weren't in love.'

'Jess, my parents are here, for crying out loud!' I retort in Jake's voice.

Then as Jess, I say, 'Babe, it's okay, your mum has seen it all before. And I just want her and you to know that I'm not marrying you because of the size of your penis, I'm marrying you *despite* that.'

It's a little uncouth to laugh at your own jokes but when I see the mixture of mortification on Jake's face and horror and blushing amusement on his mother's, then see Jess hiding behind her fingers, I burst into uncontrollable laughter.

'I'm sorry, I couldn't resist.' I look at Jake apologetically. 'I know your small penis is a real sensitive topic. Sorry, buddy, I should've been more considerate.'

He launches a sofa cushion in my direction.

There is a nanosecond where I glance across to Sarah and find her laughing, her attention focused on me. I quickly look away.

16

SARAH

Charlie is definitely avoiding me.

I have tried all night to get near him. I only wanted to talk. To tell him about the dog thing.

More than that, every time I have looked his way, he has scowled or looked right through me as though he hasn't seen me, or quickly looked the other way.

It's *rude*. It's nasty. And—

Oh God, how many times *have* I looked his way?

Despite lying on my bed in darkness, I reach for a pillow and cover my face, horrified.

What must he be thinking? What if he thinks I have been staring at him because I—?

The bedroom door opens. Slowly, on tiptoe and

with the floor around his feet illuminated by the torch light from his phone, Charlie steps inside.

'I'm awake,' I whisper, giving him the green light to make noise and turn on a light.

'Oh. Sorry, I thought you'd be sleeping by now. I'll be quick.'

He stays with the torch light only and begins to undress by the chaise longue. I can just make out his figure, wearing a white vest, underwear and socks. Socks pulled up to his *knees*.

I watch from the bed as he sets his phone down on the wash basin and washes his face, then cleans his teeth. When he's finished, he wipes his hands and face dry with a towel, then looks in the mirror. Not at himself, but back toward the bed. At me.

I suspect he can't see me in the dark, staring right back at him.

I know he can't hear me thinking, *You make a little more sense to me, Charlie.*

The mood swings, the erratic behavior. He has had such a rough upbringing.

Should I be sympathetic, rather than being mad at him?

No. People have shit to deal with. He is an adult. He knows what is socially acceptable.

As he settles under a blanket on the sofa bed and finally turns off the torch light, I sit up in bed.

'Have you been avoiding me today?'

Charlie doesn't respond, which makes me fiercely mad. *Coward.*

'Well?' I demand, furiously slapping my hand down on the bed.

Then I hear the now too familiar sound of a pig grunting, his snores.

Slapping both hands down on the bed, I let myself fall back against the pillows, too cross to sleep.

* * *

I checked my watch at two minutes past two, six minutes past three, fourteen minutes past four and must have eventually fallen asleep sometime after that, once I had decided that I don't care what Charlie thinks about anything anymore. After convincing myself that I don't want to know anything about his childhood, or his education, or his work and friends. Nothing. Not a zip.

Now, I'm awake. It is just after eight in the morning, I don't feel rested at all, and I *still* want to know why Charlie was so hideous to me yesterday. Not that

I *care*, I just think he ought to justify his ignorance. That's all.

Unfortunately, when I make to get out of bed to question him, Charlie is gone. His blanket is folded neatly on the bottom of the sofa bed.

Pulling on my robe, I go in search of him. Only when I reach the kitchen and half the guests of the house are already fully dressed and sitting around with teas and coffees, with Charlie notably absent from the group, do I realize how ridiculous I am being.

To save grace and prevent questions, I pour myself a filter coffee and tell the others I'll be back down once I am dressed.

* * *

It is the eve of the wedding and I am pleased to be leaving the house – and the men residing in it – to go to the wedding venue and spend the day and night in the spa and bridal suite with the girls. Drew's mum and sister, Jess's aunt, Cady and Amy have also been invited along to pamper themselves for the day with the bride and bridesmaids.

The wedding venue is an exclusive use, Palladian-style mansion from the eighteenth century, which has been modernized to include a small spa in what were old stables but which have retained alluring, seventeen hundred's luxury.

Our party ascends the stone steps from a gravel driveway, turning our backs on an ornate water fountain and vast country views. I imagine how beautiful Jess is going to look, standing on those steps in her dress for photographs the next day, which is set to be fine weather.

A concierge brings inside our bags and dresses, which we've been assured are going to be hung 'with urgency' by the staff to avoid creasing. I love how posh Brits speak.

'It's the King's English,' Izzy says.

Inside the mansion, the entrance has a marble floor and marble pillars. Gold trimmings finish the decorative walls, and crystal chandeliers, large and low, sparkle in the light that shines through tall, wood-trimmed windows.

The staff are dressed in period attire that screams *Downton Abbey*. A pianist – who I assume will be the pianist for the wedding – appears to be practicing alongside a concert harpist. To my ears, he needn't practice at all.

'It's magical,' Jess breathes.

I have to agree, it's magnificent. Prior to arriving

today, I have only seen it on the website, which already makes the venue look and sound incredible. It hasn't nearly done it justice.

We are shown to the bridal suite – a trove of fancy treasures and upholstery – where we take our spa attire from our bags, then head off in search of it.

The day passes in a blur of coffees, cakes, nail gels, body oils and wedding conversation. Jess giddily describes the places she wants to see whilst on honeymoon in the Philippines. Becky relays the plans she has made for the day after the wedding for her and Drew, before they go home to New York. Izzy theatrically imagines the lunch she has booked with her parents, Brooks and Cady on Sunday – *Meet the Fockers* style. Drew's mum and Jess's aunt discuss the best matinees currently showing in the West End and where best to get post-theatre food. Millie says over and over, 'I feel like my ears have fallen off' and regales us with hilarious stories about the silly things her kids do, despite being ecstatic about having some 'me time' away from them. In equal measure, she criticizes Eddie and praises him for keeping the kids in check this week.

I take it all in, excited for the others but saddened that my sight-seeing adventures around London next week are going to be undertaken alone.

No matter, I am a big girl and after a week of company – some people's more pleasant than others – some time alone might be nice.

You have plenty of solo company at home, says the black dog on my shoulder, but I choose to ignore it, as I have become so good at doing.

Bark somewhere else, hound.

After dinner, everyone except the bride and bridesmaids departs, following lots of well wishes, compliments and hugs for Jess.

'This is it,' Jess says as she stands in the lobby with Izzy, Becky and me at her side. 'I'm getting married tomorrow.'

I lean my temple against hers. 'Yeah, you are. To a great guy, too.'

I open my eyes widely, telling my tears they mustn't fall. This is *not* about me, or Danny, or loneliness, jealousy, anger, sadness, or anything else. It is about two of my best friends agreeing to spend the rest of their lives together.

For their sakes, I hope those lives are long.

17

SARAH

Chaos.

Beautiful. Energized. Emotional. Chaos.

Isn't that how every bride's wedding morning could be described?

I remember my own.

Danny and I were married in a church – his family practicing Catholics. I, like Jess, had a gorgeous bridal suite in the hotel in which we held our wedding breakfast.

I had two bridesmaids, both friends of couples Danny and I had been friends with. Neither of those women I see regularly these days.

In the months following Danny's death – after the initial weeks of people rallying and offering their eternal support to me as a new widow – I noticed my friendship circle slowly dwindle. There hadn't been malice in it, I didn't think, but being my friend in the wake of Danny's tragic accident had become too difficult.

Do we invite her out with us as a couple anymore? Can we be couple-y in front of her? Will her very presence bring down the mood? What do we say to her?

Those were just some of the questions I imagine my old friends repeatedly asked themselves, until eventually they only saw me at a yoga class or for events and activities that had been pigeon-holed for women only, like baby showers and spa days. Even then, due to the latter two questions I suspect, I don't often receive invites anymore.

The friends who did stick with me, ironically, were men. Drew, despite being Danny's best friend, hadn't abandoned me under a banner of 'too difficult'. Brooks and Jake still invited me places.

And now, I have the ladies in this bridal suite to count amongst my best friends. There's no way that I could lose them that isn't beyond my control. And I will do just about anything to keep in my life the people I love.

I am the one to call upon as Matron of Honor. I'll

be the one who buys the best and most inappropriate gifts that my godchildren will love. I'll be the one to call if they ever need to hide a body.

My peak of loss has been reached and I am not willing to lose anyone else important to me.

Thankfully, the morning passes in a blur of me topping up mimosas and orange juice, handing out pastries when people can't get up from their seats because they are being arranged by a hair stylist or beautician, finding hair grips, lost shoe boxes and mislaid items of clothing.

There isn't time for me to dwell on the past, or recent history, like yesterday and why on *earth* that lump of... lump of stupid man avoided me all day.

Does he think I am just as dumb as him? Feigning being asleep? Come on! As if I'd fall for that. As if I didn't try that trick on my mother a million times as a child.

My mind does defy me and briefly wanders to these thoughts about Charlie. When I come back to the room, standing behind Izzy and holding a box of hair grips as the stylist perfects her up-do, Izzy is looking at my reflection in the mirror.

'Penny for 'em?' she asks.

I smile. 'I'm not sure where I went there.'

More quietly, Izzy asks, 'Are you okay?'

Still smiling, I lie. 'Absolutely. I think I might be a little dehydrated. I can't remember when I last had a drink of something that wasn't a mimosa. Would you like water?'

Just like that, I busy myself with another job.

By the time the other bridesmaids and Jess are complete with make-up and hair, though still in the matching silk robes that I ordered and had personalized for the occasion, we are running massively behind schedule.

'Just do whatever you have time for, I'll be happy with anything,' I tell the hair stylist, who has agreed to work around the beautician, who is applying a limited range of products to my face, both due to time constraints and because I never feel comfortable wearing a heavy coverage.

The stylist has partially pinned up my hair and curled the ends of the rest with heated irons. The beautician has applied soft-pink color to my lips and cheeks, and nude shades everywhere else.

Just as I am proclaimed complete, the wedding photographer knocks on the suite door. Jess wanted the morning, before now, to be natural and just us girls. It has meant that we could talk freely and, I suspect, delayed the element of the day Jess is least looking forward to – being surrounded by people she doesn't consider to be her nearest and dearest.

'Can I get the Matron of Honor helping Jess into her dress?' the photographer asks after she has taken pictures of Jess's dress hanging on the antique wardrobe and her bridal shoes standing on the windowsill, the outdoor wedding set-up in the background.

We can see guests arriving and filling the rows of white iron chairs that have been decorated with bows and wildflowers. At this stage, the archway, similarly decorated, which will act as the altar, is empty. Jake and the groomsmen aren't outside yet.

I have a feeling that Jess's increasingly nervous energy would be calmed if she could see Jake. For now, I will have to be his lesser replacement.

Once the photographer has positioned Jess in front of the free-standing, floor-length mirror, I start fastening the dress. There are twenty-four buttons on the back and as I take each one in turn, my eyes begin to sting. The pace in the room has slowed and the emotion of the morning is threatening to spill out of me.

When I've finished the buttons, I look up to the mirror and the reflected image of Jess, secured into her dress. Elegant. Mesmerizing.

My tears fill my eyes now because her beauty is the straw that finally breaks the dam.

The photographer asks for the headband of wild-flowers. For the purposes of photography only, I place the headband on Jess's head and once the photographer is satisfied, I step aside to allow the hair-stylist to take over, forcing the fingers of the band into Jess's hair, accentuating the flawlessly relaxed look.

The photographer hands each of us a tissue and though we all genuinely wipe our eyes and noses, the photographer makes impromptu snaps of what I think will be the funniest picture of all – four grown women, all dressed-up, blowing their noses.

If Charlie had been in the room, I am sure he would have come up with a hilarious caption, taking the emotion out of the situation. As I smile for more pictures, I ponder how much of his use of humor is a product of him papering over a troubled youth. Not for the first time, I think: is comedy his defense mechanism?

Almost at the same time, guilt pulls my heart deep down into my abdomen.

Why am I thinking about Charlie now? Why isn't the first person I am thinking about in the circumstances Danny and what he would say on seeing me brim-full of emotion?

Thankfully, the venue's wedding coordinator, Ashley, knocks on the door at that moment. We have clawed back some time, thanks to me having shorter slots with the beautifying team and Jess calling time on photographs sooner than the photographer would have liked. We are as close as any bride can be expected to be to the planned schedule.

'Are you ready, Jess? It's time,' Ashley says. He is tall and slender, wearing a plain black three-piece suit, as opposed to period dress like the other staff at the hotel, and his hair has been slicked in a way that reminds me of Joe Elvis. 'You look a million dollars.'

Jess inhales deeply, her shoulders rising. She looks out of the window to the rows of seats, which are now full. She seems to scan the guests, pausing when her gaze lands on the three men wearing morning suits at the archway of flowers. She exhales, finding her groom, and she returns the coordinator's smile.

'I'm ready,' she says with confidence.

Jess's aunt and uncle tap on the door next. 'Is it okay to come in?' her aunt calls.

'Shall we give you guys a few minutes alone and meet you downstairs?' I suggest to Jess.

Before we leave, I am pleased to witness Jess's aunt gasp and bring her hands to her mouth, and I am warmed to hear Jess's uncle say, 'Oh stop it, you're setting me off.'

Jess was almost married once, years ago. On that day, when her uncle knocked on the door of her bridal room, he was coming to tell her that she had been jilted.

Clearly fate stepped in because today is the exact opposite. It is precisely how weddings should be. Full of love and joy.

It must be hard for Jess to be getting married without her parents present, without her father to walk her down the aisle, and her mother placing last-minute jewels around her neck. I don't believe the hole created by the loss of a loved one can ever be filled, but Jess is so incredibly loved by her aunt and uncle, it must go some way toward filling Jess's doubtless massive void today.

Izzy, Becky and I turn right out of the bridal suite and descend a bi-furcated staircase, in the manner of Rose descending the clock staircase in *Titanic*. Only at the bottom of the staircase, rather than Leonardo DiCaprio waiting, there is Cash, Will and Charlie. Three ushers waiting for their female partners to walk down the aisle.

I have been paired with Charlie, therefore he will need to acknowledge my existence at some point.

There's no getting away from me today. He'll need to link with my arms, and at least for the benefit of the other wedding guests pretend he can stand being in the same vicinity as me.

Whilst my mind focuses on my feet and not falling in my heels, now higher than I would like, my eyes glance ahead and find Charlie's eyes on me. Unlike yesterday, he does not look away, but holds my gaze with such intensity that it makes me hot around the neck.

Oh no, mister, I won't get flustered for you.

Clearly one of Charlie's other personalities is making an appearance today and apparently, I am allowed to exist.

Well, no siree, I won't allow him to play his nonsense games with me. I am a grown woman. A strong, independent woman and I won't be messed around by some... by some... man-child!

Following Cash's lead, Will and Charlie hold out hands to Becky and me respectively as we reach the bottom of the staircase. I can feel myself pouting as I glare at Charlie's hand, then back to his face, then decidedly stare across his shoulder, dismissing him entirely.

Okay, perhaps games aren't entirely beyond me but he deserves to be ignored. He deserves to feel small, the way he made me feel small and insignificant yesterday.

'Call me old fashioned but when someone extends their hand, it's polite to take it,' Charlie whispers.

'Seriously?' I snap back as best I can in a whisper. 'Call *me* old fashioned but if you've been an asshat for the last twenty-four hours, it's usually polite to apologize.'

Our bickering is halted when Jess appears from one side of the staircase, her arms linked on each side by her aunt and uncle.

She is glowing. I have honestly never seen her look happier. And any nerves I detected in the bridal suite aren't noticeable now.

'She looks incredible,' Charlie says quietly.

And solely because he is gushing about my friend, I respond. 'She's going to meet her lobster.'

Charlie smiles and nods, getting the *Friends* reference, as I expect him to. 'She is,' he agrees.

We can hear the wedding coordinator asking the guests to take their seats and I feel anticipation in the air as they await the bride's entrance.

I prepare the short train of Jess's dress and overlay the train with her cathedral veil, as Jess

braces herself behind double French doors, preparing to walk the aisle.

With Jess set, I give her a final kiss on the cheek,
then take my position at the front of the bridal party
with Charlie. Behind us, Izzy links arms with Cash,
followed by Becky and Will, and finally, most importantly, Jess with her aunt and uncle. Reluctantly, I do
the same with Charlie.

Ashley returns to our group and when Jess confirms she is ready, Elvis Presley's 'Loving You' begins
to play.

I turn to see Jess gently laughing and dabbing the
corners of her eyes.

'He's such a goof,' she says, shaking her head.
'Jake told me he chose "Pachelbel's Cannon". I should
have known he'd sneak in an Elvis track.'

My stomach twists as I feel the love my friends share.
I know the feeling because I once felt it myself, right before walking down the aisle to the man of *my* dreams.

Slowly, steadily, Charlie and I step out of the
building and walk behind the guests sitting on the
right – not specifically the groom's family and
friends, per tradition, but a mix of all the guests, as
Jake and Jess requested – then turn right, down the
aisle, toward the groom and his best men.

'Did you really call me an asshat?' Charlie asks, for my ears only.

Biting down on my tongue to stop myself from firing a retort, I brush him off and smile for the guests, many of whom are taking pictures.

'Are you ignoring me?'

'Sure am,' I reply through my teeth, beating myself up for even responding to him at all.

At the front of the aisle, I wink at Jake, who looks more nervous than I have ever seen him, then part from Charlie, moving to stand to the left of the archway, as he moves to the right.

It is done. No need to speak to him or touch him again.

La la la la laaaaaaaaa. Life is such a dreeeeeam.

As I stand in position, watching Jess glide down the aisle, I realize that, unbeknown to him, Charlie has managed to completely distract me, right at the moment my body had decided to fall into grief. Instead of internally breaking down because I can't be here with Danny, amongst my friends, enjoying this celebration of love, I was arguing with Charlie.

For the briefest moment, I soften toward him. Could he have saved me intentionally? Defended me with his humor? Then I remember he is an asshat and he couldn't possibly have done something as kind as that on purpose.

Despite my partner, I am pleased to have walked down the aisle first. I'm in prime position to see Jess walking toward her soulmate, to see the radiance in her face that has nothing to do with make-up or sparkling blusher. Better than that, I get to witness the moment Jake finally sees Jess. The moment he takes in her beauty, as outstanding on the outside as we all know her to be on the inside.

If I have one regret from my own wedding day, it is that I didn't arrange for a wedding video to be taken, because all of the photographs of this moment in my wedding are of me walking down the aisle. I have longed to see the moment when Danny first saw me walking toward him, regretted not having it captured so that I'd be able to replay it time and time again. I remember the way he looked at me. The sparkle that lit up his otherworldly eyes. The way he gently caressed my cheek with his fingertips as he lifted my veil back from my face. That first smile he gave me on our wedding day. I am terrified that my memories will one day fade.

Jake and Jess have written their own vows, which they speak with depth and honesty, authenticity. I am mostly pleased that they haven't relied on traditional words and that awful line about loving each other until parted by death. I said that line on my wedding day and now, in the wake of Danny's death, merely saying I would love him until his death is not enough. Not even forever would have been enough. I hope that, wherever he is now, he knows that I still love him and always will.

After a charming service with personal words from the officiator, Jake holds Jess's cheeks in his palms, looks into her eyes, and kisses her as if they have been apart for ten thousand nights, not one.

Everyone cheers, and under the canopy of biodegradable confetti, the newly married couple lead the bridal party and groomsmen back down the aisle.

'It was a nice service,' Charlie says as I reluctantly link my arm through his one last time.

'Please don't speak to me,' I reply.

And clearly my tone is not sufficiently or adequately conveyed, as Charlie's response is casual laughter. No matter – after thirty more steps or so, I will never have to touch him or speak to him again, for real this time.

18

CHARLIE

Oh, she's pissed off all right.

Watching Sarah actually try to express anger is almost comical. She knows how to be mardy as hell – I have witnessed her whip of the tongue – but this angry show she is putting on today is hilarious. I have to keep reminding myself that she probably thinks my ignoring her yesterday was similarly ridiculous. But she didn't know my rationale. My ignorance was reasoned. Protective. Today, she is simply playing a game of tit-for-tat.

The thing is, as I lay alone in our bedroom last night, I came to the realization that, for whatever reason, completely baffling to me, I was missing Sarah's company. It was utterly bizarre because I hate sharing my home and especially my sleeping space with other people. My bedroom, if not my entire home, is my sanctuary. Yet, last night, in the double bed (which I will not confess to Sarah so that I won't have to change the sheets tonight), I could smell her scent on the pillows and, oddly, wished that she was in the room making fun of me or issuing one of her silly jibes.

It also occurred to me that I had been staying away from her for two reasons. First, because I was told to by her mafia bosses and secondly, because I didn't want to upset her when she has already been through so much in her life.

But... after today, I won't really be seeing Drew and Brooks again, and Jake, well, I can take him, easily. Well, okay, not easily. Maybe not at all. But I know Jake and don't fear his wrath, not the way I'd fear Brooks aka The Thing from *Fantastic Four*.

As to the second point, clearly me ignoring her had made her unhappy too, so either way, she is angry with me. Ergo, I might as well get some enjoyment out of the situation. Plus, after today, I might not ever see her again. (Maybe I should encourage Jake and Jess to have kids and throw a big christening bash.)

Furthermore, and more pertinent, whenever I see

Sarah today, in moments where she doesn't realize that she is under a watchful eye, she has looked sad. More than sad. Heartbroken. She clearly still loves her husband. Of course she does. And that makes my crush on Sarah a safe space. Because, whilst I indulged a moment of flattery in which I dared to believe that Drew, Brooks and Jake were right to think Sarah might like me even the smallest amount, I know I will never be able to compete with the man she holds in such high regard, dead or alive.

All I have wanted today, in those moments of sadness I have witnessed, is to make sure Sarah is okay. To make sure someone, in amongst the wedding bliss, has thought to ask her if she is doing all right.

The wedding guests have moved on to a south-facing part of the estate whilst the ceremony area is reset for the wedding breakfast. Out of the shade of a parasol, I am hot, extremely so in a three-piece morning suit. I have escaped to the respite of a picnic table and managed to steal some moments of shade here and there but mostly I've been in or around the photographs being taken of Jake, Jess and their family and friends. The photographer has taken all the usual poses, like the groomsmen holding up the horizontal bride, the groomsmen walking in a line, as if they're about to step onto a space shuttle, much like Bruce Willis and Ben Affleck in *Armageddon* (minus the big orange spacesuits).

Throughout the taking of photographs, Sarah and the other bridesmaids have corrected Jess's clothes, repositioned her hair when it's been moved by the occasional light breeze, and generally, on the instructions of the photographer, marshalled the guests around.

True to our gender's stereotype, and despite the fact we will probably all need to detox at the end of this week, the groomsmen and ushers have managed to have bottles of beer in our hands for the duration of the photographs.

Whilst I am usually exhausted by this level of forced extroversion, today I am in great spirits and genuinely enjoying conversations and banter. Jake and Jess are like family to me, therefore, by association, I like their guests.

I sometimes wonder if Jake and Jess will one day move to the States and how their long-distance relationship with me would work but I know we'd survive. Even if I have to be a really annoying third wheel in their relationship, hounding them on FaceTime and making surprise visits.

I can tell Jess is growing weary of the limelight and being forced to smile in the direction of the photographer's twinkling finger gestures and it isn't long before I see her whisper into Jake's ear. About a second after that, time is called on the photographs. Jake and Jess are a team. They work together like Woody and Buzz Lightyear, Hans Solo and Chewy, Thelma and Louise.

I am also thrilled the pictures are done because I've seen the waiters with canapés circulating among the mass of guests and I want in on those blinis. I haven't grown up eating caviar like some people here, therefore the novelty of the salty black balls hasn't worn off for me in adulthood.

Once I'm given the green light, I make a beeline for the waiter carrying aloft a tray of blinis. Then I make a beeline for a waiter carrying a tray of goat's cheese and caramelized red onion tartlets. Shoving those into my mouth, I head directly for the waiter offering bruschetta. Now, I am not a lover of the old tomato but the bruschetta is the largest of the canapé offerings and I am bloody ravenous.

I haven't attended many weddings in my life but I always find that this is the longest and hungriest part of the day, the wait between the ceremony and the lunch, which, for some reason, they call a breakfast, despite it usually taking place in the early afternoon.

I'm doing the food rounds and pondering whether to steal some accessories from other guests in order to disguise my identity and take more than my allotted share of mini bites. As I do so, I notice that Sarah has been absent from the group for longer than it takes to make a trip to the loo, even whilst wearing a fancy dress and heels, which I'm sure adds time to the whole process.

I thought about her a lot yesterday, whilst playing golf with the guys. I haven't ever lost a spouse or even a girlfriend. I've never really been close enough to anyone to describe them as a significant other, let alone to lose them. My birth mother died so long ago that I barely remember her features; I have flash-backs, or early memories, but I can't say that's equivalent to losing someone I have chosen to love and spend my life with.

My thoughts from yesterday come back to me now as I wait outside of the loos for what feels like far too long without seeing any sign of Sarah but being looked at like a dodgy lingerer by every other woman coming or going.

I look in the room that has been set inside for the

wedding reception with no luck. I find and knock on the door of the bridal suite, receiving no answer. I even check the car park.

The one place I don't expect to find Sarah is sitting on a picnic bench designated for the hotel's staff, by the exit from the main kitchen. Though her eyes are hidden behind sunglasses, I can tell from her body language that she is flat. Her shoulders are rounded, where they are usually rolled back. Her spine is hunched over, where it is ordinarily straight. And she is staring out into the distance, not even looking at the plate of canapes in front of her, as she absentmindedly selects one and pops it whole into her mouth (my kind of woman).

'Don't mind me,' I say gently, though still managing to startle her. 'I'm looking for the loos.'

She watches me approach the table. 'Do you think there are portable toilets? They're inside.'

Though the last thing I want to do is antagonize her, I smirk. She amuses me.

'She speaks,' I say.

She pouts, clearly rattled because she has forgotten to ignore me. Her expression only serves to entertain me more.

'What do you want, Charlie? I'm just taking five to enjoy the view.'

The view is better from the reception side, I think, deciding to hold my words in my mind.

I move closer and tell her, 'Budge up,' as I lift one leg over the bench seat, straddling it as I face her, my side to the view.

Now what? I didn't think through what I'd do if I found her.

For a minute, maybe two, I admire the view silently and Sarah finishes her canapes. Then something comes to me...

'Have you ever heard of professional huggers?' I ask.

'Come again.'

'Professional huggers. Unsurprisingly, because it's weird, they're more of a thing in the States.'

I sense she is rolling her eyes behind her lenses. 'Is that right?'

I nod. 'Anyway, these men and women get paid for giving hugs.'

She looks at me now. 'What?'

'Yep. Sort of physical therapy.' We fall silent, then I clarify. 'It's not a sexual thing or anything.'

'Right.'

'Well, I'm thinking about it as a side hustle and I'm wondering if you'd let me trial it on you?'

'Trial hug—'

I lean in, tugging her to me and holding her tightly in my arms. I brace myself for a beating or at the very least a sarcastic comment.

Instead, I feel the smallest of movements as she adjusts her chin on my shoulder. I feel her lean into me, ever so slightly.

She doesn't hug me back – her arms stay rigid at her sides – but she doesn't push me away either.

'What do you think?' I ask after long seconds. 'Can I make it?'

Then I feel the best response I could have hoped for. She chuckles against my chest. 'Charlie, you're off-the-charts strange.'

I smile to myself, then sit back from her, straight faced, and say, 'That'll be fifty quid.'

'Are you joking?'

'The big guys are charging seventy-five green-backs in the States.'

Pinching the corner of the frame in her fingers, she lowers her shades and looks over the top of them. 'Charlie, no one says greenbacks.'

'That's not cool?'

'In no walk of life.'

'Damn it.'

I catch her brief and tiny grin before she turns back

to the view, exhales, and stands up, gracefully hitching up her dress as she lifts her legs across the bench and starts walking back to the wedding reception.

'You still don't exist to me,' she calls back.

My laughter dances in my chest. *Sure I don't.*

* * *

I can put some food away but after the five-course wedding breakfast, even I am fazed by the wedding cake being handed around with glasses of champagne to toast through the wedding speeches. It doesn't help that, along with the meat sweats, the extra layer of clothes I changed into between main course and dessert has me roasting like a Christmas potato.

The Top Table comprises the bride and groom, the groom's parents and the bride's aunt and uncle, and Millie, Eddie and their kids, who look edible in their page boy and flower girl outfits. I am sitting on Table One, with the other groomsmen – Brooks, Cash and Will – the bridesmaids – Sarah, Izzy and Becky – Edmond and Amy, and Brooks's daughter. There are two perks to this. First, we are *numero uno* to be served both food and drinks, after the Top Table. Secondly, Sarah is sitting directly across the table from me.

It is a large round table, which means Sarah is ideally situated – too far away for me to antagonize but perfectly placed for me to watch her smile and laugh with her friends. Not even the *Mona Lisa* could rival the sight. It isn't that I want to indulge my crush; more that I am pleased to see her looking genuinely happy.

If I ever do go into professional hugging as a business, I ought to charge a damn sight more than fifty quid. Evidentially, I have a magic touch.

Once everyone has a piece of spice cake from the bottom of the three-tiered creation – eight hundred quid now cut into tiny pieces – and a full glass of fizz, I, as designated MC, ting a fork against my glass and stand up from my seat.

'Ladies, gents, and everybody else in the room who identifies as neither a lady nor a gentleman, for whatever reason, it's that time at a wedding where we all have to listen to the groom and be well-mannered and gracious as an audience, whether or not he's sweet and funny or just a bloody twat.

'I'm just joking around, Jakey boy, you know you're perfect. Tall. Dark. Those washboard abs, all eight packs of them. The way you hold yourself, conduct yourself, dress yourself. Your unarguable charisma.'

I look to the sky wistfully as I speak, then act as if I have been startled out of a daydream about my friend.

'Sorry, where was I? Oh, that's right, Jake is a pin-up. More than that, he has sexual energy. And, believe it or not, he's not just a pretty face; he's intelligent, too.'

My sarcasm hits the spot. The wedding guests express their amusement.

I wait for the room to fall silent again, then hold up one finger, pointing to the ceiling and say, 'Except!' I labor the word. 'Jake obviously made one of the biggest mistakes of his life when he failed to ask me to be best man today.'

One wedding guest gives an 'aww'.

'Thank you, I appreciate that, man in the window over there. I won't lie, it hurt. It's like being in love with someone who just doesn't love you back, you know? He's my best mate, I'm just not his.' I wipe a fake tear from my cheek. 'In all honesty, if I thought I could have been her maid of honor, I probably would've told Jess that she was my best mate. Anyway, enough about me, it's time for the big man himself to make his speech. So, without further ado... Hang on a minute, where is he?'

I look toward Top Table now, turning my back to the rest of the room.

'Jess? Where is he?'

Jess looks genuinely perplexed. Jake told me I had to buy him some time to get changed and Jess must be wondering where her groom has gone, probably thinking I am an idiot for not having realized that the man I am introducing is not sitting at the table where he ought to be.

Suddenly, the backing music to Elvis's 'Can't Help Falling in Love' begins to play through the room's large speakers. From the door at the back of the room, Jake appears wearing Joe Elvis's leather suit, playing a six-string acoustic guitar and sporting his signature coy smile.

'Well, I have no idea where Jake is but it looks like The King has arrived,' I say. 'Take it away, Elvis!'

And as I finish speaking, Jake begins to sing.

Move aside, Tom Fletcher and all your McFlyness, you have been usurped on the list of the best ever wedding speeches.

Whilst Jake transfixes the room, I turn to watch Jess, whose eyes are the picture of love. She has sparkled like a diamond all day but right now, watching her soulmate live out her fantasy in a room full of people who are here to celebrate their relationship, she is a beacon of happiness.

But, for some reason, I feel compelled to look across the table at Sarah. She and I (mostly her) helped make this magical moment happen but I know that isn't the reason I choose to look at her now. When our eyes meet, it is as if someone is reaching inside me and squeezing my guts in their hands. I feel knotted and twisted and completely discombobulated by the woman in my sights.

I'm still watching her when I set down my microphone and, whilst her jaw hangs loose with shock, I strip out of my morning suit.

I am not alone in my stripping. Drew, Brooks, Cash and Will have all stood from their seats and started taking off their layers too.

Everyone whoops and cheers as Jake welcomes to the dance floor not one, not two but *five* Elvises in the white Las Vegas jumpsuits, complete with Elvis wigs.

Caught in the moment and relieved to be free of my layers, I take my MC microphone and strut toward Jake. As all us men form a group on the dance floor, we face Jess, Jake proud and center, and begin a rendition of 'Jailhouse Rock'.

Despite Izzy's efforts, thanks to the very short

space of time we had to secretly pull together some moves for the occasion, we are calamitous. Bumping into each other, laughing where we should be singing, but ultimately fitting in plenty of hip swinging and pelvis thrusting, we sing through a medley of 'Jailhouse Rock', 'Hound Dog' and, of course, 'Suspicious Minds'.

The room is one well-intentioned mass of guffawing, us guys laughing along with the guests. No one chortles harder than the bride. Goal achieved.

At the end of the medley, though not the usual order of things, Jake invites his bride to the dance floor for their first dance.

We groomsmen stand together and sing 'Blue Suede Shoes' (a tad pitchy), until we are rescued by a DJ, who plays the real Elvis's version of the song. At which point, Drew goes to Becky, Brooks heads over to Izzy, Cash and Will come together, and all begin to dance in couples alongside the bride and groom.

On our table, Sarah is sitting alone.

Not on my watch.

I offer her a hand. 'Come on, Matron. You can continue ignoring me in three minutes' time.'

She smiles. She actually smiles at me, and *God*, my insides are knitting and knotting once again.

She places her hand into mine and from her touch alone, I feel like I grow to seven feet tall.

As I lead her onto the dance floor, I try to control my pounding heart.

How ridiculous I would feel if she could sense my delight at her slightest touch.

19

SARAH

Endorphins from laughter. Dopamine from hearing music I love. Nostalgia reminiscing about good times had.

This is what I am feeling. Happy chemicals in my brain. And this is why, as I willingly stepped into Charlie's arms on the dance floor, I feel like I'm on cloud nine.

It has nothing to do with Charlie's touch. His gentleness. The way my body seems to fit so perfectly against his.

I daren't admit to myself the last time I felt a wave of need come over me like this. It isn't a sexual need, I don't think. It is a desire to be held. To be in someone's arms.

To be in *Charlie's* arms.

It feels like we've been standing still, in each other's hold, for an achingly long time, staring at each other and, for my part, wondering what he is thinking. In reality, only one line of 'Suspicious Minds' has lapsed.

One more line is long enough for me to move my focus from Charlie's eyes to his mouth, and to consider what it would be like to press my lips against his.

Danny...

Just as my husband enters my thoughts, Charlie sends me literally, rather than metaphorically this time, into a spin.

Holding his hand, I swirl to his right, back to the middle, to his left and back to the middle again, this time with my back pressed against his chest, where we twirl on the spot together. He dips me backward across his right arm, then switches me to his left. They are textbook moves but he executes them well and in doing so, makes me feel high on life.

We dance into 'All Shook Up', sometimes together, sometimes twisting and shaking independently. Through it all, my thoughts don't drift to anywhere other than my bouncing feet, my swinging hips, and the ache in my ribs from the enjoyment of it all.

Ignoring Charlie had been just desserts for him but I am having a lot more fun now that I've stopped.

The DJ changes the track to 'Love Me Tender', the rhythm of the music slowing to a heartbeat. Some people drift back to their tables. Others move closer to their partners.

I am the Matron of Honor. Charlie is an usher. We *can't* leave the dance floor. And so, when Charlie holds out his hand, I take little encouragement to move closer to him.

When he interlaces his fingers with mine, I go with it. When he drops his other hand to the small of my back and nudges me closer to him, until our bodies are pressed together, I don't pull away.

And when he holds my gaze, I hold my breath. Waiting. Blinded by the atmosphere. The occasion.

I feel, more than see, his proximity increase.

I close my eyes and feel my chin lift toward him, preparing, waiting.

'It's really hot in here. Shall we get a drink?' he then asks, moving me back from him with his hands on my shoulders.

What the actual?

Was he going to kiss me?

Was *I* going to kiss *him*?

And why the hell did he pull away?

I watch his back as he walks away and I feel like I have shriveled to the size of a raisin. I scan the guests around me to see if anyone else has noticed my almost indiscretion, or my rejection.

For a moment, I was floating on air. Now, I have come crashing to the ground and hit a load of tree branches on the way down, before being mowed down by a truck, like vermin.

It's been a fantastic day in many ways. It's also been one of the lowest of my life.

Right now, standing in the middle of the dance floor, alone, while couples slow dance and smooch around me, I am at my lowest point yet.

All thanks to that asshat!

Suddenly, I am raging. I feel fire blowing from my nostrils with my breath.

Like a dragon fueled by fury, I go after Charlie. He has bypassed our table, where his drink remains untouched. He doesn't make a beeline for the bar. He is heading toward a staircase that leads to the lawn outside.

I catch up to him right by a group of wedding guests who are smoking. They surreptitiously nip the ends of their cigarettes when they see me approach. They can't move inside fast enough.

I really *am* breathing fire.

'What the hell was that?' I demand.

Charlie turns to face me, his expression much like a bank robber caught in the act.

'What was what?' he asks, unable to feign nonchalance, if that is in fact what he is trying to do.

I round upon him. 'You were going to—'

Was he...? Had he been about to kiss me? Have I imagined it? Had I been about to kiss him, entirely one sided? What was I thinking? I *hadn't* been thinking.

My eyes start to sting and I'm not sure why. Anger? Remorse? Embarrassment?

'To kiss you,' he says, gentler now, dropping his hands to his sides limply. 'I'm sorry. I got carried away with the music and the whole day. I shouldn't have come near you.'

I feel my brow crease with confusion but I can't speak. I don't know what I'm feeling and I sure as hell don't know how to respond. I simply stand there. Confused. Dumbfounded.

Charlie draws a deep breath. 'When we got back the other morning, the guys told me about your husband. Danny?'

Hearing his name on another man's tongue, a man I was going to kiss, is wrong. I hate it. More than that, I hate that Charlie has called me out. What I had been about to do on that dance floor was despicable.

In sickness and in health, until death parts us.

I hadn't meant those words. Death doesn't change a thing. My eyes are burning; I can feel my tears forming.

'I promised them I won't go near you,' Charlie continues.

'Excuse me? They don't control me. They can't tell me when it's right or wrong to—'

'Wait,' Charlie says, holding up his palms. 'Don't get mad with them. They were trying to help you.'

'Help me? By deciding who I can and can't speak to? Am I that pitiful?'

'Pitiful? God, Sarah, you're anything but piti—'

A proverbial penny drops.

'*That's* why you were ignoring me?' I snipe.

Then I think about his *free-of-charge* hug earlier. About his offer to be my dance partner.

'Does everyone think I'm just some pathetic widow?' My eyes finally fill with tears.

'Pathetic?' Charlie has closed the space between us and reaches out to touch my arm. I shrug him off.

'I don't think you're pathetic, Sarah. I think you're incredible. To have been through what you have and still have your shit together. It's... commendable.'

'Oh, Charlie, fuck off. I don't need your pity.' I swipe at my wet cheeks. 'You act like you're all perfect but I know those jokes about your upbringing aren't just for the stage. Jess told me it's all true. Should I pay you the discourteous sympathy vote? How would that make *you* feel?'

He rolls his jaw tightly as he takes a step backward. He scoffs, nodding slowly.

'Haven't you? You know, I wondered what shifted between us. I wondered why suddenly hangry, cranky Sarah started to want to joke around and throw me smiles.'

We stare at each other. Motionless. Speechless. For my part, wanting the ground to swallow me whole.

Eventually, I break the silence.

'I'm sorry, Charlie. I don't know why I said that. I'm just angry and upset but that's no excuse.'

Charlie shrugs and for a moment I see a small boy, shrugging in the face of his adversity. It pulls at my heartstrings and makes me despise myself even more for the way I just brought his upbringing into our argument.

'I can't change my past any more than you can, Sarah, but I can assure you, I don't pity myself, nor do I want anyone else to. So believe me when I say, I don't pity you. I just have empathy for your loss. If that's a crime, then lock me up.'

I am speechless. I am ashamed of myself but still so mad at Drew, Brooks and Jake for telling my story and, moreover, using it to push away Charlie.

'I don't even know why we're arguing,' he says. 'You don't like me and I'm not good enough for you, so what are we fighting about here?'

'Don't put words in my mouth. I never said that.'

Charlie glances back toward the hotel, where the sounds of happiness are coming from within.

'This is one of the best days of our friends' lives and you and I should be having fun celebrating with them. What do you say we forget whatever is going on here and we go back inside and have fun? Can you fake being my friend for a few more hours?'

'Charlie—' I want to protest. I want to tell him I am his friend, that I do like him, that I fear I might like him too much. But I don't have any of that straight in my own mind yet. I'm not sure how I like Charlie, and how that can be; after all, I've only known him for a matter of days.

And this feeling, whatever it is, it's bigger than

just Charlie. This is a chink in my armor. I have convinced myself that I will never replace Danny, that I have lost the love of my life and I am willing to spend the rest of my life single, holding on to his memory. I haven't doubted that plan before tonight.

My head is all over the place and I don't want to hurt someone because I can't get my words right. I really don't want to hurt Charlie. Hasn't he been through enough in his life? I'm unsure of his whole backstory but anyone who grew up in the system must have suffered rejection.

I have already had enough drama in my life without adding to it.

So, rather than say the things I ought to say, I simply nod, smile apologetically, and watch Charlie head back inside.

'I'll be there in a minute,' I tell him.

What is happening to me this week?

I'm one of those people who has everything together, at least outwardly. Everyone tells me as much. I am organized and in control and help to organize and control everyone else in my life, but this week I am all over the place. A real hot mess.

Part of me is regretting having planned an extra week in London. If I could just get back to my life in New York, I'm sure that everything will seem better, that I'll stop feeling so out of kilter, that I will be re-centered.

Drew, Brooks and Jake were wrong to interfere with things between Charlie and me – not that there are things to interfere with, as such – but I know that their intentions will have been good.

So, I will dust myself off (metaphorically speaking) and head back inside to find my people.

20

SARAH

The rest of the evening has gone off without a hitch (pun intended).

Jake's musical speech got the evening party started early, such that it was only once the evening buffet was announced as open by Charlie that Drew and Brooks gave – or rather performed – their joint best man speech.

With dubious props, mortifying photographs and utterly laugh-out-loud stories about Jake (some squeaky clean and others borderline outrageous), their speech was memorable to say the least. Without causing offence to either the bride or groom or any of their guests, the duo managed to get buckets full of laughs and guffaws.

There was a line or two with sentimental words but honestly, Drew, Brooks, Jake and our entire gang know how much we love and are loved by one another, so the squishy notes weren't missed.

Though the wedding breakfast was sheer indulgence, I think I worked off every single calorie and more as I set aside my volatile temperament and danced the night away with my friends.

Around midnight, the remaining wedding guests (excluding a fairly comatose couple who had been drinking liquor from the free bar like water in the desert) cheered and waved off the bride and groom in a traditional-style car, a 'just married' sign covering the rear number plate of the old Jaguar and a large ivory ribbon on the bonnet.

One of the barmen called last orders shortly after that and the number of the remaining guests began to dwindle (the comatose couple escorted into a cab), until there are now only the members of our house sitting in a large circle, finishing our last drinks and remarking on what a wonderful day it has been.

It's clear that we've all had a little too much to drink (Becky excluded), and Izzy a little more so than the others.

Perhaps she didn't indulge quite as heavily in the buffet as I did.

Returning from a break to the toilet, Izzy lands with a thump in a padded chair next to mine. She leans toward me, clumsily throwing her arms around my neck, and says, 'I love you like a sister, Sarah.'

I titter and tell her, 'Right back at you, gorgeous lady.'

She bends forward to pick up a drink from the table.

I have no idea whether she realizes she is picking up my half-drunk cocktail rather than her own, which is on the opposite side of the table.

'So,' she sings, 'are you going to tell me what happened on the dance floor earlier? Did I see you and Charlie have a *moment*?'

As if that needs more explanation, she pouts her lips and smooches the air.

My skin flushes with panic and embarrassment.

'A moment?' I scoff. 'Charlie and me? Ha. As if. Absolutely not!'

'Me thinks thou doth protest too much,' Izzy teases.

'I *can't* protest enough,' I quip, reaching for the glass in Izzy's hand as a mode of distraction. 'This is mine.'

'Oh.' She falls back in her chair, giggling uncontrollably, the way a grown woman can generally only manage when heavily inebriated.

As I sip my drink, I feel a presence behind me. My stomach sinks as I see the figure move into my peripheral vision. I die a thousand times when that figure turns out to be Charlie.

Did he hear? What is wrong with me? Why do I keep being such a dick when it comes to this man?

Now I have yet another reason to apologize to Charlie. I am so sick of being a disappointment this week. I can't remember a time when I have had to repeatedly apologize to someone like this. And actually, it isn't his fault at all; it is entirely my own.

I'm pleased when a member of the hotel staff announces the arrival of the minibus I have pre-ordered to take us back to the house.

I'll be able to speak to Charlie, one on one, in our bedroom, where there are no eavesdroppers. I'll apologize for everything I've said and done in the last week and then tomorrow we can part ways on a positive note.

It's entirely possible that we will never see each other again.

That thought makes me irrationally sad, given my constant struggles with him.

Bizarre.

In the minibus, Charlie sits on the backseat with Brooks and Drew, who is wrapped around a very tired-looking Becky. If the early weeks of pregnancy feel anything like I imagine – shattering and maybe sickly too – Becky has coped remarkably well this week. Much better than me, in fact!

I sit at the front of the minibus next to Izzy, who almost immediately lays her head on my shoulder and falls asleep before the driver has even pulled away from the hotel.

There is nothing like watching someone sleep, listening to their slow heavy breaths, to make a person feel sleepy themselves. And gosh, do I feel sleepy. It has been a long, long week.

* * *

It wasn't a long ride back but I have a feeling I drifted because by the time we arrive at the house, I'm feeling groggy.

Nevertheless, I hand off Izzy to Brooks, check with the driver to ensure the payment has already been settled in advance, then say I will make a round of soft drinks and herbal teas to help everyone come morning.

The whole group – with the exception of Izzy and Charlie – enjoys drinks in the kitchen.

I'm not sure where Charlie is but I am desperate to catch him before he goes to sleep. I don't want to end the day on an argument. I want to wake up tomorrow feeling like we can at least go our separate ways without hating each other.

Taking my mint tea with me, I say my goodnights and head upstairs to our bedroom. I tap gently on the door with my knuckle, something I haven't yet done whether or not I thought Charlie was in the room. I wait but there is no response and so I creep in using the torchlight on my phone.

Doing my best to gather my pajamas and other bits, I move quietly, barefoot, into the ensuite and turn on the low lighting of the bulbs around the sink mirror. Only now do I look to the sofa bed to find that Charlie isn't here. His blankets are folded on the bottom of the chaise longue, unused.

I suppose he's decided to sleep in a more comfortable bed for the evening, most likely having moved to Jake and Jess's room.

Very disappointed, I decide that tomorrow morning will have to do. I finish my ablutions, change into my nightwear, and crawl into bed, feeling the full weight of my body sink into the mattress as I drift into a deep and necessary slumber.

* * *

The next morning, I've enjoyed such a deep sleep that on waking it takes me a few seconds to remember where I am. After a full body stretch, I reach to the side table, pick up my phone and see that it's already nearly nine. I can't believe it. I never sleep in this late.

After a quick shower and an application of my daily anti-aging skin serums, I slip into a linen jumpsuit and head downstairs.

Despite my lying in, only Edmond, Amy and Becky are awake. They are seated on stools around the island in the kitchen, each of them holding a hot drink and a pastry.

I pour myself a coffee from the machine and go to sit with them.

In the middle of the island is a plate stacked full of various pastries – pains au chocolat, pains aux raisin, cinnamon swirls and croissants. I, of course, recognize the medley of pastries that I purchased and put away into the freezer for this very purpose at the end of the long week.

I assume one of the chefs in the room has warmed them up, but as I reach for a cinnamon swirl, I see a handwritten note lying next to the tray.

Sorry I had to make an early exit but the coffee is on and I've cooked the frozen pastries as an apology. Awesome week and a pleasure to meet you all. Until next time, Charlie :-)

He's gone.

21

CHARLIE

I know myself. I know that I like plain pasta with peas and can't stand any fancy types that have creamy sauce. I know I prefer beer over cocktails. That the weather affects my mood – the sun shining makes me happy, the rain bums me out.

I know that spending time on stage and in big groups of people is fun, or at least tolerable, but that I need to spend some time alone afterward. I don't have a huge group of friends because I prefer to have a small group of people whom I know are invested. I have their back and they have mine.

Families leave, but friends choose to stick around, if they are true friends, in good times and in bad.

Sitting in my apartment, on my futon, alone, I

look around at the cardboard boxes that surround me. I know that the reason these are still packed isn't just because I have recently moved in (is six months even recent?), it's because I know nothing lasts. Homes are temporary, so why bother furnishing them and unpacking things that will need to be repacked when the next move comes along?

I'm not a dog bred from pedigree and I suppose that doesn't make me marriage material, but I'm also *not* the worst person in the world. Surely I wouldn't have such great friends if I was.

I'm good with my life. Good with all of this. My life these days is comfortable, stable, dependable. That's all I hoped to have for a very long time.

What I absolutely don't understand is why I am sitting on my futon feeling low and rubbish about myself, more so than usual. Why I actually want to be back with my friends and surrounded by people rather than enjoying my usual decompression period.

And I really can't understand why I want one of those people around me to be Sarah. After all, she's the primary reason I'm feeling shitty. She dragged up my past, she made clear she considers me to be undatable.

That isn't anything I didn't already know, but she

confirmed it. It's been a while since anyone has been so overt in giving their damning opinion of me. It's been even longer since I've put myself in a position to garner that opinion.

So why on earth am I craving her presence right now? Am I completely sadistic? Do I want to change her opinion of me? To prove myself as... what? Someone who hasn't grown up in foster care, who didn't drop out of education, who has a stable job and a structured ladder to climb? Well, I can't do any of that.

Fresh air. What I need is fresh air and distraction. I have a gig tonight, that will distract me later. For now...

I pick up my house keys, pull on my tatty old trainers and head out for a walk.

I make my way to Clapham Common. The sunshine of the last week is hidden behind wispy white clouds. When it makes an escape from cover, I walk under the shade of the trees around the lush green grass of the park, shielding my fair skin.

Kids ride past me on bikes, nearly wiping out runners and dog walkers on the track. They laugh, sing and babble away without a care in the world, not realizing that, if they're not careful, they're about to put old Joan from down the road in hospital.

I envy them. Their innocence, their ignorance, their typical lives.

A dark-brown sausage dog comes sniffing at my trainers. I can't blame the thing; my trainers probably smell feral and would be delicious to a dog. I crouch down to pet the little pooch, a sparkly collar around its neck a complete contrast to its fetish for smelly feet.

The owners – a young couple – smile politely but don't make conversation. I understand. It's Sunday, a family day, a respite from work, not a day to chat to strangers.

Ironically, most of my Tinder dates have taken place on Sundays, by my making. Sundays are good for two reasons. First, if they go badly, the fact it is traditionally a school night gives both parties, in monopoly terms, a get out of jail free card. Secondly, this day has, for single people and family-less people, the potential to be the loneliest day of the week.

In recent times, I've had gigs on Sunday nights but if I don't, it's a day I know my friends, mostly coupled, will be spending time with their partners and families. I don't want to bother them and I certainly don't want them to feel obliged to see me, their lonely mate.

Hence, I'm currently wandering around a park aimlessly, alone.

I stop at one of the sports fields, where one of the local clubs is apparently playing a cup game. I watch them for ten minutes or so, until a goal is scored and I, quite apparently, cheer the wrong team.

Under the glares of sideline supporters, I continue my pootle.

I come upon a pond, where anglers are fishing and ducks are swimming gracefully. Sitting down on the grass, I get lost in watching the fisherman casting in. Observing the ripples that span out across the vast expanse of water, despite the meeting of an infinitesimal hook with the surface.

It's funny how one small moment in life can have an infinite ripple effect, just like fly fishing in a pond.

Something has happened to me this last week. I'm not sure of the how, what and why, I just know that I am feeling different. Hating on myself and my past, where I thought I was comfortable and accepting of it. Lonely, despite being a self-confessed loner.

I am pondering this as I spot an elderly man walking a Labrador. The man and his dog are playing with a stick – throwing and retrieving. Every time the dog returns it to its owner, the owner's expressionless face turns to a beaming smile. It's happiness. True fluffing-a-dog's-ears kind of happiness. And the dog wags its tail. True having-my-ears-fluffed kind of happiness.

Maybe that's what I need in my life. Someone to come home to. Someone to walk with on Sundays.

A dog, of course, though that would never work around my lifestyle.

I rise to stand and wipe the back pockets of my jeans with my hands.

A cat, I decide. Maybe I need a cat.

22

SARAH

After Danny's motorbike accident, I made a vow to myself to make as many happy memories in life as I can. Even the longest of lives can be too short and I know only too well how from one day to the next life can change catastrophically. So, I'm willing to splurge on new experiences.

With that being said, I'm not loaded and so while my fantasy London trip involved a stay at the luxurious five-star The Savoy, I have opted to stay elsewhere in the West End. But after saying goodbye to my friends this morning, after heading into London feeling utterly like crap for the way I've treated Charlie, I find myself sitting in one of Gordon Ramsay's restaurants in The Savoy.

After a week of eating too many carbohydrates, too much meat and a lot of sweet treats, I make a bee-line for the raw bar. From my stool, perched around the focal point of the restaurant, I can see three different kinds of oysters – Jersey (presumably not New Jersey?), Carlingford (apparently somewhere in Ireland) and Cumbrae (from Gerard Butler Land).

I'm uncomplicated when it comes to oysters. A squeeze of lemon, sometimes a little vinaigrette, that is all I need for those slimy little creatures to slip down my throat and fill my tummy. In The Savoy, however, the oysters come with a choice of blood orange or rhubarb and lemongrass. It looks like I'll be trying something new.

I order half a dozen, two from each location, and a bottle of fancy sparkling water, rather than the suggested pairing of Perrier Jouet. For the price of the water, I might as well have ordered champagne.

As he is preparing my plate of oysters, the raw barman tells me that the panoramic views I can see through the windows of the restaurant are of the River Thames and Victoria Embankment. I try to appreciate the landscape. I want to appreciate the landscape. But all I can think, sitting here in a fancy hotel and looking at a river, is this is something I could do in Manhattan.

I take out my small leather notebook, with the initial S on the front – a gift from Becky as a thank you for arranging deliveries of items to her apartment one day while she was working a lunch shift. In fact, it's something I would have done for Drew anyway, as his secretary – a role that is often akin to a nanny or housekeeper more than a legal secretary – so to receive a gift in return had been a wonderful gesture.

I open the notebook to the page marked with silk ribbon, where I have a list of things I must see whilst I'm in London. It feels a little like a consolation prize that Becky and Izzy can't be with me to enjoy the sights but I'm grateful for their input into what I ought to do whilst here.

With the caveat that everything is a little bit touristy but a must see, they have given me a list of top ten sights. There's everything from a turn around the London Eye to the Natural History Museum. From shopping in Harrods and sampling the delights in the food court to a tour of the Tower of London (with an accompanying note telling me not to miss Borough Market when I visit the Tower).

The thing is, these activities require energy and motivation, both of which I am lacking today. It has been a long week but my lack of get-up and go, deep down, is more than just weariness from a week of activities.

The oysters are delicious, though in my opinion – probably controversially – the accompanying flavors of blood orange and rhubarb and lemongrass detract from the natural saltiness of the shellfish. While I'm on the subject, and again, somewhat controversially, I find The Savoy luxurious but dark. Too dark. I like the old English glamour, I get the old Hollywood vibes that I was promised from the hotel's website, I like the sheer indulgence of the fancy food, but it just isn't wowing me today.

I finish the oysters and for a nanosecond consider whether I will indulge in caviar, but at hundreds of pounds for a tablespoonful, I decide against the idea and instead order a dish of seabass ceviche, which I enjoy more than I would have enjoyed a blini with overpriced salty eggs on top, I'm sure.

'Can I get you anything else?' the barman asks.

I contemplate saying yes, purely because I can't be bothered to move just yet, but my bank balance will be better depleted elsewhere, and so I thank him and politely decline, then settle my check.

I walk back through the opulent and famous entrance of the hotel, casting a side-eye to the patisserie and wondering whether a box of macaroons would be completely unnecessary. I decide it would and head outside, where two concierges wearing top hats thank me for my visit and bid me a good day.

As I stand on the Strand, my Google Maps tells me I will get to Trafalgar Square and the National Gallery if I turn left. A quiet saunter around an art gallery is about all I can face this afternoon.

Inside, I see *The Entombment* by Michelangelo, *The Madonna of Pinks* by Raphael, *The Virgin of Rocks* by Leonardo da Vinci, all of which would usually move me in some way. But it isn't until I arrive in room forty-three (according to my free map) and I'm staring at Vincent van Gogh's *Sunflowers* that I realize none of these incredible pieces of artwork are penetrating me on anything other than a superficial level today.

I'm distracted and at the heart of my distraction is the unease I have for having left things on such a horrible note with Charlie. I'm not a bad person and I can't blame him for having left thinking that I am.

Did I drive him to leave early without saying goodbye to anyone this morning? How horrible for him to feel like he had to do that, as if he didn't fit somehow.

I have to take the Elvis suit Jake borrowed back to Camden in a couple of hours. Joe Elvis has kindly agreed to launder the suit himself provided we pay for it. Something tells me he will never launder it and that he'll pocket the cash but it's Jake's money, not mine.

I leave the National Gallery after an hour or so of mindless wandering, head past Nelson's column, which is apparently something to do with Napoleon and a Battle of Trafalgar – there was a volunteer in the National Gallery who told me as much and I had seemingly nodded, ooh'd and ahh'd in the right places to keep him talking for ten minutes.

The history is no doubt fascinating to many but I am a little underwhelmed by the column as I walk past it in the direction of the Mall. I have seen the Mall, of course, in coverage of royal events, not least the weddings of Kate and Will and Harry and Meghan. I buy a bottle of water from a street seller and wander the famous route toward Buckingham Palace.

By the time I reach the palace and stop to take a photograph, my feet are sweating, my *boobs* are sweating and I realize I have walked further away from Camden, where I now need to go.

With increasingly less enthusiasm, I decide to walk some of the way toward Camden from the palace.

I cross into Green Park, with my Google Maps open in my palm. People are enjoying Sunday strolls with their dogs. A giant stage is being erected for some kind of sunset concert. People are enjoying picnics in groups, in couples. One couple is kissing on their checked blanket, a bottle of fizz and a cheeseboard on the rug beside them. With my heart feeling just as heavy as my legs, I exit the park and see on my map that I am near the Ritz, another hotel I understand to be a must see in the city.

Actually, I am thirsty and so I head inside, up the pristine stairs, through a door held open by an immaculately dressed concierge, and into the bright marble atrium of the hotel.

Perhaps it's the idea that my legs are going to get a break, maybe it's the fact that the atrium is cool and I am sweating all over, but I find the brightness of this hotel much more appealing than The Savoy. With direction from a member of hotel staff, I locate the bar, where I am seated at a table for two, on my own, and order an elderflower spritz.

Unlike the atrium, the Rivoli Ballroom is dark and everything is finished with ornate detail, gold and mahogany furniture and trimmings. Having come from the National Gallery and Buckingham Palace, I do enjoy how the hotel oozes vintage London. My drink arrives and I sip the ice-cold beverage, feeling the fluid seep into my hot and dehydrated body. As I do, I can't help but notice that every table is full of couples and families.

I don't enjoy the rest for long, feeling uncomfortable in my surroundings and maybe even in my own body.

I leave a five-pound tip and head to Green Park Tube station to navigate my way to Camden and Joe Elvis.

Somewhere on the journey, while sitting uncomfortably on the slightly grubby seats of the train, I wonder how my friends are getting on with their last-day plans before their journeys back to New York. I wonder what Charlie is doing today.

My mind is still on Charlie when I get off the train and a very short distance from the Tube station in Camden I see a poster outside a bar. On it, Charlie's name and the time of his show, tonight. Coincidence or serendipity?

I keep walking, my legs moving me forward but my mind stuck on that poster. I don't want to spend the rest of my week in London feeling drained and miserable.

I take out my phone and locate Charlie's number, which I took from him in case I needed his help that day we were in London together. Standing still on the sidewalk, and receiving tuts and grunts as people bump into me and push my shoulders, I type out a WhatsApp message:

Hi. You left before I had a chance to say goodbye this morning. I'm in London. Can we meet?

At first, I end the message with 'x'. Then I delete it. Then I choose a smiley face emoji. Then I delete it. I don't know how to begin or end this message, so I take a deep breath, get bumped into by another passerby and press send on the limited words.

I meet Joe Elvis, whose quiff is as high and stiff as it was the first time I met him, and I hand over the suit.

Job done, I check WhatsApp and see that Charlie has read my message – in fact, the app tells me he read it thirty-six minutes ago – but he hasn't responded.

My thumb hits the call button before I really think about what I will say to him and I'm chewing my lip and tapping my foot as I wait for him to pick up.

He never does.

He's so big-headed. Nevertheless, I need some

closure on this for whatever reason. So there's only one thing left to do.

* * *

I arrive at the bar just before seven thirty, after quickly nipping back to my hotel to wash the grime of the hot day off my body and switch into a pair of skinny jeans and a designer T-shirt with a giant teddy bear on the front.

I've brought a thin blazer with me to wear on the way back, when the evening has cooled. Yet, as I take my seat at a high table in the comedy club, I feel chilly already. Not because of the temperature in the room but from the frosty reception I expect to receive from Charlie, owing to the fact he still hasn't bothered to reply to my message or call me back.

I'm pinning him down, giving him no out, because I need to apologize, whether or not he accepts it.

'Can I get you a drink?' a girl asks me. She wipes down the table in front of me and puts her washcloth back on a tray she is carrying on her hip.

I order a non-alcoholic beer and listen to the opening act while I wait for my drink. I check the room but there is no sign of Charlie. I expected him to be sitting at a table, I guess, like he had been before his show last time we were in London.

I wonder whether he's backstage and I remember how anxious he appeared to be last time. I don't want to make matters worse, so I decide to sit at the table and wait.

The club becomes increasingly busy as the warmup acts each perform their sets. While they are predictably ordered in relation to their level of success and longevity in the business – so I'm told by two people, husband and wife, who join me at my table – it is the second of the first three acts that I find most entertaining.

When the other acts have finished, I am growing increasingly nervous, waiting for Charlie to make an appearance.

He has to get here soon; he's on stage in fifteen minutes. Where is he?

I fall into conversation with the couple about London, comedy and other general chitchat but my mind is only on Charlie and his whereabouts.

My watch tells me there's one minute to go before his set and there is still no sign of him.

I order another drink. As it is placed in front of me, fashionably late, Charlie is welcomed on stage by the MC for the evening.

He bounds onto the stage full of life and pizzazz – he must have been backstage after all. He has a pint of beer in his hand, which he swigs from as the crowd applauds, then he sets the drink down on the floor next to the centralized standing microphone.

He is wearing what I know to be a signature stage shirt – Hawaiian, shockingly bright and floral. In response to the applause, Charlie pulls open this shirt and holds out his arms as if they are wings, revealing not a Marvel T-shirt beneath, as I would have expected, but a Harry Potter one instead.

'Did anybody else want to be a wizard when they were a kid?' he asks the crowd. 'Didn't you wish you could wave a wand and transport yourself to a castle where your best friend was the most uncoordinated kid in school, who went around with a rat in place of a fancy owl and diverted negative attention away from you?'

There are nods and affirmations from the audience.

'Ah man, to be a wizard, huh?'

Charlie is full of energy and spirit, and he is oozing confidence, almost cocksure. This isn't the Charlie I have seen so much of over the last week; it is the Charlie who greeted me at the airport on day one. It is the Charlie who drove me back to the

Surrey house after our night in London. It is Charlie the wedding MC.

It occurs to me now, clear as day: this is Charlie the performer.

How much of the last week was an act from him? Was the man I instantly disliked at the airport an act? Why? Why perform like an asshat when the real him can be warm and thoughtful, still funny, but naturally so?

I don't have a chance to reach a conclusion because within minutes, tears of laughter are streaming down my face. Charlie may be the funniest man I have ever met.

Danny and I had laughed. We had known each other for a long time, knew each other inside and out, such that the slightest look, a certain breath, a tone of voice could have us both doubled over with laughter.

But Charlie makes me laugh generally. We don't know each other all that well, not really, yet he can tie my insides in knots with hysterics.

He can also tie my insides with knots of guilt and unease.

But not for much longer.

There's a moment in the show where I feel like Charlie looks right at me. He pauses. Then he continues to his next joke. I think about the bright lights shining on that stage. He most likely can't see me. Probably doesn't know I'm here.

He never misses a beat in his set. Every joke lands and when he curtsies like a woman before the King at the end, the audience is whooping and cheering.

After the show, I give him a short time to appear and when he doesn't, I decide enough is enough. I have witnessed his powers of ignorance and I won't leave this club before settling the ghost I have carried around since the wedding. It's time for this little spook to go to bed.

I let myself backstage through a side door from the bar. The corridor smells musty. It's lowly lit and cold. I have no idea where Charlie will be, so I move in the direction of the stage, following a black arrow on the wall.

'It's not an open mic night.'

Charlie's voice comes from behind me. I swivel to see him standing near a door at the end of the corridor. The opposite end from the stage and me.

'Well, that's good,' I tell him. 'Because what I have to say isn't a joke.'

His mouth twitches only slightly but I catch it.

'Why are you here, Sarah?'

'Because...'

'Because?'

Think. Why didn't I rehearse this?

'Can we go somewhere to talk?' I ask.

He pushes his hands into his jean pockets and shrugs, Harry Potter moving up and down with his shoulders.

'I don't think so,' he says, gently, calmly, Dumbledore-esque.

I nod. 'Fair enough.' There's too much space between us. The distance makes me feel exposed. But I need to say what I came to say and then I can get on with my life, without Charlie and without this heaviness I've been carrying around since last night.

'My husband's name is... *was*, Danny. He died in a motorbike accident eight years ago.'

Charlie takes three steps forward but now I don't want him to. I prefer the distance.

'I'm sorry,' he says.

'Thank you. But I'm not telling you this for sympathy, I'm trying to explain some of my actions and words that might have seemed a little...'

'Mean? Cruel? Unnecessarily catty? Snide?'

'Hey!'

God, this man knows how to get my hackles up.

I physically shake him off – Taylor Swift would be proud. 'I've been quick to stop people thinking that you and I might... you know... that there might be anything romantic between us.'

'Sarah, you sound like a grandparent giving their grandchild a lesson in the birds and the bees.'

I clear my throat, which is dry and hoarse. I'm going to get it out.

'Everyone liked Danny and too many people tell me I should move on and meet someone new.' I speak quickly. I'm ripping off the band aid, as the cliché goes. 'I don't want to. I won't. Losing Danny was the hardest thing I've done in my life. I promised to be his and no other's. I won't let him down. And I won't put myself in a position to lose someone I love again. I couldn't love someone else. I couldn't.'

Charlie's eyebrows draw together and I quickly gauge his reaction.

I hold up a hand, as if to tell him to stop that train of thought. 'I'm not talking about me loving you or anything here.'

He scoffs. 'Yes, I'm aware.'

'Well, perhaps you are but the others don't get it. And I wanted to silence them or cut them off the trail before any whispering could start. So, I was profuse in my dismissal of you but it's a reflection of me, not you. You're... fine. Just not for me. Nor is anyone else.'

He guffaws this time and I have to admit, he's really getting my back up now.

'I'm trying to be serious. I'm trying to apologize and explain.'

I can't believe it happens but I find myself stamping my foot on the hard ground.

Laughing, Charlie moves closer to me and holds his arms up for a hug.

'Thanks for the explanation. You could never love me and want everyone to know it, even though I'm *fine*. You've made me feel all warm and fuzzy inside.'

For some reason, I step into his arms and feel his warmth as he cuddles me.

'I get it. Don't worry about it,' he says. 'But, Sarah, you have to open yourself up to things that come along. Hiding from possibilities to make sure you don't get your heart broken is... something I would do...' He chuckles. 'It isn't healthy. Don't let fear hold you back.'

I step back and look into his eyes. I've seen his words in action. I've seen how he pushes through fear to go on stage. But the fear of complete and utter heartbreak is too much for me.

'It's just breaking even,' I tell him. 'Maybe I don't love again but I don't get my heart broken either.'

Charlie looks confused, or contemplative, I can't tell. Then he says, 'Fancy a drink? As friends?'

After a lonely day, buried in my own head, I'll be glad of the distraction and I'm happy for the lightness I feel in my chest now that I've apologized to him. 'Yes.'

23

CHARLIE

'I find you very touchy feely,' Sarah says, still in my arms, where I am surprisingly happy to have her.

When I first saw her across the club, sitting on the high table, watching me intently on the stage, it threw me.

I'm not sure what I expected to feel when or if I ever saw Sarah again. I didn't expect that the moment I saw her my heart rate would go higher than it already was, being on stage. That my palms would be clammier, that I would want to jump right down off the stage and head over to her, even if it was to hear some negative jibe cast my way.

I shouldn't want to feel like that, I know. She left me feeling awful yesterday. But I've spent a day walking and pondering, and every time I see a happy couple my mind plays tricks on me. I want to see her. I think, on some level, I've wanted her to explain her words and whether she truly hates me or it's just a feeling I've been left with.

Her husband was called Danny. *So* American. It's nice to have a name to go with the idea of a man that I already hold in high regard.

What kind of man could've won Sarah over? What kind of man could put up with her?

I don't have the answers. All I do know is that I respect her for finding me tonight. I respect her apology. And I want to spend more time in her company. As much time as she has left in London.

It's bizarre, I know.

And she's wrong; for the record, I'm not touchy-feely. I'm generally quite the opposite, actually. I just couldn't resist, I guess.

When I hold her, I feel taller, more masculine, a little less shabby around the edges.

And who knows, maybe she'll pay me seventy-five big ones for the hug.

I have no idea where to take her – it's late but I want to hang out for a while. I don't think either one of us wants to watch people grinding up against each other in a club, where we'll have to shout over each other to speak.

I want to be able to talk to her. I'm intrigued. She's finally opening up and I want to keep her talking.

'Do you like hot chocolate?' I ask, thinking on my feet.

'Does anyone *not* like hot chocolate?'

'Good point well made. Come on.'

She follows me out of the rear exit and onto Camden High Street. Though it's a school night, the street is busy with traffic and people. It's around quarter to eleven but the temperature hasn't dropped below the need for a light jacket, which Sarah has. I left mine at the club but I don't mention it.

We turn down a side street and I hope the late-night café I have in mind still exists and is still open. I don't mention where we're headed, just in case.

Thankfully, as we near Café Butterfly, I see the lights are on.

'After you,' I tell Sarah, gesturing for her to walk inside as I hold open the door.

There are half a dozen tables in the small eatery. The menu is written on chalk boards that form an arch around the counter. Inside the glass counter there's a selection of homemade cakes and pastries and hand-painted chocolates. A large coffee machine dominates the majority of the service wall and a wooden door swings open as a waitress carries clean mugs and glasses from a behind-the-scenes kitchen.

I walk up to the counter, surprisingly not nervous to be around Sarah, and not irritable either. We've declared ourselves friends, she's said sorry for things she has said, and I guess we're just at peace.

'Can we get two of your dirtiest hot chocolates, please?' I ask.

I make the mistake of looking through the glass at the delights on offer. Then I turn to Sarah.

'What are you going to go for?'

I can tell from her face that she's torn. As was I for a nanosecond. We've had a highly indulgent week and exercise isn't really my thing. I'll happily walk around the city instead of getting the crowded Tube but you're not going to find me sweating my tits off in a spin class, that's for sure.

'Oh God, I really shouldn't,' Sarah says, pressing two hands to her tummy and confirming my suspicions.

'Yep, it would be terribly fat of us. But I read this thing once that said our bodies can only absorb so much fat and sugar in one day. Then we just shit the rest out. So why not?'

Sarah lets out the kind of laugh I love to see on people, the kind that sparkles in their eyes. And it's an intoxicating sound to my ears. I would happily make it my life's goal to hear that sound again.

As her friend, obviously. I chastise that cheeky little monkey hiding in my brain that's trying to make this something more than two friends having hot chocolate.

'Plus, you are still on holiday, aren't you?'

I know she's going to cave.

'Oh, screw it.' Then to the guy behind the counter, she says, 'I'll take a raspberry macaron and a chocolate macaron, please. Oh wait, I'll have the almond instead of the... Oh, hell, give me one raspberry, one chocolate and one almond, please.'

Now I'm smirking. 'I'm going to take the same but I know how good those pistachio macarons are, so throw me two of those on the plate as well because I know she's going to steal one.'

I'm all about managing collateral fallout.

We take a seat on two Italian-style conservatory chairs – at least that's what they look like to me, woven wood of some sort and lacquered to shine under the soft lighting. We're sitting on a table for two in the window, with a view of a boutique clothes store across the street.

'That's the first store Jess ever got her clothes into,' I tell Sarah. 'Before she got into the department store concession.'

'Oh, wow, it's cute. She's done so well for herself with her clothesline,' Sarah says.

Our drinks and macarons arrive and I immediately take the second pistachio macaron from my plate and place it onto Sarah's, so we each have four. 'Excuse my fingers. I haven't washed them for a while.'

Sarah chuckles. 'You're so gross, Charlie.'

I smile and pick up my hot chocolate, slurping it then jumping when the liquid burns my tongue, as it always does.

'You just burnt your tongue, didn't you?'

'No,' I lie.

Sarah picks up her mug in two hands and gently blows to cool the liquid, her soft pink lips forming a small O shape.

Don't go there, Charlie. Just friends.

She sips the drink, sets it down on the saucer with a ting, then rubs chocolate from the corners of her mouth. 'It really is good hot chocolate.'

'They make it by stirring actual chocolate into milk. None of that powder rubbish,' I tell her.

'It's definitely up there with my top three hot chocolates I've ever tasted.'

'Three?'

She smiles. 'I'm being coy.'

I lean my head to one side. 'Coy like you like me or coy like you're teasing me?'

We seem to fix our focus on each other for a beat, as if my playful question had too much meaning. I pursue a new, safe line of conversation. 'So, what have you been up to today, Sarah?'

'Well, I went for an extortionately priced lunch at The Savoy. Then I sauntered around the National Gallery, had a walk down to Buckingham Palace, stopped at the Ritz for a brief and overpriced drink, then went to meet Joe Elvis with the suit.'

'How is our friend? How's the quiff?'

She shakes her head. 'Very quiffy. That was when I saw a poster for your gig and decided to come and say the things I had wanted to say to you before you ran off from the house this morning.'

Maybe I was cowardly in not facing her but I've dealt with these situations enough times to know that people don't often show remorse for their words. In this case, I was wrong.

'I had to leave for my gig. I did bake pastries.'

'They went down very well with the others. You certainly left on a high note with them.'

I read between the lines. 'But not you?'

She takes another sip of her drink and this time doesn't realize that she has chocolate on her lip. I reach across the table and she doesn't pull away when I bring a napkin to her mouth.

'You've got a chocolate tash.'

She makes to take the napkin from me, fingertips grazing mine as she does so and whilst I don't want to sound as dramatic as I sometimes do, there is definitely something like a lightning bolt that snaps between her skin and mine. Either that or I've got a really bad itch.

I wonder, when she glances up at me sharply, whether she has an itchy finger too. Then she snatches the napkin from my hand.

I overstepped – understood.

'The National Gallery was really top of your list of things to do in London? Are you one of those art obsessives?' I ask, trying to move on swiftly.

It works. She turns her lips up only a tiny bit but it's an improvement.

But the smile is fleeting. She shifts to look out to the street contemplatively. I'm twitchy as I try to re-spect her space. It's uncomfortable for me but something tells me that my usual tack of cracking a joke isn't the right way to go just now.

'Charlie, I'm sorry. I don't know what's wrong with me this last week. From being snappy and irritable with you, to dredging up feelings of guilt that I haven't felt for a long time and which I don't want to feel. I don't even know why I'm here, sitting drinking hot chocolate, eating macarons and laughing with you whilst simultaneously feeling awful about it. Can I promise that if you ever come to New York and want to catch up, I'll be a different person? I'm usually fun, believe it or not.'

I smile softly. 'I can believe it. For what it's worth, I think you *are* fun.' I take a drink and then replace my mug on the saucer. 'Fun, mean, crabby when hungry and full of malice.'

She laughs and I inwardly breathe a sigh of relief.

'Whilst we are confessing, I should say sorry to you, too. I had no intention of upsetting you this week. Okay, sometimes I did, like the bath incident, but once I knew about your husband, all I wanted to do was give you space. I guess I went about it the wrong way. I should have been honest with you. Maybe. I've been in situations, at events like this, family occasions, where I've honestly had so many mixed emotions. I've been happy for my friends, whilst being envious of them being surrounded by people who love them.'

I fiddle with my spoon, uncomfortable, trying to articulate what I'm trying to tell her.

'It hurts when you see people around you having what you don't. And when I heard about Danny from the guys, I thought the week must've been as hard for you as it was for me. Harder. Way harder. I just thought that if I was feeling an ounce of the pain you must've been feeling, then I didn't want you to feel that and I certainly didn't want to make it worse. Does any of that make sense?'

She looks me in the eyes, unreadable. Eventually, she speaks.

'All of it. Thank you.'

It's true what they say: if you're honest with people, they are inclined to be honest with you.

But this new-age stuff doesn't sit easily with me. I reach for a comforting almond macaron and put it whole into my mouth.

'That's disgusting,' Sarah says.

'You're just jealous.' And when I finish chewing the delicious, large bite, I tell her, 'I think you need a London tour guide.'

I genuinely mean she needs to go on a website and find herself a guided tour but I'm not sad when she takes a mouse-sized nibble of her raspberry macaron and asks me, 'Are you offering?'

For all kinds of sensible reasons that I can't quite put my finger on right now, I should say no – I know I should say no – yet there's that cheeky little monkey again and he says, 'I'm not sure you could afford me. One hug is seventy-five greenbacks, so if we multiply that by the number of seconds in twenty-four hours and the number of days you have left in London, that's going to cost you, like... a panini and an ice cream, as a minimum.'

She is beaming at me as if she's Julia Roberts.

'At the end of this week, there will be no white limousine and red roses, or an offer of an apartment in New York,' she says. 'But I can stretch to a panini and an ice cream.'

This woman is completely on my wavelength when it comes to romantic comedy references.

'But, Charlie, I'll say it again: no one uses the term greenback. It's not cool in the slightest.'

I wink. 'I thought you'd like that.'

She rolls her eyes as she says, 'Right, if we are going to have a big day ahead of us tomorrow, I need some beauty sleep.'

I'm not tired. I could sit here until breakfast. Except the café is closing, so I can't, even if Sarah wanted to.

'I thought we were going to be honest with each other from now on?' I say. She raises one quizzical eyebrow. 'You really want to head back to your hotel to put on an elasticated waistband and let your belly hang out, don't you?'

She opens her mouth to protest, gasping as she does. Then her shock turns to a mischievous giggle. 'I totally do.'

I take her back to her hotel in a taxi, tell her I'll meet her at reception at nine thirty in the morning, watch her go through the revolving doors of the entrance, then pay the taxi driver and bid him farewell. There's no chance I'm paying to continue all the way on home to Clapham.

24

SARAH

I had the best sleep ever. After saying goodbye to Charlie, I was in my stretchy pajama bottoms and sinking into the mattress within minutes. I had a full tummy, I was comfortable and warm, and I had no negative energy on my mind.

My phone tells me that the weather is going to be seventy-two degrees Fahrenheit and sunny with little wind today, so I have dressed in a sundress and sneakers, prepared for a day of sightseeing with Charlie.

I wish I could say that I have made the most of the hotel's breakfast offering but after last night's late dessert binge and knowing that a day with Charlie is going to involve a lot of eating, I settled for a small plate of fruit, a slice of sourdough bread and a hard-boiled egg.

Now I'm making my way back downstairs, having cleaned my teeth and collected my small backpack, ready for the day ahead. As I near the hotel reception area, I see a man with his back to me, wearing a Union Jack-themed top hat – the type I have noticed being sold by street sellers with carts full of touristy merchandise. He is holding a spare hat in his hand.

Though his back is to me, I know that the T-shirt he is wearing with his khaki shorts and runners will be depicting either a Marvel or *Harry Potter* character. That knowledge makes me smile as I approach him, expecting to be overcome by embarrassment but in fact finding his outrageous get-up entertaining.

'Good morning,' I say brightly.

He rotates to show me a T-shirt hosting a Spider-Man figure in his infamous Spidey pose, except Spider-Man's usual costume has been replaced by a Union Jack, which draws even more attention to Charlie's ridiculous top hat.

'Here she is, Touristy McTourist Face.'

I have zero idea where that name has come from but this is Charlie and so I don't expect to follow his peculiar train of thought at all times. I think that's a good thing, too.

'Nice shirt,' I say.

Completely straight-faced, he replies, 'You too.'

And I laugh because I'm wearing a dress.

Charlie takes a step toward me and places the spare top hat on my head, adjusting my hair to move it out of my eyes as he does so. 'This is for you.'

'Is the hat obligatory?'

'If you want to partake in Captain Charlie's Day of Touristy Fun, then it is absolutely essential.'

I don't bother arguing. We make our way outside to the street and when we're there, I reach into my backpack and hand Charlie an almond croissant, double wrapped in cloth napkins, which I stole from the breakfast buffet.

'I know you like a pastry.'

He takes a mouthful before responding and through half-chewed croissant, he tells me, 'Yeah I do.' A little bit of food escapes from his mouth.

'Charlie, I don't want to start the day on a bad note but you're totally gross and since we're being honest with each other from now on, I think you should know that.'

He takes another bite of pastry then says, 'I'm fully aware, Touristy McTourist Face.'

Reaching into the side pocket of his shorts and handing me a flyer with a receipt stapled to the front, he says, 'And in return, this is a gift for you. It's your ride for the day.'

The receipt and flyer tell me I have a day pass for an open top, hop-on-hop-off London bus. 'This is like that episode of—'

'*Friends.*' We say the name of the sitcom simultaneously.

For some unbeknown reason, I am blushing as I ask him, 'Where do we start?'

He shakes his half-eaten croissant in the direction of travel and I follow him along the street. There are people dressed in suits still heading for work but the commuter traffic I had noticed through the window of the hotel during breakfast has died down and been replaced by tourists – notably hat-less tourists.

'Charlie, I feel a bit ridiculous in this hat.'

'In that case, I'm pleased I didn't buy you the flag to go with it.'

He laughs but I have a sense he genuinely considered it.

We head down to Victoria Embankment and he buys us each a bottle of still water from a kiosk. There are boats drifting up and down the River Thames, sunlight dancing off the ripples left in their wake. We follow the river west and as we do, I see the

London Eye across the water, on the south side of the river.

'The London Eye is on my list of things to do, Charlie. Have you incorporated that into your tour?'

'Do you like surprises?'

'I like good surprises.'

'Then stop asking questions. Captain Charlie has got your back.'

'Can I at least ask where we're going?'

Charlie rubs the back of his hand across his lips, removing remnants of his pastry. 'First, we are going to Downing Street to see if we can catch you a glimpse of the prime minister and the infamous number ten door, which you're almost guaranteed to see on the news on a weekly basis, even in the States, because that's how often we change prime minister.'

I catch the reference, amused. I am aware of the political turmoil associated with the United Kingdom at the moment and I am no stranger to the same in the US.

'You can't actually walk along Downing Street these days because it's heavily guarded by police but I have a little spidey inside who tells me that if we walk a bit faster, we'll catch a glimpse of the PM leaving this morning.'

'Oh cool. Who is the Prime Minister this week?'

'Fuck knows,' Charlie says, and we titter together.

But despite his playfulness, very soon after arriving at the heavily guarded gates on Whitehall, Charlie's source is proved correct. From our position alongside a couple of tourists and a few press cameras, we see a man wearing very shiny Prada shoes and a pinstripe suit leaving number ten Downing Street. Just at the right moment, Charlie whips out his phone and snaps a selfie of us with the prime minister standing equidistant between our top hats.

Next, he tells me we're going to Friary Court to see the beginning of the changing of the guard, which is another thing on my to do list.

'I thought the changing of the guard happens at Buckingham Palace,' I say, which is what I had found out from googling after Izzy and Becky told me I should witness it.

'Ah well, technically, the changing over does happen in the forecourt of Buckingham Palace but you told me that you walked the Mall and went to Buckingham Palace yesterday, so I thought I'd get you a better view somewhere with a few less tourists around and show you somewhere you haven't yet seen.'

I am impressed he was actually listening last night and not just scoffing macarons and drinking more hot chocolate than I'd expect from the residents of the small village of Lansquenet.

We arrive at Friary Court at St James's Palace and while there are a couple of walking tours nearby, within minutes Charlie has got us in a great spot. At precisely ten twenty-five by my watch, soldiers come together in the Court and a band starts to play.

'That's the St James's Palace Detachment of The King's Guard,' Charlie tells me, raising his voice to be heard above the sound of drums being beaten and brass instruments being blown. 'They're having their uniform inspected now and in...' He checks his watch. 'Seventeen minutes, they'll march off toward Buckingham Palace and the band will follow them the whole way.'

I have to admit, it's pretty awesome. The whole thing feels steeped in British history and looks like the kind of thing one might see in the movie *Paddington*.

'I love the fluffy hats,' I say, leaning into Charlie's ear in a quieter moment of the band's routine.

Charlie looks aghast. 'Did you just emasculate every single soldier in the history of The King's Guard?'

I chuckle. 'What? They're cute.'

He shakes his head. 'Those are bearskin hats. They're more hunter gatherer than fairy princess.'

We watch the soldiers begin to march. Next thing I know, Charlie has grabbed hold of my hand and is hurrying me through the walking tour groups and telling me something about Birdcage Walk. We walk across a bridge, through the park, and see another group of soldiers, who Charlie tells me are the New Guard, marching off in the direction of Buckingham Palace.

'So, it's up to you, we can run on down to Buckingham Palace and watch the actual change over, or we can head across to Westminster and Big Ben,' Charlie says.

'You mean to say I have a choice in how to spend my holiday?'

Charlie twists his mouth as if thinking, almost caricature-like in his expression, then says, 'You're right, this is Captain Charlie's tour; let's head on to Big Ben and Westminster. You've seen your fluffy-hat men now.'

We head to Westminster Abbey first and I recognize it as soon as I see it from the coverage of royal weddings. Charlie asks me which such wedding has been my favorite and I tell him Will and Kate's. If asked a few months ago, I might have said Harry and

Meghan's because I had loved the rags to riches story of Meghan Markle but today, I'm not feeling contentious, and so I go with the much less controversial option. Charlie agrees and we share an easy conversation about the royals, real life events and, of course, Netflix's *The Crown*. I gather that he is dubious about the factual content of the show and that he is very definitely a royalist.

Charlie seems to know something about everything, in a completely unpretentious and non-boastful way. It leads me to ask, 'Where did you learn all this stuff, Charlie?'

'You mean other than streaming services?' he jokes, but I sense some hesitation or even embarrassment and I don't know why. It's almost as if being smart is a negative character trait. Admittedly, before today, Charlie hadn't struck me as overly intelligent but like many of my initial opinions about him, I'm changing that one, too.

I decide not to let him off the hook with his usual way of avoiding questions, which is to make a joke of everything, and I wait for his truth.

'If you can believe it,' he begins, as we exit the beautiful Abbey, 'I went right through the education system by hook or by crook. I studied history at university for a couple of years, then I dropped out to do comedy full-time. Something my mother is *very* proud of.'

I hear his sarcasm but I'm mostly impressed. I'm also surprised to hear him talk about his mother. He doesn't expand and I don't know what is considered taboo when talking to someone who has had his kind of upbringing, so I decide that now, during Captain Charlie's Day of Touristy Fun, isn't the right time to pursue that line of enquiry.

'Surprised?' he asks, and I realize he's talking about his education.

'That you went to university or that you dropped out? One is more believable than the other.' I say it tongue-in-cheek and thankfully he laughs.

'Yeah, I can imagine.'

Charlie has pre-arranged tickets for us to enter Westminster and we have jumped a reasonably long queue to look around inside. The building outside is impressive but much like I have seen in movies and on the news.

'Did you always want to be a comedian?' I ask.

We head inside to the atrium.

'Did I always want to be a comedian? Not really,' he says. 'I didn't have a Mr Moon in *Sing* moment, at least.'

I get his reference to the kids' movie (which every

adult needs to see, not least for the epic music), and say, 'Such a good movie.'

'*Great* movie.'

We express our appreciation simultaneously.

When Charlie sobers, he seems to look everywhere except at me. He can pretend to be taking in the decorative ceiling or the paintings on the walls, even the fancy tiled floor, but I know he's avoiding meeting my eyes.

We head left, following a tour group, and Charlie tells me we can steal their guide for free, which gives me some insight into the type of student that Charlie was.

'I changed schools a lot as a kid,' he says, still averting his gaze. 'Every time I moved foster homes and got a new "family", I changed schools, too.' He adds inverted commas around the word with his fingers. 'The younger you are, the easier it is to come and go discreetly. Kids sort of accept you and maybe even like the new kid because he's like a shiny new toy – for five minutes, anyway. But as you get older, all it means is that you don't have time to make and keep a set of good friends.'

He shrugs and finally glances in my direction but the connection is brief.

'As you get older, you can be bullied for being a

new kid – a bit different and completely undesirable to the other kids' parents once they find out on the PTA grapevine what your background is. Or you can play the idiot, mess around in class, get kicked out of lessons, basically play up to the stereotype, which is the image the good kids have already sold to their parents on your behalf anyway.'

And suddenly, I understand. 'You started playing the role of the class clown to protect yourself.'

We follow the tour group into a room with large wooden tables, highly polished with leather tops attached by what look like press-studs. There are portraits on the walls with the names of historic prime ministers underneath. Some of the older portraits look like they would fit in the National Gallery. The name of the room escapes my attention as Charlie and I continue to talk quietly.

'I guess you could say that being the joker was my defense mechanism and when I finally got with a family and stayed with them long enough for them to convince me that I needed a good education, it was hard to break the mold I'd created for myself. So, I went to college and I got into university. I'm not stupid, believe it or not,' he says with a laugh that I don't return. I've seen enough of Charlie now to know he isn't stupid, far from it. 'But at university, I did what you might expect of me and started to piss away my grades. I was already disappointing my mother anyway, so back then I thought why not really rub salt in the wound and throw her kindness right back in her face. Two years into my degree, I quit.'

He shakes his head and looks at his feet.

'Anyway, the only thing I knew was being the class clown, so I started going to open mic nights and after a while recognized that I had a talent for reading the room and dealing the lines at the right time. Fast forward another few years and I realized the many, many, many errors of my ways and thought, shit, I have nothing else to fall back on so unless I want to pull pints for a pittance for the rest of my life, I better put some real effort into this comedy thing.'

He raises his arms out from his sides, as if to say, *this is me.*

'It sounds like one of those everything-happens-for-a-reason stories but I think you might be downplaying your talents there, Captain Charlie.'

He scoffs and I'm pleased I can lighten his mood.

I consider my next words and whether I should ask a question at all but I decide it's appropriate. 'You mentioned your mother...'

We've followed the tour group into a large dining

hall now, which ironically would be fitting for a scene from *Harry Potter*, and I tell Charlie as much. He agrees and lapses into silence.

Eventually he must register my query about his mother, or decide he is ready to talk, which he does.

'I was adopted when I was fifteen, which is pretty unlikely after more than a decade in foster care, but my parents...' He looks to the ceiling as he speaks and I can tell he's uncomfortable referring to his mother and father in this way. 'They are good people. They had fostered for years, across all the age groups. I was wild when I arrived and I don't know what it was about them but they had a huge calming influence on me. For the first time in my life, I was being spoken to like an adult. We had dinner as a "family".' He adds inverted commas around the word family, again. 'Every night we would sit at the table, their maternal kids and foster kids – three of us, including me – and discuss our days at school or whatever else we had been doing that day. They encouraged me to go out to work with my dad at weekends – he was an electrician, so I used to help him out and he'd give me some cash, which inevitably I blew on stuff I shouldn't. It was the first time I'd really had any money of my own – or any responsibility. In hindsight, they were amazing parents. I couldn't see it at the time but I do now.

'I calmed down in the home, a lot. Not at school but they recognized that and my mum is a teacher, part time in retirement now, and she saw the difference in me, so she tutored me at home and, by hook or by crook, I got enough GCSEs to get into college. I was used to change and my parents thought that moving to a college with new people would actually be a good thing for once in my life – they were right again. They formally adopted me, which had a huge impact on my view of the world. No one had ever been loyal to me before then, not even my own birth mother. So I went to college, still playing the class clown but making enough grades to get into university and the only thing I really cared about was history, so that's what I studied.'

He's shaking his head again and puts his hands in his shorts pockets, his shoulders high and tense.

'It's all worked out for the best but I don't know that I can ever repay them for their loyalty and their belief in me. For their hard work and investment in me. And I'll never shift the guilt of how I threw that back at them when I quit university.'

I look around us and see that we are now in the Commons chamber – obviously not in session. It's smaller than I would have imagined from TV but the rows of green leather upholstered benches are just as I have seen before and they line either side of the room. The Speaker's chair is at one end and it is as large and grand as I anticipated. There is a box-like piece of furniture in the middle of the room, equidistant between both sides of benches, where the prime minister opens that big fat book on the news. Charlie tells me I'm looking at the house table and a mace.

'Have you had this conversation with your parents?' I ask.

He looks at me almost with surprise on his face. 'They lived it. There's nothing to tell.'

'Charlie, I don't know your parents but I think I'm starting to get to know you better and I think you've done incredibly well for yourself. Please don't take that to be patronizing; I don't mean it that way. I think for anyone to find their passion and find their feet in the world is impressive. You keep striving and getting better and I've seen you before you go out on stage. You push yourself every time. I don't think you need to have any guilt and if your parents are as decent as they sound, I'm sure they agree.'

Charlie turns his head sharply, almost aggressively quickly, and tells me, 'With respect, Sarah, you don't know what I've put them through.'

He's misunderstood me, I think.

'I appreciate that, Charlie, I'm just saying that if you—'

'Can we just have fun today? Please?'

I know the conversation is over. I nod but he has already followed the tour group out of the chamber and away from me.

I hang back and pretend to be appreciating the room for a minute or so longer, giving Charlie space, which I think he might appreciate. All I'm actually thinking, as I look around the now empty room, right before another tour group moves inside, is how sad it is that Charlie can't appreciate the complete inaccuracies of his words.

The tour ends after one more corridor and by the time we're outside of Westminster Abbey, on the sidewalk, it's as if our conversation about his past never happened.

There's no remnants of animosity or anger as he asks, 'Hungry?'

It's early afternoon and after being on our feet since Charlie picked me up at the hotel this morning, I've worked up a good appetite.

'There's a proper British pub nearby if you fancy the full experience?'

We walk a few minutes to a traditional public

house. It has deep-red facias and gold trims on the signage outside. Inside, there are oak tables to match an oak-top bar and several booths are furnished in deep-red leather. We take one of the booths and peruse a large two-sided menu.

'Tell me, what do I need to eat to get the full British culinary experience?'

'It's got to be beer-battered fish and chips,' Charlie tells me. 'Though this is a British pub with a typically British pub grub menu, so I'm sure you'll be good with any choice.'

I turn my menu over to review the drinks options then set it down on the table, patting my hands on top of it affirmatively. 'Nope. If you tell me I need fish and chips, that's what I'm having.'

Charlie orders the same and we each order a pint-sized soft drink to replenish after our hours of activity. We end up falling down a rabbit hole of British history which then somehow burrows into movies of historic significance and their many factual discrepancies. Charlie and I agree to disagree on the fact that he is ruining Hollywood gold for me by changing the story of William Wallace that I understand from Mel Gibson, and the events of Queen Victoria's life that I've learned from Emily Blunt.

Nearly an hour and a half has passed when we

head out for stop number nine at Westminster Bridge.

We don our top hats once more and Charlie takes a selfie of us with Big Ben poking out of my head. We are near the front of the queue when the bus arrives. Charlie briefly chats to the driver and after he ushers me upstairs to the open top deck, he informs me that she's a friend; she also works the comedy circuit and this is her side hustle.

'She's good,' he tells me. 'It's just a matter of time and luck for her.'

I admire how supportive he is of other comedians, rather than competitive, like I see so often in the legal field, with men and women constantly beating each other up in the proverbial sense in order to get a jump up the ladder.

From up here, we have an amazing view as we drive through the city. There's a slight breeze in the air and when the bus picks up speed, I'm forced to hold onto my hat. The wind blows in my face, cooling against the warmth of the sun. We drive alongside Hyde Park and I tell Charlie, 'I'd like to go for a walk down there.'

'If you can trust me, I'm going to go one better than a walk but that's tomorrow, during Captain Charlie's Second Day of Touristy Fun.'

I close my eyes and tilt my face toward the sun, trying to soak in the welcome vitamin D.

'I trust you,' I say. 'But I do think you need to work on your branding. Surely you can do better than Captain Charlie's Second Day of Touristy Fun.'

'Hey, I'm not a man of many words but like most good things, it's quality over quantity, no?'

'Charlie, don't lie to me. I haven't been able to shut you up all day.'

The bus takes us past St Paul's Cathedral, which, to me, bears a resemblance to the White House but Charlie is horrified when I tell him that. He goes on to give me the history and significance of the cathedral. His passion for facts is endearing – and admittedly, in some places, boring as hell, but he is happy.

We drive past the Tower of London and I point out that this is also on my list of places to see.

'Would you stop ruining my trip? That's the first stop on tomorrow's agenda.'

I offer a superficial apology, amused by how seriously he is taking his tour guide duties.

We head across Tower Bridge to the south side of the River Thames, yet, as Charlie points out HMS *Belfast* to me, once again giving me its historic details and connection to His Majesty the King, I am suddenly overcome by a sense of gratitude. He has genuinely thought about and planned everything. He must have spent hours last night and this morning organizing the day, buying bus tickets and entrance tickets.

The bus pulls up to some traffic lights and the noise of the wind dies down.

'Thank you, Charlie. Sorry, I mean Captain Charlie. I'm having a great day and I really appreciate the effort. At some point last week, I think I stopped looking forward to sightseeing around London and started to see it as more of a chore than a holiday. You've changed that. I've not stopped laughing and smiling all day and that's truly thanks to you.'

I think I take us both by surprise when I lean into him and press a kiss to his cheek.

'You're a sweetheart,' I say.

He is clearly taken aback by my forwardness as he stares at me and I wish I could see his eyes behind his sunglasses to get a better read on his thoughts. As I am looking, we end up locked in a gaze that I hadn't intended but which I feel compelled not to break.

Eventually, Charlie says, simply, 'You're welcome.'

Then he clears his throat, as if the pollution we are breathing in up here on the top deck of the bus is taking its toll.

25

CHARLIE

I had intended to end the day here, on the last stop of the Red Route, on the south side of Westminster Bridge, but I can't.

Not after that look. Not after feeling her lips on my skin.

The crush I was harboring last week. The crush that was devastated by Sarah's words to Izzy after the wedding. It has reignited and its flames are burning like a bonfire on Guy Fawkes' Night.

The thought of leaving her here and heading back to my empty apartment... I just don't want to.

Should I dare to hope?

Probably not. Since our tour of Westminster

Palace, Sarah knows even more about my undesirable past.

But that look. I can't get it out of my head and I haven't been able to for the entire bus ride along the Southbank. I've been talking, I think, as normal, filling her in on some useless trivia I have acquired over the years about the sites and buildings we were driving past, but there's been a knot deep in the pit of my abdomen, ever since that kiss on my cheek.

Her proximity is overwhelming, such that I'm almost – not quite – relieved to alight the bus and put a few more inches between us.

But all at once I am feeling relieved and bereft by the loss of her hip next to mine, the occasional graze of her knee or nudge of her elbow.

And so I ask, 'Are you tired? Do you want to go back to your hotel?'

Her sunglasses are now on top of her head as the sun has very slowly started to hide behind tall buildings and I register the absolutely aghast look on her face. I realize the error of my words.

'Shit, no, not like that. I didn't mean us... I just thought it's been a long day and you might want to go home but if not—'

I'm speaking too quickly, rambling, but I need to think on my feet because I don't want her to go back to the hotel right now. I recalculate the next few days' activities I have planned. 'I'm wondering if you're up for the London Eye as the sun starts to go down?'

Maybe I shouldn't have mentioned the sun going down. Does that imply romance? I hope not. I didn't mean it to. I just thought—

Christ, I'm even rambling in my own head.

Sarah purses her lips, like she's mocking me. 'It is on my list of things to do, provided I'm not going to get into trouble for saying so on this occasion.'

My hands have found their way into the pockets of my shorts and I'm staring at my shoes, grinning like a bashful child. I nod.

I pull myself together and tell her, 'On this occasion, Captain Charlie will let it slide.' Gesturing with my head to the path that runs alongside the River Thames, I say, 'It's this way.'

She's pouting again and I figure it's because the London Eye is so blatantly that way, it hardly needed me to point that out.

'Following your lead, Captain Charlie.'

We queue for around thirty minutes, which isn't bad. I had intended to book us queue jump tickets but as this wasn't on my agenda for today, we have to wait. Sarah doesn't seem to care in the slightest. I buy us each a bottle of water and we chat through the wait.

She seems lighter today than she's been since we met and, in the back of my mind, I'm wondering if it's because the wedding has been and gone. The thoughts of her husband that must have been haunting her last week – they would have got to anyone with half a heart – maybe aren't as painful now as they were.

This version of Sarah is incredible. She's funny. So funny. Actually in quite a dry, British way... for an American. She's intelligent and witty. Not half as needy as she seemed at times last week.

One thing hasn't changed. She is still as strikingly beautiful as she was the moment she stepped out of the airport at Heathrow.

My mobile has been receiving notifications all afternoon – I've felt the vibrations in my pocket and when Sarah has taken toilet trips, I've looked at the messages. They're all from a WhatsApp group Jess set up for those who stayed in the house in Surrey. She's just sent the group a picture of an immaculate beach, with long stretches of white sand, and a cocktail in her hand. She thanked everyone for making her and Jake's wedding day special. Then she gave particular thanks to Sarah for being the best Matron of Honor and organizing the entire week.

I was wrong about Sarah's relationship with those guys earlier. She *is* a people pleaser, 100 per cent. But now I think I understand that more than I did then. She just doesn't want to lose people she cares about in her life. Maybe staying busy with administration also kept her mind off her husband, too.

But I was wrong about her friends not appreciating it. They love her. Spending days in their company showed it. In hindsight, the way the lads were so quick to get on my back when they thought I was trying it on with her proved it. And the stream of messages from everyone in the WhatsApp group, an outpouring of love and thanks for Sarah, has reaffirmed it.

What's more, I totally get it. They know, as I've come to appreciate, that she's amazing.

She would be amazing anyway but to have loved someone enough to marry them, expect to spend the rest of her life with them, then lose them the way she has and be able to carry on? *Wow*.

Once we are standing in the window of our panoramic glass capsule, rather than taking in the views, I find myself staring at Sarah. I find myself thinking what a lucky man Danny was to have been adored by her. (And, admittedly, a very unlucky man to have died in his twenties.)

'What is it you say to me?' Sarah asks. 'Penny for your thoughts?'

Oops. Caught red-handed.

'I was just thinking... ah... that the London Eye is the tallest cantilevered observation wheel in the world.'

As our capsule slowly ascends, Sarah and I stand side by side, soaking up the view. There are other people in here but everyone has their own area, and they are speaking quietly, staying segregated. It's a well-behaved capsule crowd.

I point out sites and buildings, like the Shard, the Cheese Grater, the Oxo Tower and the Old Bailey. Facts, histories and architectural design details are rolling off my tongue. I even astonish myself with the wealth of knowledge I have amassed in my thirty-one years on this planet.

As I'm speaking, mostly I'm thinking about impressing Sarah but sporadically, I question whether I am quite as stupid as I have been told over the years – quite as stupid as I have played the role of being. A new idea occurs to me: to create a sketch for my shows based on places of interest and random facts about history. Grown-up and funnier *Horrible Histories*.

But now, as we pause at the very highest peak of the observation wheel, I am staring at Sarah's hands on the safety rail. The sun is shining from behind a rogue cloud to the west of us, low and glowing orange across the river. All I can think about is how much I would like to be able to slide my hand on top of hers, to stand behind her, my chest pressed to her back, my chin on her shoulder, the scent of her hair consuming me with every breath I take.

Whoa, knock it off, Charlie!

I'm letting this crush, this fantasy, this overpowering feeling run away with itself.

I need to remember the reasons I left the house in Surrey without saying goodbye.

I'm not good enough for her, her friends made that clear, but even if I were, she doesn't want a relationship with anyone, let alone me.

We descend to the ground and I walk with Sarah in the direction of her hotel, happy for the company and not at all bothered that I've been on my feet for most of the day.

She offers to walk the rest of the way herself when we are on the north side of the river, in a place she recognizes, but she doesn't protest when I say I'll happily continue on.

'So what's the plan for tomorrow?' she asks.

I'm already giddy thinking about another day with her.

'I'll collect you around nine thirty again, then we can head to the Tower of London for a tour. Does that sound okay?'

Her sunglasses are now resting on her head, holding back strands of her hair, so I can see her quizzical look and it makes me smile.

'Don't act like I have any say in the tour schedule.'

I chuckle. 'You're right. Be ready for nine thirty, that's an order. Then I've booked us tickets to a matinee performance in the West End and a table for dinner afterwards.'

She opens her mouth in, I think, happy shock. 'That's all on my list! Which show? And more importantly, how much do I owe you?'

Now I really need to book a show.

'It's a surprise and nothing.'

We reach her hotel and we're standing on the pavement outside, facing each other, staring at each other, and I am blinded by an insatiable desire to kiss her.

I don't know what to do but I know I need to leave. Now.

I thrust out my hand; I've no idea why. For her to shake?

She moves in to hug me or kiss me on the cheek, I'm not sure.

It all happens in the blink of an eye and I sort of poke her in the stomach and she lands a blow to my check with her hand.

Now we are hugging, kind of. Not quite shaking hands and hugging. Shugging.

Oh God, this is awful.

I leave, watching my feet as I go.

'Night then!' I call, not looking back and walking in entirely the wrong direction for my Tube station.

'Nine thirty then?' she calls in response.

'Yep! Goodnight!'

I don't hear anything else as I weave between two small groups of people and hope she can't see me when I reflexively slap my palm to my forehead.

Total. Loser.

26

SARAH

The slightly confused ending to the day aside – I
went in to kiss Charlie's cheek; I think he, oddly, went
to shake my hand – yesterday was a great day. We saw
the city's sights, I laughed so hard I was sore, and last
night I passed out in bed, physically exhausted in the
best way.

I woke just after 6 a.m. and for the first time since
arriving in England, I didn't struggle to peel myself
off the mattress. Both because I had the deepest,
most peaceful slumber, and because I'm super excited for the day ahead.

I struggled to wait until 8 a.m. for breakfast,
trying to pace my morning, taking a mug of English
breakfast tea in bed before washing my hair and

taking time to dress. I drank more tea over breakfast – a pot, in fact – in place of my usual coffee, and I enjoyed a continental breakfast.

Now I'm walking slow circles around the hotel's atrium, waiting for Charlie to come by. It's nine twenty-nine and I'm eager to get on with our plans.

Precisely as my watch flips to nine thirty, Charlie walks through the entrance to the hotel. My heart leaps in my chest, as if his presence has startled me, despite my waiting for him for a quarter of an hour.

'Hi!' I almost sing, a little too cheery.

He gives me the biggest smile and holds up two take-out reusable coffee cups that say *Monmouth Coffee* on the front.

'Good morning,' he says. 'This, I assure you, is the best coffee in the city. And the mug is a gift – we shouldn't keep getting disposables.'

'I agree,' I tell him, tempering myself now. 'Thank you for yet another gift.'

While we stand on the spot, I take a taste. 'Not bad at all,' I say, 'and thank you for remembering how I take my coffee.'

'The basics of lasting friendship. Ready?'

I nod and follow him out of the hotel, warmed by his words.

I've been pushing to the back of my mind the fact

that today is Tuesday and Friday will be our last day together, but knowing he wants to stay friends beyond that is... like a big bear hug. I won't tell him because he'll probably try to charge me seventy-five bucks again – or worse, *greenbacks*.

We walk to the Tower of London, my heart racing most of the way. But whether that's from the strong Monmouth coffee or something else, I don't know. It's a lengthy walk but we talk non-stop, and when we arrive we take a self-guided audio tour of the tower. Despite the wealth of information provided, Charlie manages to entertain me with some extra bits of history, some of which seem too hilarious to be true and some of which he eventually confesses to maybe having embellished somewhat.

After the tour, we stroll around St Katherine's Dock, discussing the docked boats – which ones we'd live on, the reasons people live on boats (divorced men, we decide, are top candidates), and where we would sail if there were no boundaries. Charlie tells me about *Gloriana*, Queen Elizabeth II's row-barge, built to commemorate her diamond jubilee.

He asks if I want to take the bus or the Tube back to the West End for our trip to the Savoy Theatre, which happens to be right by my hotel. We decide we have enough time to walk.

I'm not sure whether Charlie offers his arm, or I take it, but we end up strolling with my arm linked in his.

It turns out Charlie has booked us tickets to see Ivo Van Hove's adaptation of *A Little Life* by Hanya Yanagihara. We've both read the book and so we pass most of the walk discussing the merits and our criticisms of it.

I'm nervous when we near the theatre because I remember being emotionally drained by the book, but I'm buzzed to be seeing the production.

'I have to give you the money for the tickets, Charlie. This must have cost a small fortune.'

'Why don't you buy dinner?' he suggests, and we agree to settle the discussion with that, but I know he's drawing the financial short straw.

The show starts at one thirty. We order popcorn and soft drinks using the in-seat ordering tool from our spot in the stalls. It transpires that Charlie had to book two individual seats and there's a man booked to sit between us. When he arrives, Charlie politely asks if we can shuffle to sit together and, happily, the man obliges.

'It was pretty last minute and most showings of this are sold out,' Charlie tells me.

The effort he has gone to again, his kindness, it

all threatens to overawe me. But when I express my gratitude, in true Charlie fashion, he dismisses it all as nothing.

The show lasts for around four hours. There are multiple moments when I sneak a glance at Charlie and see him discreetly wiping a thumb under his eyes. Meanwhile, tears roll freely down my cheeks. At one point, I audibly sob, quickly silencing myself with my fingertips pressed to my lips.

Charlie slips his hand over mine on my thigh and gives it a comforting squeeze. I stare at it, wondering if it's okay for him to touch me like this, openly, unabashed. But if Izzy was here and crying, or Becky, or Jess, or one of the guys, I'd do the same thing for them.

So I wrap my fingers around his and leave our hands there, on my leg, occasionally glancing down and reminding myself that Charlie and I are friends now. We have a connection. A strong connection. We can talk endlessly, we enjoy many of the same things, we laugh *a lot*. I'm crazy happy in his company. I feel more myself than I have for eight years. Old me. When I still had Danny physically in my life.

We are in the very last scenes of the play when I become conscious that I'm comparing life when I'm with Charlie to life when I had Danny.

I slide my hand out from under Charlie's and pretend to need a drink. I don't return my hand to my thigh.

Outside on the Strand, I'm feeling discombobulated. The show was incredible but it tied my emotions up in knots. Charlie's presence was welcome, his touch was calming. Yet, both were... too much.

What if I've thrown him a wrong signal? What if he thinks there's something more than friendship between us? What if Danny can somehow see us?

I'm by myself out on the street – Charlie hung back to go to the toilet – and now he exits the theatre, walking toward me. I can see his shoulders are high, his hands are in his pockets and his exhale is long and slow, purposeful.

We are facing each other, neither of us speaking.

Charlie exhales again, then says, 'That was a lot, wasn't it?'

He has no idea.

'A lot,' I agree. 'But great,' I'm quick to add, not wanting to seem ungrateful. 'The cast were amazing.'

He nods. 'They were. And the story was—'

'Really on point. So close to the book.'

'That's what I was going to say.'

We are both nodding and not speaking. It's awkward and my mind is about to spiral as it chews over the reasons why when Charlie says, 'I understand if you just want to chill tonight, after that.'

Oh. The thought had occurred to me but now that he's said it first, I don't know what to think. Have we crossed a line holding hands, linking arms, kissing on cheeks?

'Right. Yeah. Well, same for you, obviously.'

'No, I'm good,' he says. 'I think I need some comfort food but if you want to join me, I'm all for it. I just wanted to give you an easy out if you need one.'

Huh. I might be even more confused now but I'm not sure I want to be left alone with my thoughts, so I ask, 'Do you know a good burger place?'

'My kind of woman,' he says, smiling, then immediately follows up with, 'to have as a friend. I'm wary of people who don't like a good burger.'

Then he's gone, moving away from me along the Strand. I watch him, unsure whether I'm supposed to be following.

After long seconds, he turns and calls, 'Are you coming? I'm starving.'

I do a short-stepped run to catch up to him and we walk speedily to a burger bar, which gives me time to brush off the play, the theatre and any idea that there was awkwardness between us.

We both order beers and burgers – halloumi and

Portobello mushroom for me, beef for Charlie – agree to *not* talk about the show for fear of giving ourselves the blues, and wind up sharing our best burger experiences instead.

By the end of our feast, we are full and, at least for my part, contented again with our state of friendship.

As I'm settling the check, I wonder how we should say goodbye in order to avoid the shaking-hug scenario we had outside the hotel last night.

But Charlie prevents the situation entirely.

'The Tube is closer than the hotel for me, so are you okay to get back yourself, if I head to the Tube?'

'Absolutely,' I tell him, relieved. 'Same time tomorrow?'

'Great. See you then.' He's already backing away from me when he waves a hand and calls, 'Thanks for dinner!'

'Thanks for the entire day,' I say, but he's already lost in the bodies of people walking on the street.

* * *

'Oops, sorry!'

I apologize to a fellow hotel guest as I realize I've been holding a slotted spoon over a bowl of fruit for longer than is necessary to decide which fruit I might like on my Greek yoghurt. I scoop up halved peaches and put the spoon down on a side plate, ready for the stranger to use.

This is symbolic of how my morning has been. Everything feels a little hazy and confused.

I woke with a start around five thirty-five and I don't think I went back to sleep, not properly.

I had been dreaming about a gorgeous, deep, loving, sexy-as-hell kiss with a man. I think that man was Danny, or at least in my mind it had started out as Danny, but when I forced myself to stop dreaming, that man was most definitely Charlie.

My pulse racing, I sprang upright in bed. I hadn't meant to dream about kissing Charlie, of course I hadn't. I wouldn't. But I couldn't get that kiss out of my mind. It was exactly how kissing Danny in the early days used to feel. Full of passion.

And so I spent another thirty minutes or so, I think, in a sort of semi-lucid state, trying to get back to that feeling, to that kiss, trying to force myself to see Charlie in my mind... No, Danny. I was trying to see and feel kissing *Danny*.

'Would you like more tea, madam?'

I love the way the hotel-service personnel speak like it's the nineteenth century. It feels quintessentially British and makes me want to accept more English breakfast tea in fine-bone china but I say no because it's almost time for Charlie to pick me up in the way I am becoming used to now.

The thing is, I'm nervous. If I see Charlie and I think about that kiss, will my dream be written all over my face? The heat of it. My desire for more. The unrelenting guilt that is threatening to take over my every thought?

I make quick work of cleaning my teeth and grabbing my backpack, then I hotfoot it downstairs to the atrium.

And every negative thought I have experienced over the last four hours disappears with one look, one smile, one good morning from Charlie.

He hands me a Monmouth coffee again in the cup he took back from me yesterday morning with the intention of reusing today. It's so hard to remedy the Charlie I met at the beginning of last week and the Charlie I know now. I met the performer last week and this version of Charlie is, I believe, the real him.

I sip my coffee and thank him again for his generosity. Then I am transfixed as I watch him drink from his own cup. I watch his lips gently maneuver around the edge, then softly press together as the coffee passes his tongue and he swallows, the move-ment moving his Adam's apple up and down his lightly stubbled neck. In this moment, I can't deny that the lips I kissed in my dream were his. I know because my body is responding in the same way as it did in my sleep. My throat is tightening, my heart is pounding, there is a knot in my stomach, and some-where south of that is fizzing like an effervescent bath bomb.

Oh my God, I have a thing for Charlie.

He's talking to me, telling me about the day ahead and I hear something about Hyde Park being on the agenda but I am silently distracted by panic. I don't want to have a thing for anyone, especially not Charlie, whose company I am enjoying beyond measure.

By the time we reach Trafalgar Square, I'm feeling more rational. It's Wednesday. Friday is our last day together and there's every chance I will never see him again. It's a brutal way to end a beautiful friendship but it will be my saving grace.

Plus, Charlie said it himself, we are friends. We are both on the same page. Or I can pretend to be for three more days, I'm sure.

I am out of New York, away from things and places that Danny and I enjoyed together, away from our home. And people have these sort of holiday blips, right? That's all this is. A blip.

With a newfound calm, I re-engage in conversation.

'I'm happy to walk,' I tell him when he asks me if we should go by foot or take public transport from the square. I'm used to walking in Manhattan and I know that Charlie prefers being in the open air too, so we make a happy pair as we traverse Piccadilly and arrive at the corner of Hyde Park.

Charlie points out Wellington Arch and gives me the history of the statue on top of it. We stroll inside and both comment on the beautiful scents coming from the rose garden, then we make it to the Serpentine pier, where a row of blue pedal boats is loosely docked.

Charlie takes my empty coffee cup and shakes out the last drips, then replaces the lids and puts both cups in his backpack, presumably for coffee tomorrow morning.

Then he walks up to a young man selling tickets to the pedal boats. He comes back to me looking triumphant and nudges me in the direction of the mini vessels.

The guy in charge tries to hold the boat steady as Charlie lets me climb on first but I still end up squealing as it rocks under my weight. I eventually come to sit with a bang, holding a hand to my chest as I catch my breath. Charlie is laughing at me but gets his comeuppance when he unsteadily flops into his seat, making the boat rock far more than I did.

The guy pushes us away from the dock and we fall into a steady pedal together. The sky is scattered sparingly with clouds that make the sun come and go but the air is warm and it's another day of very little breeze.

The surrounding trees are lush green and full with large leaves. The grass is as vibrant as I have ever seen and people in the park are joyful as they walk, work out and play. It isn't the school holidays in England, so I'm told, but there are lots of young children out, squealing and giggling.

For a while, we pedal in comfortable silence, taking in our surroundings.

Then Charlie asks me, 'How do you know Jake and the others?'

'Well, Drew and my husband went to college together and I became Drew's legal secretary early in his career, which is how Danny and I met. Brooks is one of Drew's oldest friends from school and Jake is obviously Drew's brother. The girls are additions in more recent years. Edmond is the executive chef at the restaurant where Becky works and Drew and Edmond already knew each other, mostly because Drew likes steak.'

'So it's all a bit incestuous really,' Charlie says.

I laugh. 'It sounds weird. But actually we're just a close group of friends with a lot in common, and I guess that means we tend to like the same people.'

Charlie seems to take a beat to process my answer. 'I understand why the guys are so protective over you, what with your relationship with Danny.'

'How do you mean?'

'Well, initially I thought they were warning me to stay away from you purely to protect you but maybe if they were close with your husband too, there is an element of them not wanting to see you with another guy. I don't just mean me, obviously.'

I've found that generally, when there is an awkward conversation to be had in life, it's easier to be sitting side by side than to be facing each other. Perhaps that's why I engage in a conversation I might have avoided another day. I stare at a duck that's swimming on top of the water and the circles spanning out from its body as it moves.

'Maybe they were concerned that there could be something between us and they weren't sure how legitimate it would be on your part.'

If I had been looking into Charlie's eyes as I spoke those words, I would have been cringing inside because I know they're leading words. Just like Drew might try to give when cross examining a client in court. But there's no one here to object to my leading question. No one to protect me from myself.

I can sense Charlie's attention is on me. It's heating my skin just like the sun that has presented itself from behind the clouds.

'I can understand their concern, if that had been the case.'

My body feels like it slips into the seat of the pedal boat. I know that physically it doesn't, but internally I fall, not because of Charlie's words but because of the things he hasn't said.

'I'm not frivolous when it comes to women, Sarah, I want you to know that. The guy you see on stage and in social groups, he's a social extrovert. He wants to please people to keep them around, just like you. And his way of doing that is to use humor. That version of me uses humor to make friends and defend myself. Maybe when he's on stage that guy jokes about frequently swiping left and right on Tinder and one-night stands, but the real me isn't like that. I'm not going to pretend I haven't done it, because we all have needs and I've not been in long-term relationships before – not because I haven't thought about that but I guess I'm just not a long-term relationship kind of guy. At least, I haven't been in the past.'

I'm not sure whether Charlie is trying to tell me something, to get me to decipher a hidden meaning in his words, or if it's just because I would really like to find one, but I'm incited enough to ask.

'Are you the kind of guy who would like a long-term relationship now?' I ask, genuinely intrigued by the answer.

He shrugs. I'm watching him now.

'I didn't like returning to my empty apartment on Sunday, after a week in the house in Surrey. I didn't like that my flat felt void of a presence, warmth, that the boxes of my things were still packed and, in all likelihood, probably will stay that way for a long time. I didn't like walking around Clapham Common and seeing families and couples out and about together.'

He turns to look at me and we both stop pedaling. 'All I can say is that those feelings haven't infiltrated me very often, if at all, in the past.'

We look away from each other again and begin to pedal, moving aimlessly around the lake, avoiding other fellow boaters. But there is a sense that this conversation hasn't finished. There are unspoken words and I'm not sure either of us know what they are.

'It's not the place of Drew, Brooks or Jake to decide if or when I can be in a relationship with someone,' I finally proffer. 'But the truth is, Charlie, I have already given away my whole heart once, and when someone dies they never give you your heart back. I'll always love Danny, so I'm not sure it would be fair to any other man, or to Danny, for me to be in another relationship.'

As I say those words, I remember my dream, and I think it's a good thing for both Charlie and me that I have made my position clear. Charlie said we were friends. We *are* friends and I need to remind myself that we won't be anything more than that.

'Understood,' Charlie says. 'And for the record, even though the guys allowed me briefly to entertain the crazy idea that you might like me even a little bit *like that*, I know I wouldn't be the kind of man you would go for, even if you were open to the idea of a relationship.'

He's right. Grumpy, rude, constantly angling for the big laugh, that's not the kind of guy I'd usually go for. But sweet, thoughtful, knowledgeable and funny without trying too hard Charlie? Maybe that's the kind of guy I'd go for.

'What was he like, your husband?' he asks.

I smile at Danny's memory. 'He was warm, passionate, ambitious. He and I used to bounce off each other, I guess, like a double act, and we found each other amusing. He was handsome, in a clean-shaven, suave kind of way, but he could surprise people too. The weekend version of Danny didn't wear suits; he wore leathers and rode a motorbike too fast. *Too* fast.'

I close my eyes as images of Danny lying in a hospital bed, cut and bruised, on life-support fill my brain. They are images I try never to see and I don't want them now; they are never welcome.

'He sounds pretty incredible,' Charlie says.

He's right, again. My husband was – *is* – an incredible man and thoughts like I was having in my dreams last night aren't right. They are not okay. Guilt fills my eyes with tears and I'm grateful to be hidden behind shades as I can only nod, swallowing down emotion.

'For what it's worth, Sarah, I'm sorry that the world can be so shit sometimes. I'm sorry Danny was taken from you too young and too soon.'

With Charlie's words, I can't help silent tears falling from my eyes.

'Thank you,' I say, not able to hide the croak in my words and not able to continue pedaling.

I expect Charlie to say something – like, he's sorry for upsetting me – but what he does is so much bigger than words. He reaches across the boat and takes hold of my hand, squeezing it as he looks into my eyes.

'You don't have to hide your true self from me, Sarah. I know how toxic it can be to keep negative thoughts bottled up in your head, just to prevent somebody else's discomfort. You're not making me feel uncomfortable.'

I feel my chin tremble because Charlie has un-knowingly spoken words that are resonating deeply. My tears over Danny, our lost life, our plans for a family that will never come to fruition, usually come when I'm alone, in the privacy of the home I shared with my husband. I don't want to lose friends by showing them my true feelings. I need my friends. Making people uncomfortable is the reason many of mine and Danny's couple friends no longer see me, except by accident.

Charlie is giving me the freedom to cry and I've not felt like anyone has given me that freedom, not even my own parents, since Danny died.

I'm breathing out, making raspberries with my

lips as I try not to let go too fully and scare him, but his words have opened a floodgate of quiet emotion. He holds my hand until I finally pull myself together and say, once again, 'Thank you.'

I start turning my legs around the pedals, which encourages Charlie to do the same, and we move across the water in silence, for my part, just trying to breathe.

Eventually, I say, 'We had so many plans that we will never get to do. We wanted to travel all over the world. London was one of the places we wanted to visit and we never got around to it. We wanted to have a family and move out of Manhattan to the sub-urbs. Two boys and a dog, Danny wanted. I used to tell him we had to have at least one girl that I could dress up and take to afternoon tea.'

I exhale audibly again, steadying myself.

'I look back over our years together and think how ridiculous it was to have spent extra time in the office or keeping other people happy, talking about plans and never taking vacation time from work. I think about all of the things we could've done with those hours, all of the conversations we could've had, that we didn't get to. And I wonder all of the time how different life might have been if we had taken a vacation that very weekend that Danny had his accident. Would I still have him now or would something else have driven us apart? Were we always destined to have a short yet beautiful time together?

'And if that's it, if that was my love and now it's done, what does life hold for me now? Just more of the same? The same job, the same friends? It occurred to me last week that all of my friends are moving on. New relationships, starting families. And I'm just me. Still Sarah, but somehow a lesser version. I'm the Matron of Honor, maybe a godmother-to-be, but I'll never again be the wife, I'll never be the mother.'

'Sarah, I don't know Danny but he sounds like a really great guy and I don't think he would want you to feel like the best years of your life have been and gone.'

I shuffle on my seat to face him, still pedaling. 'The thing is, Charlie, I couldn't go through that again. And if you never open yourself up, you can never get hurt.'

Charlie opens his mouth to speak but before he does, we jerk forward, colliding with another pedal boat, crashing into their side.

'Oh my God, sorry,' I tell the young couple opposite us. 'I was distracted.'

'Don't say that,' Charlie says. 'They'll be suing us

for the clothes off our backs if you admit liability. Have you seen how jazzy my Harry Potter T-shirt is today?'

The young couple start to laugh. 'Don't worry about it!' the young man says. 'We're totally uncoordinated.'

'But I probably *would* sue for that T-shirt if it had been Hufflepuff rather than Gryffindor,' the young woman says. 'I'm a *Harry Potter* fanatic. Have you visited the studios?'

'Not yet,' Charlie says, 'but we're going.'

'We are?' I ask, delighted. 'I've read all the books.'

Charlie looks at me. 'You have?'

'There's not an age restriction on wanting to be a wizard,' I tell him.

The young woman is smiling at us.

'You guys are couple goals,' she says. Then she nudges her partner and the couple pedal away from us, calling 'Goodbye' and telling us to enjoy the studios.

Charlie and I look at each other and laugh, deciding to call it time on our calamitous boating experience.

* * *

Ironically, following my unexpected emotional meltdown in the pedal boat, I feel like the proverbial weight I've been carrying around since I've been in England has lifted.

Charlie and I have spent the most random and amazing day together, finishing the adventures at London Zoo. We spent a lot of our visit making wild animal noises and comparing each other's features to those of the animals around us: Charlie's wild hair to a lion's mane. My long legs to a giraffe. Charlie's laugh to a gelada. And my long feet to a flamingo.

We bought sandwiches and had a picnic on the grass. We chose ice creams for each other based on personality types. Charlie chose a Calippo for me, telling me I'm icy at first glance but the longer I'm held, the more I melt, which I thought a fair reflection of my time spent with Charlie. I chose Charlie a Smarties ice cream – bold and gregarious on the outside but calm, soft and mellow once those crazy candies have been bitten through.

We're on the underground heading back toward Covent Garden, where we plan to watch street artists perform and grab some dinner at a pub, but I notice Charlie, sitting opposite me, rolling his jaw to stifle a yawn. Then I catch it and I am less subtle as I hold my hand over my open mouth.

'Please don't feel like you can't cancel on me tonight,' he tells me.

He's giving me an out again and maybe he wants one too. We've had a big few days. My legs and feet are tired and I'd like nothing more than to put on some loungewear and eat room service from the big bed in my hotel room. But I'm happy in Charlie's company.

With little thought, I suggest, 'How would you feel about getting room service at my hotel tonight?'

As soon as the words have left my mouth, I'm conscious they could be taken as suggestive and I feel my clumsiness heat my cheeks.

'Do you have good movie channels?' Charlie asks, not taking my words to be suggestive at all, thankfully.

'There's a box office and I'm willing to splurge for a movie in my stretchy pants.'

'I'm sold.'

27

CHARLIE

I'm lying on a large hotel bed, next to the woman I have undeniably fallen head over heels for. And the fact that she's switched from her summer dress – which she looked stunning in, again – into her stretchy loungewear, isn't off-putting at all. It's only serving to make her more endearing to me.

I shouldn't be allowing my mind to do so but it's imagining lazy weekend days spent lounging around our home, lying in bed, having a late brunch and binge-watching our latest addiction on Netflix. I can see it all.

In the past, if I even got to a place of starting to imagine days like this with someone, it would've made me twitchy. But lying here, with my arms behind my head and at full stretch on the bed, with Sarah sitting cross-legged next to me deciding what to order from the room service menu, I'm not twitchy at all.

Maybe that's because I know there can't be anything more than friendship between us. With her words, Sarah keeps making that clear, despite all the subtle touches here and there, arm links, kisses on the cheek, knee grazes. There are moments, minuscule moments, where I wonder for the briefest time whether I might not just be imagining mutual feelings.

Then she'll completely squash that idea, like she did on the pedal boat earlier today.

So, I'm not twitchy but that's because I know my feelings are not reciprocated.

It's good, really, because I'm completely at ease. I'm more myself around Sarah than I would be around any other girl.

Even when I'm alone, I tend to have restless energy. I need to be thinking about something, analyzing something I've done, questioning what my next life or career move should be. My legs jump reflexively with unburned energy.

Right now, I'm still.

Maybe I'm being corny, as Sarah would say, but I

seem to have this sort of inner peace when I'm around her.

'I'm going to have the butternut squash and grilled goats cheese salad,' she says. 'How about you?' She holds out the menu for me to take.

'Is there a burger on there?' I ask, turning my head to look at her but staying in the comfortable position I'm in, reclined on her medium-firm pillows.

'There's a burger.'

'Then I don't need to look at the menu.'

'Don't you want to know what it comes with?'

'Nope. Any form of potato is grand by me and I'm sure it comes with potato.'

She reaches for the old-fashioned telephone-on-a-box style handset and presses a number for room service. She orders our food and makes a request for two brownies with ice cream to be sent up thirty minutes after the main meal. Just before she hangs up, she asks if they have popcorn. I can tell from her wide grin that they do. She asks for popcorn to be brought up with the brownies and ice cream.

I guess we are pigging out again. This woman is a dream.

I've got control of the TV remote and now that Sarah is paying attention, I move to the section 'Box Office Movies'.

'Oh, they have *Top Gun: Maverick*. Have you seen it?' she asks excitedly.

'Have I seen it? Every time I have a movie night with Cash and Will, we have to watch the original, then *Maverick*, too. I must have watched that volley-ball scene with them more times than the number of hours I've been alive. Even though Tom has got older, they still find him easy on the eye.'

'And, of course, now there's Glen Powell, too.'

'Ooh, got yourself a little crush, have you?' I tease, irrationally jealous.

'Shut up,' she tells me, rolling her eyes.

'*Maverick* it is, then.' I select the movie, check the budget with Sarah, since it will be going directly onto her room bill, and press play.

Sarah leans back on her side, knees bent, her head propped up on her hand, her hair flowing down to the pillow on one side, her neck bare on the other.

My mind falls to the gutter for as long as it takes for me to wonder how the skin of her neck would taste on my lips.

Then I snap out of it as we hum and sing through the opening sequence, which is the same as the original.

When Tom Cruise appears on screen, Sarah says, 'You know, if it wasn't for the crazy stuff he's said and done in his personal life, he could still be a hot older guy.'

Of course, because people who have checkered histories just aren't attractive prospects.

Before I have a chance to go into my usual analytical mode and get lost in some level of self-destruction, there's a knock on the door.

'Room service!' a voice calls.

'Pause it,' Sarah says, eagerly springing on bare feet to answer the door.

I can smell my burger and thrice-cooked chips before she's back in the main room.

With my mouth wrapped around the hefty brioche bun, I manage to tell her, 'This is an epic night!'

She laughs, forking goat's cheese into her mouth and nodding. 'Now we really are couple goals.'

She has no idea how happy those words make me feel.

After the main course, we have ten minutes of uninterrupted fighter-jet action before the brownies, ice cream and popcorn arrive.

'Sarah, you are one top gal,' I say, greedily accepting the bowl of brownie and ice cream she hands to me.

Somehow, we manage to share the popcorn too, taking turns to dip our hands in the large bucket.

We spend the last forty minutes of the movie moaning about being full, while at the same time gripped by the completely unreal events onscreen.

At some point, relaxed, full, sleepy, the proverbial lights go out for me.

* * *

I rouse in a blur of confusion. I've been dreaming about things a man can't help dreaming about when he's lying next to a very attractive woman with whom he is madly in lust.

But when I open my eyes, that woman is still there, right beside me, albeit now under the bed covers.

The television has been turned off and the only light in the room comes from blue floor lights.

It's enough to allow me to see the white towel dressing gown that Sarah must have placed across me when I fell asleep.

It's enough to allow me to watch her sleep. Angelic. Peaceful. Insanely beautiful.

Her breaths are soft, whispered. Her chest hardly

rises and falls. She's almost still, like a flawless painting of a woman.

I'm not sure how long I've been watching her when she murmurs.

I'm definitely confused because I allow myself to hear her whisper my name from her exquisite lips.

Of course she doesn't.

Then she stirs.

Her eyes shoot open.

She's looking right back at me and it's now that I realize I've been sporting a hard weapon under my shorts since I woke up.

Jesus!

I jump up and run into the bathroom, taking my erection to hide with me. Hoping Sarah didn't notice.

FFS! I'm Jim Levenstein!

I lock the bathroom door behind me and now I need to take a leak but I can't go until Captain Charlie calms the heck down.

I'm thinking about pineapples. Pineapples. Coconuts. Coconut bras. Coconut bras and grass skirts. Sarah on a Hawaiian beach in a coconut—

Damn!

Jake. I'm thinking about Jake.

There we go. Down goes Captain Charlie.

I lift up the seat and stand in front of the pot but

as my wee comes, it sends a green light to my arse and now I need to break wind.

Damn my meat eating!

Please don't, Charlie. Please don't. Sarah's just on the other side of that door.

The need goes off, thankfully, and I resume my—

Noooooooooo!

The wind comes out. It's an audible release.

I squeeze my arse cheeks together but it's too late.

Oh God.

There's nowhere to hide.

She must have heard.

Maybe she went back to sleep.

Please let her have gone back to sleep.

I tiptoe out of the bathroom, turning out the light. I reach the bed and thank the heavens that Sarah's eyes are closed.

I lie back down on the bed, pull the dressing gown back over me and will my mortified self back to sleep.

Just when I think I've got away with the wind break and erection combo, Sarah says, 'Nice fart.'

Kill me.

Kill me now.

I want an asteroid from outer space to fall to earth and strike only me.

The floor lighting allows me to see her silhouette and I notice her shoulders are shaking with laughter.

'Like you've never farted,' I say in the manner of a petulant child. It only makes her laugh harder and all I can do is go with it, until the entire bed is vibrating with our amusement.

When we calm, I ask, 'Would you like me to go home?'

'Because you farted? It's 2 a.m. Go back to sleep.' She rolls over so that her back is to me. 'If you promise to keep that ass away from me, you can come under the covers.'

I slip off my combat shorts, roll up the dressing gown and put it under the sheets to act as a divider between us, then climb under the duvet.

I don't sleep a wink. I can't. She's right *there*. And when she rolls around to face me in the night and her arm slides on top of mine, our hands touching, I don't dare move.

28

SARAH

Charlie is snoring. Not like a hippopotamus snore, more like accidentally over-sucking through a straw in your soft drink, but it's enough to rouse me. I open my eyes to see his mouth wide open, his chin hanging low. He looks both comical and peaceful at the same time. It makes me smile.

Now I notice my fingers are touching his, despite the dressing gown that has been rolled like a sausage and placed between us. His attempt to secure physical distance between us is hilarious.

The interesting thing is, for the first time in years I have woken up with a man in my bed and I don't feel guilty. Charlie has made clear to me that we are friends – his comfort level around me is much more friendly than intimate, hence farting in the bathroom last night and sleeping partially clothed but with a towel robe between us. I also don't believe he would have made the level of comments about the male bodies in *Top Gun* that he did last night if he were trying to pursue me.

It's actually nice to not wake up alone.

I peel back the covers and quietly move around the room, picking out my burnt-orange playsuit from the wardrobe – short with long sleeves – and underwear. I take a very quick shower and dress in the bathroom.

Charlie has changed position when I come back in, so he must be in a light phase of sleep, but his eyes are still closed.

I fill the water container on the back of the coffee machine then set it away heating up. I head back into the bathroom and apply a base layer of sunscreen and a little eye make-up before making us drinks.

Charlie must smell the coffee – no pun intended – because as he reaches up his arms and enjoys a full body stretch, he opens his eyes and makes one of those noises you're allowed to make every time you move once you've reached your thirties.

'Good morning, snorer,' I say, mockingly. 'I've made coffee.'

Charlie reaches for his khaki shorts and comes to sit on the edge of the bed, the duvet still around him, and pulls on his shorts. I hand him his cup.

Now that we're both up and dressed, I open the curtains to let in the natural light, revealing the view of the street below – not yet too busy with commuters, and very little sign of tourists. I turn off the lights in the room and turn off the air-conditioning unit, too.

'Charlie, would you mind if we built some shopping time into today?' I ask. 'I'd like to pick up some gifts and maybe check out some British fashion.'

Charlie swallows a mouthful of hot coffee. 'Oh, that's good.' He takes another mouthful, as if his mouth is heat resistant. 'Not at all, actually. I thought you might want some shopping time and I kept today flexible for that reason. Plus, I couldn't get us tickets to the Harry Potter studio until tomorrow. I'm thinking we can meet at platform nine and three quarters around eight thirty tomorrow morning. Is that too early?'

I blow on then slurp my coffee, resting back against the small desk in the room.

'No time is too early for wizards and witches,' I tell him.

'I agree, wholeheartedly.'

'Would you like to have breakfast with me here at the hotel?'

'Actually, I might leave you to it this morning. You've probably seen enough of me for a while anyway.' He chuckles, then scratches his head. 'Plus, shopping gets my heckles up like nothing else. Crowds. People bumping into you.'

'Men are so weak,' I tell him. 'I wouldn't have asked you to stay for breakfast if I'd had enough of you but given you slept in your clothes, you probably do need a shower. I can smell you from here.'

He laughs into his coffee cup. 'There's no need for insults. How about we meet for dinner tonight?'

'Sure, but only if you let me organize this one.'

'You're on. Shall I meet you back here later?'

I'm already pondering where to book a table, if they have space. There is still one place left to visit on my to-do list, after the Harrods food hall.

'I'll message you later,' I say.

* * *

I get back to my hotel just after four in the afternoon, arms aching from carrying bags of gifts for my friends and parents. It's the Harrods ceramic jar of cookies that's weighing me down but my mom would never forgive me if I forgot her 'fancy British biscuits'. I bought the same for Danny's mom, too, and have been carrying a jar in each hand, alongside the other gifts, for hours. How I'm going to fit all of this stuff in my luggage, I've no idea.

As I walk past the reception desk, the guest concierge confirms there was a cancellation at the restaurant I had in mind. Charlie and I are booked for dinner at 9 p.m. We have a bar seat for cocktails from eight.

Back in my room, now cleaned and made up by the hotel staff, I make myself a coffee, indulge in the delicious homemade cookies that are replenished each day, and put my feet up in a wingback chair in the window, watching the street below.

I'm excited for dinner tonight. So much so, I have bought a new dress for the occasion.

After coffee, I'm going to beautify and indulge in the getting-ready process for a change.

A huge yawn visits me as I finish my cookie.

Or maybe I'll beautify after a nap.

* * *

The dash in the cab informs me it's 7.58 p.m.

I step out of my ride outside the towering entrance of The Shard. I look up but even craning my neck, I get no sense of the height of the building from down here.

I'm not a stranger to skyscrapers but I've been looking forward to going up The Shard and looking down over the city. It's a clear night, the sun is going down, and when I bring my gaze back to the entrance, standing in front of me, wearing a royal-blue suit with a flowery blue and white shirt, is Charlie.

The next things that happen to me have been written into every romantic comedy. They are reactions we read or hear acted out and allow ourselves to believe are for dramatic purposes but in reality, think, yeah right. But it's true: my heart is doing star jumps in my chest, my hands are trembling with excitement, and I'm a ball of nervous anticipation... with clammy hands.

Charlie makes strides toward me and when we are face to face, he tells me, 'You look incredible.' His voice is barely more than a whisper.

In an instant, my qualms about spending two hundred pounds on my halter neck, silk red dress are dispersed.

'You too.' My words struggle to leave my dry mouth.

One side of Charlie's mouth curves up and he

shifts to my side, holding out his arm for me to loop my hand through.

'Shall we, madam?' he asks, faking a Hugh Grant in *Love Actually* style British accent.

We ride the elevator up to level thirty-three of the tower and are greeted by a waiter, who guides us to Hutong's Shanghai Bar.

I can feel my body starting to relax but neither Charlie nor I have spoken since meeting outside.

We order cocktails. A Chinese Lantern for me and a Tropical Negroni for Charlie – the bar's take on a typical Aperol Spritz and a Negroni.

The cocktail is delicious and goes a small way toward settling my unexplainable edginess tonight. I don't know what it is but it feels like Charlie is Bella in *Twilight*, exuding some kind of protective field that stops me from speaking or taking any action. I am stupid with nerves.

Perhaps it's because I know the answer to certain questions running through my mind. Why did I choose to visit The Shard with Charlie? Why did I book the most romantic restaurant in London? And why did I splurge on a special dress for the occasion?

Charlie puts an end to my boundless concerns by asking, 'So, what has been the highlight of your trip so far?'

It feels like forced conversation and makes me wonder whether his cocktail has had a similar effect on his thoughts. Did he wear a suit tonight because it's appropriate for The Shard or is the suit for me? I doubt very much that he went out and bought one for the occasion, though it would make me feel better about buying my dress.

'The wedding, of course,' I say, 'but this view isn't bad and riding an open top bus in a Union Jack hat was pretty good fun.'

'Don't forget the soldiers in fluffy hats,' Charlie says, smirking.

'Ha ha. I get it, it's bearskin. Uber masculine. Every-man-wrestling-a-bear-for-himself kind of mas-culinity.'

He laughs. My anxiety is beginning to fade and I realize how much I've enjoyed listening to his laughter over the last week or two. It's a sound that comes from deep in his stomach but it's also quite high-pitched and childish. Infectious.

'But honestly, the biggest highlight of this whole trip for me has been...' The word on the tip of my tongue is *you*.

Meeting you, Charlie. Waking up to you this morning. Not feeling as lonely as I so often do because of you.

He's staring at me, waiting for my response

through what is an unnecessarily long pause on my behalf.

'...meeting Joe Elvis. It has to be number one.'

He laughs heartily this time, throwing his head back.

I'm laughing with him when the maître d' heads over to us and says, 'Mr and Mrs Cooper, your table is ready.'

'Oh, that's not us,' I say.

'I'm so sorry,' the maître d' says. 'You look very much like a picture of a newlywed couple and I just assumed it was your celebration tonight.'

We smile politely and watch the maître d' move to another couple at the bar, who are perhaps in their fifties or sixties, her in a cream dress and him in a three-piece black suit with a gold tie that reflects the gold belt on the lady's dress. They are in fact the newlyweds, the Coopers.

Given their age, I wonder whether they might be divorcees or widower and widow. It seems, for some people, that life does move on and some people are open to finding love again.

Charlie slurps his drink as his straw makes contact with the ice in the bottom.

'That was a rookie error, Sarah,' he says. 'You should have at least waited to see if they had a prepaid dinner and a free bottle of champagne on the table before telling him we aren't the Coopers.'

Still somewhat lost in thought, I tell him, 'You're terrible.'

Do we look like we make a good couple?

When we are taken to our table, we ask the waiter to take a photograph of us in the window, with the cityscape our backdrop. Charlie offers for me to have my photographs alone, which I decline because I'd like to look back on this time in London and see Charlie in my photographs. He has made my week and alone is precisely what I don't feel when I'm around him. So we lean in to have a photograph together, our backs to the lights of London, against the backdrop of dusk.

I don't know how close to get to Charlie or where to put my hands but he takes the decision away, pressing his side against mine. Then he slips his arm around my waist, his left hand holding my left hip through the thin, smooth material of my dress. I feel his touch in a way that has me remembering that kiss in my dream and our almost kiss at Jake and Jess's wedding, the last time we were wearing a fancy dress and a fancy suit. My body is responding on reflex. Charged with desire and anticipation. I can't control it.

I feel that energy, that physical connection to Charlie even when we are sitting adjacent, at a square table for two, forming a V shape, looking out to the impressive view.

We are presented with a feast of Asian delights and ordinarily I would be gobbling it up just as quickly as Charlie, but tonight we both seem to be picking our way through the dishes slowly.

We order a bottle of wine with dinner and after main course, though we decline desserts, we decide to have one more cocktail at the bar.

It's busier now and when we sit on our stools, our knees are pressed together. There's a moment, a joke, and then Charlie's hand is on my knee and I don't push it away. My instinct isn't to flinch; I enjoy the contact.

When we are sitting in a black cab, Charlie his usual gentlemanly self, dropping me to my hotel before heading home himself, I am overcome with the need to explore that kiss. We pull up to my hotel entrance and the driver stops to let me out.

I don't immediately reach for the door; I look at Charlie. I don't know what I'm thinking or what I'm trying to convey in this look but I don't think I'm telling him to stay in the cab and go home.

'I'll see you at eight thirty on platform nine and

three quarters, then?' Charlie asks, but his voice is uncertain and, I think, asking a very different question.

He has mentioned tomorrow, our last day together. The thought of not seeing him again makes what I am about to say both necessary and possibly excusable.

'Would you like a nightcap?'

I'm tense; my mouth is dry. He wants to be friends but I think maybe there's something more between us tonight, and I'm terrified. I'm terrified he'll say no. I'm terrified he'll say yes.

* * *

As we walk through the hotel foyer, my heels click against the tiled floor. It feels incredibly loud. As if it would draw the attention of every person in the reception area and in the residents' bar as we pass. I don't dare look, keeping my focus on the elevator ahead.

I'm as nervous as the night I lost my virginity, which is crazy.

This is Charlie.

I can back out of this at any time, pretend I really meant a nightcap, that it wasn't a clichéd innuendo.

There's zero pressure and I know that.

Yet, I don't call it off. There's a small, quiet voice in my head saying this is a bad idea. There's a huge, loud voice telling me I want this. I want Charlie.

My thoughts are in danger of spiraling, I feel Charlie's fingers graze mine. Then our fingers interlock, our arms are pressed together, and we step inside the elevator.

I watch the floor number increase on the digital sign above the doors, my body on fire, feeling like I'm about to explode from the inside out, until finally, we reach my floor.

Letting go of Charlie's hand, I slide the room card from my purse and the door light flashes green.

This is it. I can still back out.

I push the door open. Room service has been to turn down the bed and there's a lamp light on in the main room.

Stepping inside, I set my purse down on the side table and turn to face Charlie. He's right there, in front of me, asking me in a look if this is what I want.

With a steadying breath, I nod.

He brings his fingertips to my face and traces the line of my jaw, then places his palm where his fingertips have been.

Finally, my lips meet his with a sigh. The tension

I have been carrying all night melts away as I lean into him. It's not like my dream. It's better. Bigger, somehow.

And it scares me.

I'm back in my head, weighing up those two voices, and I pull away from Charlie's kiss, unable to look at him.

Then he holds my chin gently between his index finger and thumb, slowly encouraging me to raise my eyes to his. I do.

And I'm no longer in my own head as he kisses me again. Firmer, longer.

I moan with pleasure, my fingers moving into his hair, my palms caressing the base of his neck.

His tongue gently parts my lips and meets mine, our kiss deepening.

There's no going back because I am in this. I'm insatiable with lust, taking his jacket down his arms, pulling out his shirt and feeling his warm skin.

He walks backward as we kiss, moving us toward the bed as I unbutton his trousers.

When he can walk backward no longer, he breaks our contact and my lips feel the loss. He encourages my shoulders to turn away from him, then he's un-clasping my halter neck and I pull down the zip at the side of the dress, allowing the garment to fall to the floor.

Standing in my heels, in the new red, lace panties I bought to match the dress, I know without doubt that I dressed with Charlie in mind tonight.

I dressed for this.

My chin falls when his now naked chest meets my back and my breathing quickens.

He runs his hands down my stomach, holding my hips as he presses his crotch against the small of my back, placing soft kisses on my neck.

'I've never met anyone like you, Sarah,' he whispers. 'The way you make me feel...'

He leaves his words lingering there and I answer them with my own desire, turning to face him and kissing him greedily now.

He slips off his shoes and I push down his trousers to reveal Marvel boxer briefs and Marvel socks.

'You have got to be kidding me,' I say, laughing. 'You brought Spider-Man to bed with us?'

He shrugs. 'I didn't know this was going to happen.'

The bizarre thing is, I want him even more for being unpresumptuous, for being his true self. For wearing Marvel underwear.

29

CHARLIE

I roll onto my back, breathless, my heart racing. Not because what we just did was a cardio workout; it wasn't. It was slow. Passionate. Incredible.

It's the best time I've ever spent with a woman. From the touch of her hand in mine in the hotel lobby to the feel of her body under her silk dress. The way her hair fell into my face and the weight of her body on top of mine.

I roll onto my side, not sure how much of this I should say aloud. I want her to understand how much that meant to me but I know she was hesitant at first. I don't want to overwhelm her.

She's lying on her back but turns her head in my direction. Her eyes meet mine and silence me before

I speak because I can tell she isn't feeling the things I'm feeling.

I don't know what to say. I can't beg her to fall for me the way I have for her.

But I know her. I think. She wouldn't have done this if she didn't care about me.

The look in her eyes tells me otherwise. She looks... haunted. Regretful.

She looks away from me, casting her eyes to the ceiling. Then she flops one arm over her face and I see her mouth twist with sadness.

I don't know how to fix this and I don't get a chance to, because Sarah gets out of bed, heads into the ensuite, and locks the door behind her.

She turns on a tap and it sounds like she's splashing water on her face.

How did this go so wrong? We just had the most amazing night, both before and when we got back here. Now I'm lying on a bed, wondering what I'm supposed to do. Do I comfort her in her clear distress, her horror over spending the night with me?

I don't want her to hurt – not if it feels remotely as bad as I feel right now.

Taking a sheet with me – feeling too exposed to be entirely naked – I tap on the bathroom door.

'Sarah?'

She's crying, I can hear it now.

God, I've made her cry.

How could we have shared that experience and felt so wildly differently about it?

'I'm sorry, Charlie.' She sniffs. 'Please go home.'

'Sarah, if I've done something or said something wrong, please tell me. I thought—'

'You haven't done anything, it's me. I shouldn't have... Please go before I say something I can't take back. Please.'

I don't know what else to do, so I say, 'Okay.'

I'm gutted. Confused. Devastated. Blindsided.

I can't think straight but I do know that I don't want to upset her more than I already have.

Grabbing items of clothing from the floor, I dress.

Can I just leave? I don't want to but she doesn't want me here.

I tap on the bathroom door again. 'Sarah... I can't leave you like this. Let me see you.'

'Please, Charlie,' she sobs.

I sigh. I want to break down myself.

'I'll go but please let me know you're okay.'

'I'm fine. I promise.'

There's nothing else I can do, so I leave. On my way to the door, I hear her turn on the shower. She's going to wash me off her when, just minutes ago, I was happily drunk on the scent of her perfume on me.

* * *

I haven't slept a wink. A taxi dropped me home around 2 a.m. and I sat on the futon in my lounge, staring at a spot on the wall where any other person might have hung a family photo-graph or even just a mirror. How can two people have shared the same experience and one end up elated whilst the other is crying in a bathroom?

It's Friday. Sarah's last day in London. Tonight she'll be staying in an airport hotel waiting for her early flight back to America tomorrow morning. And I doubt I'll ever see her again.

Last night, at dinner, I knew – or I thought I knew – that we had mutual feelings. I let my mind get car-ried away with the idea that I might see her again. That there might be something between us that could last beyond these two short weeks we have spent together.

I got the first Tube to King's Cross this morning.

Now, armed with a triple-shot coffee, leaning against the wall outside of Caffè Nero because it has a view of the trains coming and going on platforms nine to eleven, I wait for Sarah.

It's my second coffee. The first was a single shot and it didn't hit the spot. I couldn't face breakfast, which is so unlike me it beggars belief. I also thought that if I got another coffee, a very strong one, it might give an explanation for my nervous energy.

My watch tells me it's 8.03. I've looked at every tall, long-haired brunette who has walked past me, but none of the women have been Sarah. At one point, I moved position because a group of holiday-makers was obscuring my view, then went back to my preferred spot.

I'm trying to convince myself that it is still early, too early for an agreed meeting time of eight thirty, and that's why I haven't seen her yet. The alternative is unbearable.

I can't wait any longer.

But what if she's early?

So I take the last remaining dregs of my coffee and walk over to platform nine and three quarters.

Of course, it's a fictitious platform. It's a sign that only states what it is, situated between platforms nine and ten, but I have to go regardless, because it is our agreed meeting place.

I don't care about the Warner Brothers' studio

anymore. I don't care if Sarah turns up here just to shout some kind of derogatory words at me and tell me how much she regrets me, because at least she'll have been thinking about me too, rather than trying to forget that our time together ever happened.

There are already tourists – mostly young students, who seem to be on an international trip – taking photographs of one another under the small sign for the fictitious platform.

It's 8.11 now. Still no sign of her.

I watch a train depart for Cambridge and another coming to replace it, ultimately bound for Ely.

If Sarah were here, I'd be telling her cool facts about where some of the *Harry Potter* scenes were shot on location around England. I'd maybe ask her if she wanted to visit them next time she is in the country.

But it's 8.24 a.m. and Sarah still isn't here.

It isn't our meeting time yet. She has six minutes. *We* have six minutes.

As the six minutes count down on my watch face, as I check every few seconds in desperation, my heart begins to travel south.

Eight thirty. I'm still alone.

There's a ball of emotion in my throat now. My gut is churning with fear.

I could call her, I know. Yet I don't, because I want her to *want* to come.

Or maybe I'm afraid she won't answer.

Maybe I'm scared she will and that she'll tell me what I don't want to hear.

The train to Ely signals that its doors are about to close for departure. As the train moves out of the station, I look across the platforms that have become visible. Perhaps Sarah is struggling to find platform nine and three quarters. Maybe she didn't think to ask anyone where it is and she is wondering aimlessly around King's Cross. Maybe she's even in the archway between platforms four and five, where the *Harry Potter* scenes were actually shot. Or at the fake platform on the concourse, which isn't actually a train track at all but where half a Hogwarts luggage trolley is stuck to the wall. Regardless, I check. There's a line of tourists waiting to take pictures with the trolley but none of them are Sarah.

I don't see her.

At 8.49, having witnessed the comings and goings of commuters on numerous trains around me, I decide to wander the station. Just in case. Just in case she's somewhere looking for me.

I don't see her. I even look in the cafés and

eateries on the ground floor, on the mezzanine. She isn't here.

As I descend the staircases, I keep an eye across, looking at the moving heads in the station.

It's 9.11 and I'm back at platform nine and three quarters. She hasn't come.

Whatever I thought was happening between us, whatever magic I have been imagining, hoping for and simultaneously disbelieving, it was nothing.

I was right not to believe. I've learned my lesson over the years.

Hope is just something people who have never been hurt repeatedly hold on to. It's pointless.

I leave the station and decide I might as well walk all the way back to Clapham because I really have nothing better to do.

She's going back to America and I meant nothing to her. As I've meant nothing to most people for most of my life.

30

SARAH

I am exhausted. Physically and mentally wiped out. I missed my usual Monday morning yoga session with Izzy and Becky because I just can't face them. I don't want to answer questions about my London trip.

And the last thing I want to do is be trudging into our office on Lexington Avenue, all of my limbs heavy with guilt, hurt. Drew is my boss and one of my best friends but right now, he's also one of the very last people I want to see or speak to.

I contemplated calling in sick for what might have been the fifth or sixth time in my entire career but I learned after Danny died that life continues and I have to continue with it.

After pushing through the revolving glass doors into the firm's high-rise building, I quickly switch out my sandals for my work heels and stand taller than I feel, straightening my back for what feels like the first time in three days. The first time since London. And only because I have to.

Marty, one of the named partners, steps into the lift just as the doors are about to close. I decide to leave my shades over my eyes for now.

It is completely innocuous when he asks, 'How was the wedding? How was your vacation?'

He doesn't prefix with a good morning because frankly, Marty isn't particularly well mannered, but he is asking standard questions that anybody else in the firm might ask me on my first few days back from holiday.

I ought to have rehearsed a response but my mind has been elsewhere. Since turning my head to face Charlie in bed and realizing that he wasn't Danny. He wasn't my husband. He was a man I had wanted to go to bed with, had desired, and whom I was ultimately going to hurt.

That night, that week, our entire time together had been some of the best time I've spent in my life.

The few men I've slept with since Danny meant

nothing to me. They satisfied a drunken, physical need and no more. Those times, I still felt shame but nothing like I feel now.

I feel like I've let down Danny's memory. I know I haven't had an affair but it sure feels close. And it's worse than that: I've not cheated on a relationship that was ending or fractious, I've cheated on my husband, whom I loved deeply, whom I still love.

This time, I have also hurt another man. A good man. A wonderful man. Different in every way to Danny, except that he means so much to me.

I went to King's Cross on Friday morning. I saw him standing there, tired, a little disheveled, coffee in hand, waiting. I saw him with his back to me, through the windows of two parked trains. When he started to turn in my direction, presumably looking for me, I was cowardly and hid behind a brick pillar.

I waited until he left the platform and when I was sure I would be out of sight, I left too. I headed straight back to my hotel, packed my bags, checked out early and went to my airport hotel, where I spent the rest of the day in bed.

Charlie didn't deserve more excuses from me. He didn't deserve ramblings about my husband. The band-aid had already been ripped off and to apply another one, just to rip that off too, would have been unfair.

So I left him in the train station, alone. And as punishment, I spent the day alone, the weekend alone, and if I had a choice, I would have spent today alone, too.

'Fine, thanks,' I tell Marty. 'The wedding was gorgeous.'

Thankfully, Marty goes on to talk about himself, and I walk with him to my desk, which is nestled in a pod with three other secretaries outside of Drew's office. I let him monologue at me. I make noises and gestures in the right places, making him think I give a damn about whatever he did at the weekend.

Drew is sitting behind his desk. I can see through the glass walls of his office. He glances my way, holding up a hand in greeting, and I notice that he is speaking into a headset, taking a call.

Relieved to put off our meeting for now, and relieved that I've arrived before the other legal secretaries, I set down my things, start up my laptop and turn on the large monitor the laptop is plugged into. I take off my shades and replace them with reading glasses in a bid to hide the dark-grey clouds underneath and the red vessels on the whites of my eyes.

Then I start working through my full inbox, trying and failing to concentrate.

* * *

The problem with being a staple figure in the office for as long as I have been is that everyone knows you and likes to know your business.

I've had an abysmal day, full of people bouncing up to me, sprightly as hell, asking about my trip.

Everyone since Marty has received the same response.

'Fine, thanks. The wedding was gorgeous.'

An hour before lunchtime, I got a notification from my calendar telling me there was a leaving lunch for one of the associates who's going on maternity leave. I remember getting the initial invitation – I even made suggestions as to the best place to host the event – but I sent an email on the back of that notification today, declining the event on grounds of having too much work to do.

Thankfully, Drew was busy for most of the morning, so we had limited interactions and he spent the afternoon prepping a client who has been subpoenaed to appear in court later this week.

I left work at five thirty on the buzzer. As soon as I

got back to my apartment, I stripped out of my tailored dress and put on my comfy loungewear. I heated up a carton of soup that I'd grabbed on the way home, which promised me two of my five a day, and now I'm sitting on the sofa, forcing myself to eat it despite having had no appetite all day.

Succession is re-running on my television, though I'm not watching it. The voices of Logan and Roman are merely providing some presence in my empty home, some background noise to drown out the voices in my head.

I discard what is left of the soup and put my crockery in the dishwasher to turn on when I have a full load.

I lie back on the sofa and pick up my phone, opening the photos app.

Charlie was completely on top of taking selfies of us and I'm grateful for the memories because I was so engrossed in sightseeing that I kept forgetting to take pictures. Of course, now most of my London memories involve him and that's a catch twenty-two.

I had such an amazing time with him that I want to look back and remember our time together fondly but looking at these pictures is a slow form of torture. A reminder of what I did to him, a reminder of what I did to Danny.

As if a secondary thought, I start scrolling back quickly to find pictures of me and Danny, to look at our memories together, but before I get too far back, I see a picture of myself. I'm standing on the back of the open-top London bus, the wind blowing my hair away from my face, looking up at the sun. Charlie must've taken it without my knowing. I wonder if he knew then that we would end up in bed together. He never gave that inclination. He said he wanted to be friends, but he must have cared about me. Our night together couldn't have felt as deep, as meaningful as it did, if he hadn't been into it.

When I close my eyes, I see him standing at platform nine and three quarters. Waiting for me.

I hate myself.

I scroll back to pictures of Danny and me. Drinking cocktails on Manhattan rooftops, frolicking on a beach on vacation, playing with Cady when she was a girl, laughing with his arms around Drew and me.

We were such good friends, all of us.

I set my phone down on the floor and close my eyes.

Charlie and I have so much in common, yet so many differences, which made for great conversation and a great friendship this last week. We were completely opposite to Danny and me.

Charlie and I forged a friendship first, then connected physically, whereas with Danny it was the other way around.

Regardless, I miss them both.

31

CHARLIE

I knew it wasn't my best performance tonight. I'm surprised I didn't get heckled, in all honesty. I said all the right things in all the right places but I just didn't have the energy I normally have to land my jokes the way I like to. When I picked up my guitar, I just didn't play it with any sort of oomph.

A few people in the audience are kind enough to congratulate me on my show as I head back into the Piccadilly-based club after my set.

I would have gone straight home but Jake and Jess are back from honeymoon and they are sitting on one of the front tables, right by the stage.

They have ordered me a pint and it's sitting on

top of the table, where there's a spare stool, waiting for me.

Jake and Jess are looking at me like I have twelve heads.

Ignoring their expressions, I ask, 'How was the honeymoon, lovebirds?'

I can't even ask my friends about the best two weeks of their lives and sound chirpy about it.

'Okay, where is funny-guy Charlie? What have you done with him?' Jess asks.

'I don't know what you're talking about.'

'Charlie, man, I love you but that is the worst I've ever seen you on stage,' Jake says.

It's a good thing I have an affection for his honesty because he is truly tactless.

'I'm just having a bad night, I guess.' I shrug, then change topic. 'Weather was nice, I take it? You two look golden delicious, positively glowing.'

They look at each other then back to me and Jess says, 'We wish we could say the same, buddy.'

'Listen, we love you, man, but we've been back from honeymoon less than forty-eight hours and have dragged ourselves away from two new comfy his and hers towel robes to come here and make sure you're OK,' Jake says.

I feel my face contort with confusion. 'Why would you do that?'

'Because Cash and Will have told me you've been ignoring their calls. That you won't go out anywhere or even have a movie night in with them,' he adds.

'They only ever want to watch *Top Gun* and I wasn't in the mood,' I lie.

'You love *Top Gun*, come off it,' Jess says.

She's got me there.

'See, the funny thing is, I spoke to my brother today and it turns out Sarah is as miserable as he's ever seen her. Moping around work, not going to her exercise classes or socials, which is so not Sarah. So, why don't you level with us? What went down between you two?'

I take a drink of my beer, which empties nearly half the glass, then plant it back down on the table and give them the abbreviated version of my time spent with Sarah in London. I leave out any romantic details because these guys are her friends and I don't want to embarrass her any more than I already have.

When I'm finished, I find myself shaking my head. 'What can I say except I'm an idiot? I knew she'd have no interest in a guy like me but I fell for her.'

I allowed myself to hope in the way I used to

when I was a child every time I got a new foster home that I liked. I would hope that my latest mum and dad would want to keep me but they always cast me aside when I became too difficult for them or they just didn't want me anymore.

Sarah crushed me, rejected me, in just the same way. I was an idiot for putting myself in that situation when I knew she wasn't interested.

Hope. What a ridiculous thing to harbor.

I can count on my fingers the number of people who haven't let me down in life. Two of them are sitting at the table with me now. And the others, I'm only recently coming to appreciate, are my parents. It has finally dawned on me how immensely grateful I am and should be that they took me into their family, into their lives.

And it dawns on me how pathetic I must look and sound now.

'Charlie, do you know that there was a point in our relationship where Jake and I felt completely miserable? It was right before we realized that we are meant to be together.'

I try to smile at her sweetness. I don't think I manage.

'I'm not good enough for her, Jess. I'm not Danny. She knows it and that's why I'm getting on with my life in London and she's getting on with her life in New York.'

Now Jake is shaking his head. 'Charlie, Sarah hasn't been in a relationship with anyone since Danny died. She is fiercely loyal, to the point of putting the needs of others above her own most of the time. Have you thought for a second that her feelings aren't negative toward you but a reflection of how she feels about being with someone she cares about for the first time since her husband? I know Sarah and I know it will be eating her up inside that she thinks she isn't being loyal to Danny's memory.'

I know Sarah is loyal; it's one of the things I admire about her.

Could Jake be right? Was she crying because she feels disloyal to her husband?

I'm not letting myself get tied up in knots over nothing again.

'Guys, I appreciate you being here, but Sarah's being upset because she feels like she mistreated her husband's memory by having a holiday fling with some guy she knew for two weeks doesn't make me feel any better.'

'Oh my God, you are really stupid, Charlie,' Jess says.

'Hey! Kick a guy when he's down, won't you?'

Jess bangs me on the head with a flat palm. 'Don't you get it? If you had had a meaningless holiday fling, she wouldn't still be devastated about it two weeks later. She cares about you, Charlie. She's hurting because she actually likes someone who isn't Danny and because now she's hurt you too.'

I want to make some kind of petulant remark, like I would have as a child, like *I'm not hurt*, or *I don't care* but I don't have the energy for it. I am hurt. I'm hurting. And I give a massive shit about Sarah.

'I can't let you get in my head like this, guys. Even if I let myself believe for a second that she likes me, it would never work. She'd find me out. I let people down, that's what I do. And even if she did like me, she's in New York and I'm in London. It's done. Over. And it's 100 per cent the best outcome for both of us. Why start something that's going to end anyway? She said as much herself; I just chose not to listen.'

Before they can continue their protest, my manager comes over to the table and asks for a word. I tell Jake and Jess that I'll catch them another time and stand.

Jake stops me with a hand on my shoulder. 'Hey. You've *never* let us down. *Never*. You're a fucking decent man, Charlie. The best. Try believing it once in a while.'

* * *

It's Sunday and I've been invited to my parents' house for lunch. It's an open invitation every week. My mum always makes a Sunday roast and she always sends me a message to remind me of the invitation. I doubt she does the same with her biological kids because they actually turn up every once in a while.

I walk up the driveway to the suburban Georgian terrace and knock on the door.

My mother answers, initially surprised to see me, then her face breaks into the sweet smile I love. 'Why on earth are you knocking on the door?'

She's an angel.

I climb the two concrete steps in front of the door and wrap my arms around her, holding on to her like my life depends on her. It did at one time.

'Is everything okay, Charlie?' she asks, still in my hold.

'I just want to say thank you.'

She pulls back from me, her hands on my shoulders, looking at me as if she's reading me like a book. 'Thank you for what, darling?'

'For being you.'

She waves her hand flippantly and gives me a dismissive 'pfft', then tells me to follow her to the kitchen, straightening her paisley cooking apron as she goes.

In the kitchen, my adoptive brother Dave and sister Lila are sitting at the dining table with their partners. My sister's kids are building Lego in the conservatory off to the side of the kitchen and my dad is on the sofa, supervising. He holds up a hand in greeting and I do the same in return.

'Hello stranger,' my sister says, getting up from the table and coming to give me a quick hug. 'I heard a rumor you were gracing us with your presence today.'

'What's up, little bro?' Dave asks. 'I keep hearing your name about town. I'm going to bring Jenny to one of your gigs.'

Jenny and Dave are recently engaged. I sent a bottle of champagne and a large bouquet of flowers in lieu of attending their engagement dinner a few months back. At the time, I was grateful I had a gig that night as an excuse not to go but here, now, I feel bad.

I take a bottle of red wine and my mother's favorite white from my backpack and set them down on the bench.

'Put the white in the fridge please, darling,' my

mother says as she takes out a tray of incredible-smelling roast potatoes from the oven. I know they'll have been roasted in goose fat because that's how she always makes the potatoes. The smell is nostalgic. Reminding me of Sundays and holidays when I was a teenager. In those days I'd have been grumbling outwardly about being forced to sit at a table to eat but even then, secretly delighting in the comforting food and normalcy of a family who would sit around asking one another mundane details about their day or week. I'd never had that in my life before.

I help serve lunch dishes to the table, which we all sit around, the kids included, and we eat as a family for the first time in years. I expected it to be awkward, strained, but it's not at all. Conversation flows and I feel brighter than I have since Sarah left.

After we've eaten, Lila is the first to leave with her kids. After Dave and his fiancée leave, I stay to help clear up. My dad makes three coffees whilst I dry the dishes my mother is washing in the sink, then the three of us sit down at the table.

Finally, I can say what I came here to say.

'I'm sorry to you both for how I've behaved all these years. I was a shitty kid and I know I let you down when I dropped out of university. Believe it or not, as a thirty-odd-year-old man, I've finally come to understand and appreciate everything you did for me. I'm sorry it's taken so long.'

My parents look at each other, confused. Of course they are; I should have said these things years ago. I should've changed my ways by now and not let them down again, after everything they've done for me.

'Charlie,' my dad says, 'you've never let us down. I overheard you earlier telling your brother about your new tour and TV news. You've taken everything life has thrown at you and turned it into something great.'

'University wasn't for you, darling. It's not for everyone,' my mother adds. 'We respect your conviction in finding something you love and pursuing it and now you're reaping the rewards.'

'We aren't disappointed in you, son. We're proud of you. The only thing we wish is that we could see you more.'

I look at my dad and my jaw feels tight, my eyes feel dry, and I can't swallow.

I look at my mother and she is reaching for a tissue from a box in the middle of the table and wiping her eyes.

That does it. I press my lips tightly together but I can't stop myself from crying.

I don't remember anyone ever saying that they are proud of me and me believing it. Never before today.

My mother gets up from her seat and comes around to my side of the table. She cuddles me from behind, wrapping her arms around my neck and kissing my head. The act is so maternal that it makes me cry more.

My dad reaches out to hold my hand and I hear him say, as he squeezes my fingers, 'You're a good man, Charlie. You're a good man, son.'

* * *

I have every intention of getting back to my flat and flopping onto the futon, emotionally depleted.

Yet, when I arrive home and sit down, I am the exact opposite of depleted. I'm completely energized by doing something I should have done a long time ago and being blown away by the outcome.

My parents don't think that I let them down. I feel like a barrier between me and them, which I created, has been removed.

What's revolutionary is that I'm starting to believe that I've made something of myself. I'll be headlining my own UK tour next year and I've been invited onto a comedy television show that I have respected and watched for years.

Maybe I'm not as big a disappointment as I've been telling myself.

And maybe it's time that I emptied these god-damn boxes and decided to commit to something for a change, starting with the place I'm supposed to call home.

32

SARAH

I've been putting off taking the jar of Harrods cookies I bought for Danny's mom, Greta, to her house. The thought of having to sit with her and talk to her about her son, the way we always do, when I have betrayed his memory, has been enough to keep me in hiding.

But she is Danny's mom and she is alone these days, since her husband died three years ago. For Danny's sake, I need to visit. If nothing else, the cookies don't have an indefinite shelf life. I need to face the music.

Greta is sitting in her usual armchair in the bay window of her home in the suburbs. I've let myself in to save her the trouble of coming to the door because she has osteoporosis and recently walking even short distances is a struggle for her.

Despite my protests, she pushes herself up from the chair and welcomes me with open arms. Her hold is weak of late but always warming and welcome.

'It's wonderful to see you,' she says, as she always does. 'Shall I make tea?'

'I'd love tea,' I tell her, 'but I'll make it. You settle yourself back down and open the gift I've bought you. It might be useful to have alongside your tea.'

I wink and she smiles, making the appropriate noises and rubbing her tummy.

I leave her opening her gift from the presentation bag I have put it in, her crochet now set aside on the coffee table, and head into the kitchen to make, ironically, a pot of English breakfast tea.

I use the time to gather myself because just *seeing* Greta has got me on edge.

When I return to the lounge, she is already chewing on a soft, crumbly cookie.

'These are delicious,' she says. 'You have to try one.'

I accept a cookie and dunk it in my tea. As I do, I hear Charlie's voice telling me that people have got etiquette all wrong and it's actually criminal to *not* dunk a biscuit (as he would say) in your brew.

'How was your trip?' Greta asks.

Out of respect for my mother-in-law, I don't give her the mundane, rehearsed response I have given to everyone else. I give her the details. I talk her through our days in the house, my trip to London with Charlie to get the Elvis suit from Joe Elvis – this makes her laugh and say, affectionately, 'That's Jake, always acting the fool.' I tell her about the wedding and about my time in London the following week.

I watch her expressions closely as I repeatedly mention Charlie's name and I desperately want to know her thoughts. I end the story at dinner in The Shard, then leave out the details of what came afterward.

When I finish speaking, Greta rests back in her seat, her fingers interlaced and resting on her stomach. I can almost hear the cogs whirring in her mind.

I need her to speak. I need her to speak on behalf of Danny. Part of me wants her to be cross with me because then I'll know she's being honest. I love Greta. I love Danny. I'd hate to upset either of them. Greta is his mother and right now, I feel like she is his voice too and I know that is why it has taken me three weeks to deliver a jar of cookies to her.

I sip my tea and place my china cup back down on the matching saucer in my hand, the way Greta insists we drink our tea. The crockery chimes, exposing my trembling fingers.

Eventually, she reaches for the jar of cookies and holds it out to me with both hands. I take another cookie, still waiting and watching.

She sits back in her chair again and I hold my breath as she opens her mouth for the first time in a while.

'Is he a nice man, this Charlie?'

I'm not sure how to respond. I opt for honesty.

'He's sweet and thoughtful. Insanely grouchy. Eats and drinks too much. And he makes me laugh, all the time.'

'Then, I think it's time you gave another man a chance.'

I exhale. I wasn't sure what I expected to hear but I don't think that was it.

'I love my son, Sarah, but I also love you as my daughter. I've been waiting a long time to hear you talk about another man and I won't pretend it's not painful to hear. I wish that you and Danny could have lived a long and happy life together but God had a different plan for our boy. That doesn't mean that you should be alone for the rest of your days.

'My husband died too late in life for me to have another companion but you're a young girl with a long life ahead of you. All that I would ask, and all that Danny would ask, is that you meet a good man, who makes you smile and laugh.'

I bite my lip in a bid to suppress the overwhelming guilt, grief and joy because someone who loves me and who loves Danny is finally seeing me. Someone who understands the trepidation and conflict I feel and doesn't hate me for it.

'Do you know how I know that Charlie is a good man, Sarah?' Greta says.

I shake my head.

'Because you've never mentioned another man to me before and the second you did, I knew that you have fallen in love again.'

I have?

I have.

'I'm happy for you, darling, I truly am. And I know that Danny wouldn't have wanted you to spend the rest of your life alone. He would've wanted you to go on and have the family that you always wanted. You deserve to be happy and you deserve to be a mother one day. When that day comes, God forbid you ever have to, you will tell your son or daughter the same things that I am telling you now.'

Now I'm not just crying, I'm audibly sobbing. I move to Greta's chair and kneel in front of her, let it all out as she wraps her arms around me.

'I'm so sorry, Greta,' I cry.

She presses her lips to my head as she tells me, 'You've done nothing wrong, my sweet girl. You can't change God's plan, none of us can. We have to make the most of the path we've been given. I love you.'

33

SARAH

It's Sunday and I'm at home in my apartment, cleaning in a pair of yellow rubber gloves because I have nothing better to do, though I am intermittently flirting with the idea of applying for the Office Manager position at work.

Since my talk with Greta, I've been thinking I need change. I've been stuck in a rut. I *am* stuck in a rut.

Maybe I do need the people around me to be dependent on me, like Charlie said, because it gives me purpose.

But my people are moving on with their lives and it might be time I let them go... A little, at least.

Baby steps. The first of which might be to apply for old Gerald's job.

There's a buzz through the intercom just as I finish shining the glass top of my coffee table.

'It's Drew. We need you to stop watching sad movies and cleaning your kitchen in your stretchy pants, get dressed and get down here ASAP. We are parked illegally so don't argue and don't make us wait. This is your intervention, misery guts.'

I gasp. How rude.

Then I run to the window and see Drew getting into the back of Brooks's truck. Brooks is in the driving seat and I think I can see Becky in the front passenger seat. And is that...? Yes, Izzy's in the back next to Drew. They start waving at me when they see me looking down from my lounge window. They are, in fact, parked illegally at the curbside outside my apartment.

I rush into my bedroom and change out of the stretchy pants Drew just called me out on and into a pair of jean shorts and a T-shirt.

As I hurry down the steps from my apartment building, Drew gets out of the truck and tells me, 'Last in gets the middle seat.'

'What is this? Where are you taking me?'

'Stop asking so many questions and get in the truck,' Brooks says.

I climb into the truck and sidle up to Izzy, asking, 'What's going on?'

'It's a surprise,' Becky says from the front passenger seat. 'Don't you dare utter a word, Izzy.'

Izzy shrugs. 'My lips are sealed, I'm afraid, but you brought this on yourself, Sarah, that's all I'll say.'

No one will tell me anything and I have no idea where we're going, except that we're driving out of the city and in the direction of New Jersey. I worry that I might have missed someone's birthday but I run through everyone's in my mind and I know I haven't. I might have been out of it for a few weeks but I would never miss one of my friends' birthdays. So where the hell are we going?

The others talk amongst themselves. The topics of conversation are so mundane that I know they're only chatting to avoid telling me where we're headed.

After forty minutes or so of listening to their nonsense chitchat, we pull up to the gates of a private airfield. Drew gets out of the truck and walks up to the security box, where a man sits inside. I hear him name drop one of our largest aviation clients – the CEO of Gold Miles – then he comes back to the truck and the electric gates open to let us onto the airfield.

I am beyond perplexed.

We drive past a fleet of Gold Mile private jets, which I recognize from brochures because there is no branding on the discreet aircraft. They are reserved for the world's most secretive passengers – Hollywood A-listers, managers of hedge funds, the CEOs of the largest banks.

We drive along a track that runs parallel to the primary runway and head in the direction of an old airplane hangar. The entire front is open and inside is what I know to be an old fighter jet, one which Gold Miles had something to do with procuring for some prestigious client. The details are hazy but I recognize the old F-14 Tomcat.

Then, I am not quite sure I believe my eyes. To the right of the hanger is a man, dressed in a Navy fighter pilot jacket, wearing a pair of aviators and leaning back against a motorbike, which I also recognize as a Kawasaki, arms folded across his chest.

'Charlie?' I say disbelievingly.

I look to Izzy, then to Brooks, and they're both giving me a coy smile.

Brooks turns off the engine and everyone gets out of the truck. The others hang back as I walk toward Charlie, utterly baffled but with a knot in my stomach that I've had ever since Greta pointed out what should be plainly obvious – that I am in love. I am in love with this man who's dressed as Tom Cruise in *Top Gun* and is standing right in front of me.

Then, oddly, I hear Jake's voice calling, 'Have I missed it?'

I turn to look back at the others and locate the sound of Jake's voice coming from Drew's phone, which he is holding up on video call to show whatever the hell is going on here.

I keep moving toward Charlie until there are maybe five strides between us and I watch one side of his mouth curve up.

'The get up was Jake's idea. He promised I'd get the girl if I said what I've got to say dressed as Tom Cruise.'

From over my shoulder, I hear Jake shout through the phone, 'Yeah, I did! Sorry, don't mean to interrupt. You go ahead, big man. Get your girl!'

Charlie chuckles and I freaking love that sound. It takes away the anxiety I've been chewing over for weeks.

I take two steps closer to him. 'How many times have you tried this stunt, Captain?' I ask.

'Once or twice.'

'And how has it worked out for you?' I take one more step toward him.

He smirks. 'The first time, I crashed and burned.'

'How about the second?' I take the final step, so close I can smell his cologne. So close, I am desperate to feel his touch.

I can't take my eyes off his lips as he says, 'I know I'll never be Danny, Sarah, and I also promise that I'll never try to be. I also know that I am far from the perfect catch. But over the last few weeks, I've decided that I'm not that bad a catch either, and the thing is...' He raises his fingertips to my cheek and I lean into his warmth. 'You make me feel like I'm a thousand times the person I am without you and there's no one else I'd rather watch reruns of *Top Gun* with in my stretchy pants.'

I smile and then I close my eyes as he gently kisses the tip of my nose.

From over my shoulder, I hear Jess whoop and Jake call out, 'I freaking told you, man.'

I can tell Charlie is smiling without needing to see. My eyes are still closed, blissed out by his touch, but his torso vibrates under my hands.

'I love you, Sarah,' he whispers.

I smile and open my eyes to find his peering into mine.

'I love you too, Captain Charlie. And I promise never to compare you to Danny. I promise to love you as you.'

He presses his lips to mine. Slow, long, and oh-so sweet.

'How did you pull all of this off?' I ask when we part.

'I had a few helping hands, which I took to be their seals of approval.' He looks across my shoulder to where the others are now cheering behind us.

But right now, I only have eyes and ears for one man.

'Charlie, I don't want to put a downer on this but I live in New York and you live in London.'

'I thought you might say that but you know, I think this is going to be a real slow burn romance and whilst we're figuring it all out, maybe flying between the two cities will give us the time we need to get it right.'

I nod.

Baby steps.

'Will you leave a pair of Spider-Man underpants in my apartment so that I know you'll come back each time?'

'I'll leave the pair I'm wearing.' He raises his eyebrows suggestively.

He's crass and funny and I wouldn't expect anything else.

He kisses me again and holds me tightly against his chest. One of the jokers behind us is playing Berlin's 'Take My Breath Away' and Charlie and I are laughing as we kiss, as seems to be our way.

I hope this time I'll get to laugh with the man I love until I'm old and gray.

ACKNOWLEDGMENTS

I want to start with you, wonderful readers. Thank you for picking up my books, for reading this series and taking the characters into your hearts. Mostly, thank you for asking me to write Sarah's story. I was nervous about writing this one because Sarah has been such a pivotal character in the other books in the series and I wanted to do her justice. Seven years after beginning this series, I think, or hope, that I have given Sarah the book she deserves.

I owe an enormous thank you to my youngest child for allowing me to write and edit this book during your nap times. And thank you for finally sleeping through the night so that I had the energy to finish the story! To all three of my greatest loves, thank you for providing me with so much love and humor, the key ingredients required to write this book. I love you all to infinity and beyond. Please keep loving me and making me laugh.

I may have been the author of this book but I am

one cog in a very well-oiled machine. Moving this series to Boldwood Books has been one of the best decisions my fantastic agent and I have made together. Thank you, Tanera (and Laura and the wider DA team) for your endless and faithful support. To the vibrant, smart, slick team at Boldwood... Massive thanks to my editor and champion, Emily Y, for believing in this entire series and helping me shape four romcoms into books I am proud to be publishing with you. To Rachel for the outrageously brilliant cover designs. Emily R, Arbaiah and Jennifer, your attention to detail is superhuman. Jenna, Nia, Amanda, Ben, Claire and Casey, you are a fabulous marketing, production and sales team, whom I am both grateful for and excited to be working with on this series and our books to come. And to the wider Boldwood team, I know you contribute hugely to the overall picture, even if we aren't always in contact. Thank you for your unwavering efforts and for being so welcoming.

Finally, and by no means least, thank you to Donna, series champion and fact checker, and Sarah's biggest cheerleader, for all your help and support.

Until next time... With love, Laura x

ABOUT THE AUTHOR

Laura Carter is the bestselling author of several rom-coms including the series *Brits in Manhattan* which she is relaunching and expanding with Boldwood. She lives in Jersey.

Sign up to Laura Carter's mailing list for news, competitions and updates on future books.

Visit Laura's website: www.lauracarterauthor.com

Follow Laura on social media:

ALSO BY LAURA CARTER

The Law of Attraction

Two to Tango

Friends With Benefits

Always the Bridesmaid

Boldwood

Boldwood Books is an award-winning fiction publishing company seeking out the best stories from around the world.

Find out more at www.boldwoodbooks.com

Join our reader community for brilliant books, competitions and offers!

Follow us
@BoldwoodBooks
@TheBoldBookClub

Sign up to our weekly deals newsletter

https://bit.ly/BoldwoodBNewsletter